PENGUIN BOOKS

THE SEAHORSE

Tania Unsworth lives in Boston, Massachusetts. This is her first novel.

The Seahorse

TANIA UNSWORTH

PENGUIN BOOKS

PENGUIN BOOKS

Published by the Penguin Group
Penguin Books Ltd, 80 Strand, London WC2R ORL, England
Penguin Putnam Inc., 375 Hudson Street, New York, New York 10014, USA
Penguin Books Australia Ltd, 250 Camberwell Road,
Camberwell, Victoria 3124, Australia
Penguin Books Canada Ltd, 10 Alcorn Avenue, Toronto, Ontario, Canada M4V 3B2
Penguin Books India (P) Ltd, 11 Community Centre,
Panchsheel Park, New Delhi – 110 017, India
Penguin Books (NZ) Ltd, Cnr Rosedale and Airborne Roads,
Albany, Auckland, New Zealand
Penguin Books (South Africa) (Pty) Ltd, 24 Sturdee Avenue,
Rosebank 2196, South Africa

Penguin Books Ltd, Registered Offices: 80 Strand, London WC2R ORL, England

www.penguin.com

First published by Viking 2002
Published in Penguin Books 2003
1

Copyright © Tania Unsworth, 2002
All rights reserved

The moral right of the author has been asserted

Set in Monotype Dante
Printed in England by Clays Ltd, St Ives plc

For my husband David and my sister Madeleine
And for my mother

PART ONE

Arrival

•

There were four children, perhaps five. But Marion West did not look at them long enough for an accurate headcount. She gained only a vague impression of a number of small backbones hunched low to the ground, a sudden clotting of tiny fists at the hem of her trousers and the feel of their hands running over her ankles with a touch both papery and determined: the confident, almost reverential, fingering of appraisers examining some rare item of porcelain. She risked another quick glance. They were so very *small*, she thought. Really hardly more than babies. How had they got there? From what feverish cranny or damp, unlikely gap had they crept, so predatory, so helpless? The sound they made was without words, a steady drizzle of entreaty, only separated from the din all around by its proximity and sense of purpose. Marion looked about her, down the long, dimly lit railway platform, with its pall of smoke, its seething, unquiet corners, its endless crowds of people indistinguishable from their own massed debris, and knew that the infants might have come from anywhere. She lifted one distressed hand in their direction. A strange, involuntary gesture both pitying and repulsed, caught somewhere between caress and protest.

'Have we got any . . . pennies?' she said.

'We used up our coins buying the biscuits, remember?' Vanessa said.

'I wish the train would come. When did you say the train would come?'

Vanessa ignored the question. She leaned forward slightly

3

on the bench and peered with interest at the begging children. Unlike her mother, the misfortunes of others had always held a certain fascination for her. She had been a child who stared. Openly, without inhibition, long after the age at which a childish lack of tact might be laughed away.

'Do you think they'll have stand-up loos in the train? The ones where you can see the train tracks rushing along underneath you?' asked Marion. 'I'm always so frightened I'll fall through.'

'Considering how only this morning you were complaining about the weight you'd put on, I don't think that's very likely.'

'Why are you being mean?'

Vanessa wasn't sure, but she suspected it had something to do with her mother's handbag. It was large and rather shiny. Snakeskin with a jaunty silver buckle holding it shut.

'I bet the beggars honed in on your bag,' she said. 'That bag was a mistake.'

'But I bought it specially for this trip.'

'You might as well write *steal me* on the side of it and be done.'

'I got it from Liberty's,' Marion said.

'You just don't take a *handbag* to India.' Vanessa regarded the neat nylon pouch strapped around her waist with satisfaction. It was roomy, yet discreet, with just enough space for passports and essential documents. When she looked at it, it reminded her that she was, after all, in control. Although she wouldn't have admitted it to her mother, the last couple of days had been, in the words of her colleagues back home at T. W. Pryce, 'a challenge'. Which was nothing but a euphemism for a bloody nightmare, thought Vanessa savagely.

She should have known what it would be like from the sight of the airport alone. That huge neon sign over the terminal building with its missing letter. 'CALCUTT' it read;

4

the last 'a' vanished like a breath suddenly cut short. And the smell of the place and the greyness and her mother trotting along behind her saying 'I don't mind, I don't mind' when she asked her where she wanted to go. The sky was brown with pollution and the streets drenched with monsoon effluvium and the horribly thin yellow dogs on Sudder Street took up no more space than stains on the ground. No time to explore, thought Vanessa, no time to really look around because they had had to change money and had wasted a whole Sunday looking for a bank that was open, and then there was that Banarjhee character who had frittered away even more of their time. As if they had come to India merely to sit and stare at the back of his lacquered head.

At least the bank had been cool. Marble-floored with large fans circulating air over the heads of the tellers behind their small metal screens and the more privileged managers who had their own desks. Mr Banarjhee belonged to the latter group. He was a tidy-looking individual with slicked down hair and white, starched cuffs. He listened to Vanessa's request to change traveller's cheques with his eyes fixed on the ceiling as though wearied beyond measure by such mundanity.

'Yes, yes,' he said impatiently. 'We can do this.' He picked up his coffee cup and took a leisurely sip. But when Vanessa put the cheques down on the table, he waved them away. 'Yes, yes,' he said again, 'these can be changed. In a minute or two.'

Vanessa and Marion sat down opposite and waited expectantly. Banarjhee finished his coffee and placed the cup on his empty desk with an air of regret. He sighed, sat immobile for a second or two, then opened a drawer and withdrew a single sheet of paper. He laid this paper delicately on the desk in front of him, shot his cuffs, sighed once more, then selected a pen from a smart-looking pen holder.

Vanessa glanced at her watch. It was early afternoon already. What was wrong with the man? Banarjhee spent a while looking at the piece of paper without touching it. He put down his pen. He opened another drawer, half pulled out a file, then replaced it. As though regretting the exertion of this action, he carefully patted the flat of his hand against his fringe to check all was still firmly in place. He turned back to the paper and, with an air of great resolve, shot his cuffs once more.

'Is this going to take a long time?' asked Vanessa.

Someone brought Mr Banarjhee another cup of coffee and he spent a while debating as to which side of the desk it should be placed. He picked up his pen and made a small, decisive mark on the paper in front of him. He sighed, he sipped his coffee, he patted his fringe.

'Is there a problem?' asked Vanessa. But her withering tone seemed lost on the man.

Marion was predictably oblivious to the delay. She seemed mesmerized by Mr Banarjhee, by the whiteness of his cuffs, by the elegant diligence he brought to the task of doing nothing whatsoever.

'Perhaps you should go to another bank,' Banarjhee said.

A young woman by the desk interrupted him. 'I'm sorry,' she told Vanessa, 'we haven't got the exchange rate in yet. My assistant is phoning Delhi for this information.'

'Yes,' said Banarjhee, 'if you cannot wait, you must go to another bank.'

'I would, but you seem to be the only place open today.'

The ceiling fans whirred. Mr Banarjhee put his piece of paper in his in-tray, removed it, then put it back again. Women in high heels made a brisk, clacking noise on the marble floor. To and fro they went. An hour passed. Vanessa thought about the itinerary for the day. There were places they needed to go. Important sites her mother needed to revisit. At this rate they would barely make it to the Victoria Memorial.

Another hour passed and somebody brought Mr Banarjhee a slip of paper. He glanced at it quickly then turned his head and looked at the two women, seeming surprised to find them still there, as though he had forgotten all about their presence in the hurly burly of carrying out the great work of the bank.

'Traveller's cheques,' he said. 'Did you want to change some traveller's cheques?'

What had made the whole episode even more infuriating was the fact that her mother had seemed unaware that they had just wasted most of the afternoon. She looked bemused, yet still vaguely willing. As though the whole enterprise was some kind of grand entertainment whose point eluded her somewhat, but would eventually be revealed. She was staring at the bank clerks counting out cash. The banknotes were stapled together in great wedges and the clerks kept licking the tips of their fingers to keep a grip on the slippery paper, flicking through it with such swiftness that the money blurred beneath their hands.

'How often do you think they lose count?' asked Marion.

'Lose count of what?' Vanessa said snappishly.

Banarjhee was presenting her now with forms to sign. 'Where are your passports, your passports?' he said impatiently, as though they were the tardy ones.

'I have mine here *somewhere*,' Marion said, removing most of the contents of her bag on to the desk. 'I know I put it in here this morning. Didn't I, Vanessa? Do you remember me putting it in this morning?'

●

But Marion had also had enough of Calcutta. She sat very still on the bench at the railway station and longed for the train to come. These two things – the arrival of the train and her stillness – seemed connected. As though she could, by willing herself to utter immobility – despite the pleading scrabbling of the beggars at her feet, the panting of her own breath made heavy by heat and distress – somehow make a kind of space for the train's arrival. She was too old for this, she thought. She was too old for Calcutta. Had the city always been this way? She couldn't remember. It had been fifty years ago after all. The heat, the noise, the speed with which her daughter walked had undone her.

It had been hard to think clearly about anything. Hard to look at anything for longer than a second or two. There were so many people in the streets and they all seemed to be in odd positions. Some sat, some lay, some squatted at knee level and sold strange corners of things: parts of flip-flops and small tin toys that jerked on the end of a thread. The ground was covered with scraps of one sort or another. Pieces of metal, rags, peelings. And some of the people who sat in the street were working these scraps; beating them, scrubbing them, collecting them up. A man flattened bottle-tops with a stone. A toddler squatted intently over a puddle as he washed a collection of plastic straws. At another puddle, a woman scrubbed at some rags. She hung them on a railing where a jackdaw perched and pecked at them, somehow finding nutrition among the meagre drapes. Only the poorest, thought

Marion, could understand the economic significance of such labour; the shaving of minute profit from the seemingly profit-less. And it seemed to her suddenly shaming that she should be there – a tourist – in this hell.

From a distance, the Victoria Memorial looked as pristine as it must have done when she had been a child. Its great dome was still white and it seemed to hover above the dirty haze of the Maidan, magically separated from the mêlée below where skeletal buses, crammed with passengers, shrieked and swerved. From a distance, the monument looked as it must always have done. The balloons and the children on ponies and two mon-keys in scarlet jackets capering over the shoulders of the post-card vendor. But when she came closer, Marion could see that nothing was the same. The balloons were splattered with mud and the postcards dog-eared and the pet monkeys mangy and subdued, and the lips of the ponies stretched so far from their teeth that they seemed to be retching. There was grass growing in the gravel around the monument. Above it all loomed the statue of Queen Victoria, toad-faced and reproachful.

Marion sat down to rest on the concrete edge of one of the ornamental ponds and stared down at her swollen feet and thought again of Ashagiri, seeking again that small, sudden throb of comfort that the memory had always brought her. But even this had changed, submerged by a sensation in which dread and hope were so tightly fused together that they had become indistinguishable from each other. It was a kind of betrayal, she thought. Another betrayal. But she would not think of that. Not there, with the lumpen, indifferent figure of Victoria at her back, and the smell of Calcutta deep in her throat, thick with the rotting of indefinable things. Marion hugged her handbag a little closer to her chest, lost for a moment in a struggle in which the wish to forget and the need to remember seemed suddenly confused.

It was so very hard to think clearly.

The thunderous arrival of the train was met by an equally powerful surge forward of passengers waiting to embark. Whistles blew, people called out, hands thumped hard against metal. It was only with great difficulty that Vanessa located their carriage and, carrying both hers and her mother's luggage, forced her way on board.

'A sleeper all to ourselves!' said Marion, sinking down with relief. 'That's a stroke of luck.'

'Luck? What has luck got to do with it? I bought the tickets remember?' Vanessa knew her tone was harsh and hated herself a little for it. The discrepancy between the way she imagined behaving towards her mother – with friendship, understanding, true equality – and the impatience she invariably displayed towards the older woman left a smear of self loathing. It wasn't merely that her mother was vague. It was her hapless, unshakeable assumption that things simply happened all by themselves. In her mother's world, job opportunities came about by sheer coincidence, friendship was a matter of fate and sleepers on trains were miraculously bestowed without needing to be asked for.

Her mother loved to feel lucky, thought Vanessa. She loved to imagine that life was a series of gifts: unasked for, unsought. As though all the best things that came to a person should arrive serendipitously and that everything that needed to be planned for and organized and anticipated was of a lesser value. This trip was no different. How blankly her mother had looked at the maps Vanessa had placed before her. How indifferent to the various itineraries proposed and the phone calls Vanessa had made to airlines and hotels.

'We'll find somewhere to stay,' she had said blithely as she packed her bag. Vanessa stared at the luggage on her mother's bed. Piles of unsuitable clothes, tins of pear drops, a quart of rehydration fluid, three loo rolls and an ancient hardback copy of *The Thousand Greatest Poems in the English Language*.

'I can't believe you're even thinking of taking half this stuff.'

'I may need it.'

'You may need silver loafers? In *India*?'

'You never know.'

Now she watched as her mother settled herself on the stained plastic bench of the train. In the weak light of the compartment, Marion's face had an ill, greenish cast.

'Are you all right?' Vanessa said, marvelling a little at the speed with which she could swing from annoyance to tenderness when she was with her mother. She wanted Marion to enjoy this trip. That was the whole point of it. Or so she had told herself. To cheer her mother up after her father's death. There was a look, an expression that people had when they travelled on the Underground. Blank, inward-looking, almost trance-like. In recent months she had seen that expression on her mother's face. As though she was simply being carried along.

'Yes, fine. A bit tired.'

'I'm sorry if I've been . . . pushing things. It's just been harder than I thought to get everything organized.'

Marion shook her head. 'I'm fine. Honestly.'

She rummaged in the side pocket of her main bag and brought out the packet of biscuits they had bought on the way to the station and a quarter bottle of whisky, laying both items carefully beside her on the bench.

'Provisions,' she said bravely.

●

The train had barely left the station when the door of the Wests' carriage was thrust open abruptly. A middle-aged woman stood in the doorway staring in at them. She had a flat, pale face, free of make-up and shoulder-length hair so dry and frizzy in appearance it seemed each strand was in shocked flight from her scalp.

'There must be some mistake,' the woman said tightly, fixing them with an accusing look as though quite certain that the Wests were to blame. 'I was allocated this carriage. At the ticket office.' Her mouth had a frayed, uneven look, the lips very red as though she had been sucking on something of a particularly staining nature.

'Oh dear,' Marion said, starting guiltily. 'I'm terribly sorry.' She stood up hurriedly. A tall woman, but one who carried her height without conviction.

'Are you *sure*?' Vanessa asked sceptically. 'I was certain these were our seats.'

'Of course.' The woman thrust out her ticket. 'It says eleven here quite clearly. That is the number of this carriage. I was allocated it when I made the booking. I must have a carriage to myself. I made that very clear when I made the booking.' She spoke slowly, with great precision, as though unused to ordinary conversation.

Vanessa looked at the ticket. 'You're right. I'm really sorry. I'll have to sort this out.' She went out into the corridor of the train and hailed the conductor who took her ticket and disappeared with a frazzled air.

'He's going to find our seats,' Vanessa said. 'It won't take long.'

'Please, sit down,' Marion said to the stranger. 'I'm so sorry about this.'

Although she appeared somewhat mollified, the woman hesitated for a second before perching on the bench, keeping a fastidious distance from the Wests' luggage lying heaped on the floor.

'Are you going far?' Marion asked politely. 'We're going to Ashagiri. The train doesn't go all the way there of course. We'll have to take a car or something at the other end. Where are you heading for?'

'Ashagiri also,' the woman admitted, a touch unwillingly.

Marion was delighted. 'What a coincidence! We can travel together perhaps.'

'I have much work to do. I'm not travelling for . . . pleasure.'

'Oh,' Marion said, a little cast down by the other's tone.

'What work are you doing?'

'Research. My own research. I am preparing material for a book. That is why I need quiet. I have simple tastes, but I must have quiet.'

She was obviously one of those people who imagined that everyone took as much interest in her likes and dislikes as she did, thought Vanessa, casting an expert eye over the woman. Her sweater looked hand-knitted and her boots clearly expensive. So much for simple tastes, Vanessa thought scornfully.

'I am a hard-working person,' the woman insisted.

Marion smiled hesitantly, unsure quite how to respond to such an assertion.

'Well . . . it's nice to meet you. Perhaps we should introduce ourselves properly. I'm Marion West and this is my daughter –' She broke off.

The woman was shaking her head, holding one hand up in protest.

'Please, no introductions. It is a policy of mine. When I'm travelling, I do not take names or give my own. Otherwise . . . there is an obligation. An obligation is created. In the past I have found myself receiving letters and even phone calls when I return home from people wishing to continue their acquaintance. It has been very awkward. The contacts I form as I travel are transitory. That is their nature.'

'They're just a bunch of tourists, in other words,' Vanessa said, unable to keep the sarcasm out of her voice.

The woman stared at her as though forming a judgement, which, although made in an instant, was set for ever. Her eyes flickered away.

The conductor appeared in the doorway. 'Next one,' he said, banging on the door of the neighbouring carriage. 'Empty.'

The woman sat back in her seat with a relieved air as Marion and Vanessa scrambled to collect their luggage.

'What a self-important old bag,' Vanessa said once they were installed in their new carriage. 'She must have seen you were tired and she still made us shift all our stuff.'

'Keep your voice down. She might be able to hear.'

•

But the woman could hear nothing but the sound of the train. There was something soothing in the endless, rhythmic beat of wheels against track and she focused on the noise, allowing her clenched fists to unfold themselves gradually on her lap. For most of her life, she had held the sense – never openly acknowledged, even to herself – that everything she did or thought or attempted was somehow not as important as the thoughts and actions of other people. She had no real evidence for this suspicion and no explanation for it either, but it was as though she had been born carrying no weight. She cast no shadow, left no footprints behind to mark where she had been and, for this reason, the relatively small matter of claiming one's assigned seat on a train assumed a vital importance in her mind.

What a lot of questions the two women had asked her! It came as no surprise. It did not surprise her that others should be so interested in her every move. But it had been annoying all the same. She closed her eyes and listened to the sound of the train, thinking of her neatly packed bags full of her note-books and specimen jars. A new start, she thought. A new life. She had earned it. Nobody knew that better than her.

Ashagiri was to be her starting off point, the logical place to begin. A known place. It had been a long, unpleasant journey, but distance was an irrelevance. There was power in return. One knew the path to take. Despite all the aggravating details of organization, the sheer friction of travel, return was a simple thing at heart. As simple as opening the back door of her mother's house and walking again down the path to the hydrangea bush at the far end where Nesbitt lay muffled by earth.

How many times had she taken that small journey? A hundred, maybe more. On winter evenings mostly. Times when the night, darkening the heels of afternoon, truncates the day, dispatching it like an ill-formed thing, born with too much haste. It took only a moment or two to reach the bush where she would stand for a while before retracing her steps back to the house. Sometimes, if the ground was not too wet, she might kneel down and put her ear to the earth as if to listen. The first time she had done this, there was a reason for the action. Repeating it later served no purpose other than a certain humorous satisfaction which was as close as she ever came to irony.

She had dug the hole first, anticipating struggle, an amount of mess. But she should have known Nesbitt would offer no resistance. He reminded her of nothing so much as a joint of pork. The same pallid beige colour, the same trussed appearance in his small harness, worn in place of a collar since he had no neck. Nesbitt wheezed even when he was quite still. He was incapable of vertical movement. She must lift him on to her mother's lap. 'Bring me Nesbitt, I want Nesbitt,' her mother called a dozen times a day. And she was obliged to follow him as he waddled away, nails scratching frantically against the wooden floor – kept free of rugs to allow unobstructed travel for her mother's wheelchair – his legs sliding out from under him. He never came at her call. His black bug-eyes almost burst their sockets in reproach at her very presence.

'My itty Nes-bitty,' her mother said, scratching at the folds of his flesh with her one good hand. 'My fat Puglet.'

You couldn't call Nesbitt a *dog*. You couldn't call him anything at all.

The decision to deal with him had not come in a single moment. It was rather more like a chore she had been meaning to do for some time. A tidying up. Then, one evening, for no particular reason, the time came. She had lifted him on to the kitchen table and thrown a towel over him while she decided on the best approach. He stood for a moment or two underneath his cover and then sat down abruptly without complaint. Nesbitt's instincts were always towards the horizontal, no matter what the circumstances. It was only by accident – or cosmic prank – that he had been born a dog. His soul was that of a cushion. Needlepoint, she thought. Overstuffed, with ugly tassels on the corners.

She picked up the bundle and went outside, still undecided. One of Nesbitt's legs came free and kicked against her. She paused to wrap him more tightly, tucking in the edges of the towel so that all further movement was impossible. She could hear him wheezing through the fabric, the sound muffled, very rapid. It was dark outside. Wet leaves on the path. She had dug the hole already. She had not planned her next move, but now it came to her. It was simply a matter of relocation.

A brief sense of warmth against her chest removed. A placing in. As she made the transfer she thought she saw the bundle squirm a fraction, but this might have only been her imagination. She squatted on her heels and reached for the wet handle of the trowel. He was wheezing still. She could hear him as she filled in the earth. His wheezing and her own breath. The two sounds seeming connected. One fading as the other – fuelled by physical exertion – grew. She put down the trowel and patted the earth flat with her bare hands. Not to conceal, but rather to mark the ground.

She needed to be sure of finding the exact place again.

Yes, return was a simple matter, if preparation had been made and landmarks placed.

She brought her hand up to her mouth and began tearing at the nail of her index finger. Within a few seconds she had bitten off a satisfyingly large scrap. She retrieved it from between her teeth and fished for the small, enamelled box kept in the pocket of her jacket. She opened the lid carefully and placed the nail inside with all the others.

The train journey would take all night. The Wests lay in their berths and stared up at the light that swayed to and fro above their heads and at the small blue sparks of electricity crackling and shooting out about the mess of wiring on the ceiling. Outside, the dark lapped against the windows of the train like a warm, black sea. Every few hours the train stopped and doors banged and voices were heard on quiet platforms where dim lights glimmered like fluorescent fish. The stations with no names advanced and fell away again as the train rattled onwards. There was nothing to do but think. For a long time, Vanessa's mind revolved around practicalities, at the necessity of holding everything together. It had not been the best of beginnings.

She had been unkind to her mother, she thought remorsefully. She had let irritation overcome her. What was the point of bringing Marion here if all she was going to do was nag at her? Instead of mocking her handbag she should have been thinking about what they would eat during the train ride. The biscuits were already gone, despite their extreme dryness, their faint flavour of street disinfectant. She should have brought a supply of Power Bars, but her mother had already packed too much. She had had to pare everything down to a minimum. Their lack of food made her think of the child beggars again. How she had leaned forward to stare at them and then how one of them – as though aware of her scrutiny – had suddenly stilled himself and looked up at her with a gaze as direct and curious as her own. It had lasted only a second, this mutual inspection, but there seemed to Vanessa to be something profound about it. As though she and this child had formed a kind of alliance. It reminded her suddenly of the episode with the Christmas boy. She had not thought about it for years.

Seven-year-old Vanessa had only made friends with Karen Christmas because of her name. 'What if your mum had called you Mary?' she asked her. Karen stood under the almond tree in the school playground in a strange, old-fashioned-looking frock and smiled at Vanessa without answering. She had large, babyish blue eyes in which full comprehension seemed always just about to dawn and a brother called Theodore whom her parents kept shut upstairs in a bedroom.

'Not all the time,' she said, 'just when people come over.'

'But why? Is he dangerous?'

'I don't think so,' said Karen, sounding unsure.

'I bet he is,' Vanessa said with confidence. She imagined Theodore Christmas, half feral, alone in his room, gnawing at the skirting boards. 'I bet he'd attack someone if they let him out.'

'I don't think so,' Karen said again. She smiled. 'Do you want to come to my party?'

'Can I see Theodore?' Vanessa asked hopefully. But on the day of the party, although she and the other guests – more than twenty girls her own age – had free range of most of Karen's house, Theodore's room was off limits.

Vanessa's disappointment at being denied the opportunity to stare at this mythical child was soon overcome by the fact that Karen's party was the best she had ever been to. She had not had very high expectations of the event, imagining it would be the usual restrained affair of pass the parcel and musical statues in which all the guests won prizes even if they happened to land on one leg when the music stopped and ended up toppling over, when she, Vanessa, was still standing

20

in plain sight, as still as a stone, rigid with effort and the desire to win. 'But you've already won three prizes,' the parents said when she protested the unfairness of it. 'Give someone else a chance.' And they would look at her in a way which Vanessa was beginning to recognize. With the unmistakable dislike that adults felt towards certain children.

Karen's party was not like this at all. There was a wildness to it. Nobody seemed to care how many crisps, Kit Kat fingers or banana sandwiches the guests ate or when. Nobody told them to stop yelling or minded when they popped the balloons or presented them with trays of dull objects on the pretext of playing a fun memory game. But the best thing about the party, in Vanessa's opinion, was the String Race. Everyone had to run around collecting pieces of string which had been cut to different lengths and hidden around the house. After the time was up, everyone sat down, tied their pieces together and whoever had the longest length was the winner. They all stood out on the lawn while Karen's father made everyone stretch out their lengths so he could measure them with his steel tape. How meagre some looked! Vanessa's stretched almost to the rose bushes at the bottom of the garden. She thought she had won. She *would* have won except that another girl's string was five centimetres longer. If only she had tied the knots more carefully, she thought enviously.

At Karen's next party, a year later, Vanessa wanted very much to do two things. To win the String Race and to catch a glimpse of Theodore Christmas. But, at first, it seemed as though one of these goals could only come at the expense of the other. She thought the only chance of entering the forbidden room would come during the game, when everyone was scattered about the house. But if she did so, she wouldn't have time to collect enough string to win. When the time came to decide, she hovered uncertainly at the foot of the stairs, torn between competitive keenness and desperate curiosity. The thought that she was about to do something which wasn't allowed also gave her pause. Karen's father had told everyone at the start of the game that there were no pieces of string upstairs. He had said this with great emphasis. But maybe, she told herself, maybe he had *forgotten* hiding a few pieces. Maybe he had dropped one or two on his way downstairs. The more she thought about it, the more plausible this seemed.

She ran up the stairs and along the landing. Theodore's room had a handwritten sign taped to the door. DO NOT ENTER, it said. Vanessa stopped, trembling with excitement and fear at the power of her own daring. She put an ear up to the door, listening for growling. If she heard growling, she decided, she would run away. But there was silence. Not even a grunt. She put her hand on the door knob and turned it quietly. One small look, she thought. She wouldn't need to move anything more than her head around the door. That way she wouldn't even be doing anything bad, since the sign said DO NOT ENTER. Did it count if only your head entered? Vanessa didn't think so. She thought what it probably meant was if your feet went inside. Or at least more than half your body. Otherwise you were just looking and, after all, the sign didn't say anything about not *looking*.

But when she opened the door and peered inside, what she saw made her forget all about these subtle distinctions. The first thing she thought was that the room didn't look anything like a cage, but just like an ordinary bedroom. An ordinary desk and chair, ordinary carpet and ordinary bed, on which a most extraordinary-looking boy was sitting and calmly staring at her. Vanessa closed the door behind her and stared straight back at him.

Theodore Christmas was small. So small that his feet dangled over the edge of the bed without touching the ground.

He was wearing a pair of tiny black patent-leather shoes and a tank top with a diamond pattern on the chest. His dark, glossy hair was cut in a bowl around his face, as smooth and solid as the hair on a Lego man. His hands were twin bowls on his lap; the fingers cupped as though to hold something, transfixed with calm and secret portent. But it was the boy's eyes that drew immediate attention. Theodore Christmas had eyes the size and shape of ping-pong balls. Vast and protuberant and unblinking, they dwarfed his other features, made a mockery of his nose and his red, infant's mouth. When people saw the boy, they always looked away immediately, shocked by the sight of those great bulging orbs. They no more looked for meaning there than they might look for expression in the headlights of a car. Instead, they found themselves blinking, rapidly, helplessly, as though to reassure themselves that their own eyes were still nestled firmly in their sockets. But Vanessa didn't blink. She looked into Theodore's eyes and saw there a curiosity as great as her own.

'How come you're not at the party?' she said abruptly. Theodore's hands curled a fraction but he said nothing.

'You're wearing party shoes,' Vanessa said. 'How come you're wearing party shoes if you can't go to the party?'

The boy turned his peculiar gaze downwards and regarded his dapper footgear as though seeing it for the first time. Vanessa watched him, wondering what to say next. She wanted to ask him why he had such big eyes and whether he could see better with them than other people but she hesitated, aware suddenly of the silence of the room and the injustice of the closed door. Faint sounds from the party below reached her. Running feet and distant laughter. She wondered how long the boy had been sitting there, listening, with his great big eyes fixed on nothing in particular and his party shoes swinging and swinging.

'I bet you wouldn't like it anyway,' she said at last. 'It's only girls. There aren't any boys there, you know.'

Theodore Christmas turned his gaze back at her. Even from the other side of the room she could clearly see her own reflection in each bulbous disc.

'Lots of string,' the boy said suddenly.

Vanessa looked down at her hand still clutching the few scraps she had managed to find before her foray upstairs. 'Not enough. It doesn't matter.'

Theodore shook his head. 'Lots and lots!' He pointed to the desk in the corner of the room where a large ball of string and a pair of scissors lay, overlooked by Vanessa in the surprise of meeting Theodore. This must have been the place his father had cut up the pieces in readiness for the game. Her eyes widened. Theodore's tiny fingers made a scissoring motion in the air.

'Cut it,' he ordered. 'Cut up lots and lots of string!'

And she had. Cunningly slicing it into different lengths so that nobody would be able to tell the difference between it and the pieces hidden downstairs. She must have won the game, although the moment of victory was forgotten. What she remembered now was only the joy of cutting those illegal scraps, intent on her task, with Theodore Christmas watching her, his fingers scissoring the air with each snip of the blades.

Remembering the episode brought a rush of self-criticism. Didn't she always end up allying herself with misfits of one sort or another? It had never occurred to Vanessa to think of her former boyfriends in this way, but now she imagined there was a pattern to her relationships. A reason for their failure. Peculiar, all of them, she thought. Except that unlike poor Theodore, they carried their oddities hidden. As the train lurched and rattled through the night, Vanessa ran through the list in her mind.

There was Alan who she had met at college. Funny, clever Alan who, a year into their relationship and while he was in the process of giving her a back massage one afternoon, told her he couldn't decide whether he was gay or simply one of those people who didn't like sex very much. The announcement coming out quite conversationally, his hands still busy kneading her shoulders. As though he expected her to go on lying there until he had arrived at some conclusion.

Then there was Pot-Holing Mark. A man who never felt more alive than when he was six feet underground. She could still hear his voice, reverberating off the dank walls of the limestone cave, which, in a moment of bravado, she had been persuaded to crawl into during a doomed weekend in Yorkshire. They had entered the cave through a horrifically small hole by the side of a stream, a manoeuvre made doubly tricky owing to the three bulky jumpers she wore due to Mark's theory that wet wool trapped body heat. Inside it was pitch dark and the air smelled quite dead. She had to stop for a moment or two to fight a surge of panic.

'Keep going, Vanessa!' came Mark's voice from the depths. *'Where's your bottle?'*

It wasn't so much the lack of sympathy in his words that had struck the death blow to the relationship. It was the terrifying cheerfulness of his voice. Almost demented, she had thought.

And then there was Michael who she had lived with until six months ago. She wondered whether there was anything worse than to fall out of love. That long, inexorable descent into certainty, slowed by all the small handholds of hope; the narrow, precarious ledges where love had been able to perch for a while and tell itself that everything was as it had always been.

The real trouble with Michael was that he was all passion without any courage. It was a dreadful combination. He was always on fire with one thing or another. A business scheme, a plan to go back to college, a trip to South America to save some apparently endangered species of sloth. And none of it ever happened. All the resolve and enthusiasm undone sooner or later by some profound failure of conviction that ran through him like a faultline. But he didn't seem to know this. Instead, he blamed others for his disappointments. Vanessa wasn't sure which was more depressing; listening to Michael talk about all the things he wanted to do – *intended* to do – or hearing him start blaming everyone and everything that was supposedly preventing him from his goals. But it had been hard to give up on him, to include herself and their relationship among all the half-baked efforts that defined his life.

Odd, how once the decision had been made, how he seemed to lose substantiality. Those last few times she had held him had been like holding something without solidity, nothing more than a shape, the simple outline of a person. And all the will gone out of him too. 'How can you be so ruthless?' he said. The words more a statement than a question. No protest or fight. He turned his wet face against her neck, like a sorrowful child. 'How can you be so . . . ruthless?'

Vanessa looked into the dark window of the train and saw her reflection. Yellowed by the weak light, expressionless, like the face of an outsider, looking in on herself. Perhaps it was true, she thought. Perhaps she *was* ruthless. More like Terry Pryce than she wanted to admit.

'What the fuck do you think you're doing?' he'd half screamed at her, bow tie jerking in outrage, when she told him she was taking this trip. She hated that bow tie of his. Alpha-male red, the badge of a bully who fancied it gave him the air of a maverick.

'You can't go,' he said. 'We've got the Lever account next month.'

She said nothing, knowing from long experience that silence was the best way of dealing with the chairman's rages.

'You can't go,' he repeated.

'It's all booked up.'

He leaned closer towards her. 'You know your job won't be waiting for you when you decide to come back, don't you?'

She nodded. She had always been one of his favourites, one of the few people who treated him without deference or fear. Others were not so fortunate. The company was rich with anecdotes about Terry's relish for reducing employees to frightened children. Through the thin walls of the office she would hear him talking. The words muffled and indistinct. Only his tone coming through. An angry *'bar bar bar'* noise punched out almost without interruption. It didn't matter what he was actually saying. The tone was enough.

Vanessa had always been a little flattered to escape such

treatment, but recently she had found dissatisfaction creeping over her. To be valued by one's ability to stand up to a petty tyrant seemed a somewhat pointless measure of success. She looked at him with new dislike.

'India of all places,' he said. 'Jesus. I didn't put you down as someone who needed to find themselves. I thought all that hippie crap went out decades ago.'

'I'm not going to find myself, Terry. I'm taking my mother on a trip. That's all.'

He shrugged and she wondered why she suddenly cared so little about displeasing him. And why her work, which she had always convinced herself was satisfying and purposeful, had begun to inspire a new feeling. A strange kind of fear, elusive and sourceless, that caught her only at solitary moments. As it did now, in the quiet of a night train, moving through a strange country, with only her own face as witness. It was the fear that what she worked at, day after day, was an empty thing. And running below this fear, a deeper one: that she too was empty. A hollow person, without core.

If Michael was all passion and no courage, wasn't the reverse true of her? For all her boldness, her energy, her ability to get things done when she wanted, in the way she wanted, didn't she nevertheless lack something fundamental? A lasting passion for a person, a place, a cause.

The irony of it, thought Vanessa, was that she had done everything she was meant to do; college and then a succession of carefully chosen jobs that had positioned her securely on an upward career trajectory. She had never allowed herself a moment of indecision, unlike many of her friends who had spent their early twenties working on never-to-be finished dissertations or stuck in menial jobs while they tried to fathom out what to do next.

She had always felt a little sorry for these people but then, mysteriously and seemingly overnight, they all seemed to have found what it was they had been looking for. Gathering husbands and jobs in television or the law. Illustrating children's books for a living, or disappearing to Sudan to work with civil-war victims, or starting families. It was not their achievements that Vanessa envied, but their apparent conviction. It was as if they had all been through some process – passed some kind of test – that she had quite missed.

Vanessa looked at herself – at her wide-set eyes, the strong, authoritative lines of her nose and mouth – and she wondered suddenly whether other people ever saw, as she did now, the face of someone secretly empty, the face of a fraud.

'Tell me again about Ashagiri,' she said.

Marion didn't respond. She was stretched out on her bunk with her eyes closed. The only movement about her person, the rhythmic amber swell of what remained in the bottle of whisky that was resting on her stomach. Her handbag had slipped down on to the floor of the carriage. She would reach for it the instant she awoke, thought Vanessa. She would find it gone and there would be a flicker of panic before she located it again. Sometimes it seemed her mother only believed in the existence of something as long as she could see or touch it.

'Are you awake?' she said loudly.

Marion shifted and opened her eyes.

'Tell me about Ashagiri,' repeated Vanessa.

'I've told you everything. I've told you hundreds of times.'

'I know you have.'

Marion was silent for a moment. 'Then you know what the best thing about it was,' she said. 'The best thing about Ashagiri was that it was so far from home. I wasn't *unhappy* at home, but I was overlooked. Three brothers to compete with. And I think my parents . . . favoured them. I don't think they meant to, they just couldn't help it. The boys were so good at sports. It was the sort of thing my parents admired.'

It was perhaps the reason why she only had one child herself, thought Marion. She hadn't realized until she held her for the first time how much she had wanted a girl. Such a white little thing, with those pale eyes, looking nothing like Pete who was dark, nor herself, with her big bones and thick, unmanageable hair. She had endured the burdensome countdown of pregnancy, the agony of labour, all thought consumed in the blind, wet workings of her own body and yet, when she held her daughter, she found herself wondering – with a sense of almost unendurable marvel – quite where the baby had come from. It had been weeks before she had been able to call the child by her given name. The idea had seemed a little preposterous. Like naming the wind.

'It must have been hard for my parents to send us all away for most of the year, but they didn't have much choice. The local cemetery was full of the graves of children who had died from malaria. Ashagiri was high up and cool. The sky was always blue there and the air so clean you could smell the trees growing on the hill above my school. And, of course, there were the mountains.' Marion paused. 'It's hard for me to tell you what the mountains were like. They were bigger than you could possibly imagine, and they stretched further than you could ever see. But there was something else too. Even though they were so impossibly grand, they gave you the feeling, I don't quite know how, that they . . . belonged to you. As if you were the first and the last person to have ever seen them. We did a lot of walking. Around and about the upper part of the town. That was where all the schools were. The Indians all lived further down. We weren't allowed in the market or the streets further down. We had to walk in a long line, single file. A crocodile. My father came to visit once and saw us walking around like that and he laughed. He said he liked the way we looked. He liked order. I think that's why he was a tea planter. There's nothing more ordered than a well-kept tea plantation. The bushes look like little green sheep all grazing tidily together.'

As she spoke, Marion looked at her daughter. Vanessa lay with her head to one side. One finger plucking at a crack in the plastic covering of the bunk, making a tiny scratching noise as she listened. Always restless, thought Marion. Such a voracious little girl and now, at twenty-eight, still the same way. At her age, she had already been married for seven years. She wondered again exactly what it was that had caused her daughter to give up her job so abruptly and devote so much energy and expense to this trip. Perhaps some problem at work. Marion would never have dared to ask her daughter outright. 'You *still* don't really know what I do,' she would say. 'I don't know why I bother explaining it to you. Go on, admit it, you haven't got a clue.'

She had never worked. These days, you were meant to add 'outside the home' to that phrase, as though those three words could convince you that you counted for something. The truth was that the large house and garden that she had made beautiful had never been her home. She had believed it was, but she knew better now. She had never worked either outside or inside the home in the true sense of the word. Marion wasn't sure there was a neat phrase to describe exactly what she had been doing all these years.

She thought of the garden. Herself kneeling by the bed of nasturtiums in the late spring of last year, with a paper towel in one hand, wiping the underside of the leaves free of the tiny black insects that gathered there and, if left alone, would destroy the plants. You couldn't use ordinary insect sprays on nasturtiums. You had to clear infestations by hand. Pete sat in the Adirondack chair a few yards away. Since the sentence of death, passed on him six weeks before, he had done little but sit. Before, during times of crisis or grief, he had always managed to divert himself with activity, finding through busyness a way to avoid talking about anything unpleasant. But now, seeing ludicrously little point in improving his golf game or researching the pros and cons of sprinkler systems for the lawn and having long ago lost the habit of sharing his thoughts, Pete had become almost entirely inert.

As she worked, Marion watched him out of the corner of her eye. She was thinking – with a kind of distant, numbed wonder – of the forces at work within him, despite his outward immobility. The drive and bustle of his cancer. The sheer energy of it. He would never see the flowers she was taking such care to protect, but still she worked, scraping at the insect eggs on each leaf with the concentrated tenderness of someone who does not know what else to do with themselves.

'There's something I have to tell you,' Pete said. Just like that. With no other preamble. Out of his silence on a spring afternoon. The affair, he said, had been over decades ago. He had not even thought about it for years. But now . . . his voice trembled a fraction. She had not raised her head from the bed of nasturtiums.

'When?' she asked.

'A long time ago,' he said again. Just after Vanessa's birth. 'In that difficult year. Do you remember how difficult things were?' He paused. 'I wanted you to understand.'

Marion wasn't sure whether he was referring to that time or asking for understanding now, at this late stage, with everything almost over and done. She had not heard this pleading in his voice for years, not since before they were married and he still unsure of her. He looked younger too, his face turned up to her, a young man's face, despite the thickening pull of middle-age. Full of a kind of hopeless faith. That she could, with everything almost over and done, still somehow save him. Turning back time for him with her absolution.

'Yes,' she said, 'I do understand.' She stood by his chair and held his head close to her, pulling him in against her waist. 'Don't worry. You mustn't worry.'

His head stilled as she touched him. 'I just wanted you to understand,' he said again. Calmly, almost happily.

'I do,' she mouthed, 'I do.' It seemed to be enough.

He did not speak of the matter again. Dying, without further discussion, a month later.

In the short space between his confession and his dying there had been no room for further questions. He must have known it would be this way. Choosing to unburden himself when there could be no chance of anything other than acceptance. You could hardly accuse a dying person of being selfish, she thought. The accusation seemed absurd in the face of the far greater selfishness of death itself. He had died mistaking her pity for true forgiveness but what did that matter to him? He wanted solace. He did not care where or how it came.

Alone, she wept for herself and for her mocked life. It was not so much the fact of his affair, but the timing of it. That year – the year she became a mother – had been one of the happiest of her whole existence. An ordinary sort of happiness, she supposed, the sort most people might reasonably expect. Nothing dramatic or different about it. But it was the year she measured all others against. And now Pete had taken it from her. She would never, ever, think cleanly of that time again. Each memory now contaminated by doubt, rotten with self ridicule. She had always thought the past was fixed inside a person, but now she saw that she had never owned it, could never trust her memory again. Someone had been able – so quickly, so easily – to take her past and tell her, no, it had not been like that at all. Not at all. And where did that leave all that happiness she had felt? wondered Marion.

As she spoke of the mountains, of butterfly hunts under blue skies, the orchid-clambered trees, of monkeys and pony rides and the sweet, dusty scent of marigolds, of herself in a navy gymslip sitting on the top of Dreaming Rock, on the brink of everything to come, Marion knew that her memories were like drawings in a book. Outlined and re-outlined a hundred times, until the original shapes had become obscured, mere approximations of what they used to be. Over fifty years had passed. Surely everything would have changed.

But Ashagiri was still a real place. She had seen it on a map. Not one of the old maps her father had kept for years, framed on the wall until his death, lined in territorial red with the configurations of a pre-independent India, the old boundaries of his world. But a new map, bought by Vanessa only a month before. The place was too small to merit even a dot on this map, but the word was there, tiny, italicized, surrounded by the markings of mountains. *Ashagiri*.

Hope rose in her again. The train was taking them nearer. From the tangle and dirt of Calcutta, across the plains, through all the small, mysterious towns where unknown people lived their unaccountable lives, it was taking them.

'I SAID, YOU'RE DRIVING TOO FAST! SLOW DOWN!'
Vanessa shrieked at the jeep driver, wondering if he could hear her over the death rattle of the vehicle's engine. To the perils of the road, narrow, precipitous and scattered with rocks from recent landslides, was added the driver's jaunty bandanna, which he wore, Kamikaze pilot-style, low across his forehead, virtually covering his eyes. Blind as well as deaf, thought Vanessa bitterly. The driver took one hand off the wheel and fiddled with the radio, settling at last on a demented rap consisting of eight words repeated over and over to a sanity shaking beat. *North! South! East! West! Ind-i-a is the Best!* The driver turned up the volume and grinned hugely at Vanessa. 'No worries,' he yelled. 'No worries!'

Behind her, Marion bounced and lurched in silence. She was concentrating very hard on blocking out all the racket. She listened instead for another sound, one that came from outside. At the bottom of the hill, where the road started, the sound had been easier to detect. Their route had wound through dense forest, splintered by sunlight, out of which came a low, urgent humming that seemed to spring from somewhere deep within the trees or far beneath the ground. But as they climbed higher and left the jungle behind, the sound altered, became quieter. Its tone changed too. No longer a humming noise, thought Marion, but a kind of *tingling*. More felt than actually perceived. A keen, pulling note like the sound a magnet might make if one could only hear it. It is Ashagiri, she thought, and she rolled down her window to hear it better.

The weather had changed. A mist had rolled in. Tentative and straggling at first, coiling in thin wisps about the ferns on the side of the road. As they climbed, it grew thicker, clotting the branches of the trees, obscuring all view but a short stretch of road immediately ahead. It began to rain.

'Do you *have* to keep the window open?' Vanessa asked.

'I'm listening.'

'I don't see how getting drenched will help.'

The jeep driver fumbled in the breast pocket of his grubby shirt and pulled out a packet of Marlboro.

'On second thought, better keep it open,' Vanessa said. 'Jesus, I don't believe this. Where are the famous mountains anyway?'

She was grumpy from lack of sleep and the effort of negotiating over the price of the jeep ride. 'One hundred rupees,' the driver had told them in the railway station. It was very early in the morning. The only other people she saw getting off the train was a trio of student types with ratty hair and backpacks. Of the disagreeable woman from the compartment next door there was no sign. She must have disembarked and found transport while they were still struggling to gather their belongings.

Vanessa shook her head. 'Twenty-five,' she said firmly. She knew from her guide book that this was an appropriate price.

'One hundred rupees,' repeated the driver. 'Each.'

'I'm sorry,' said Vanessa. 'That's just too much.' She looked at the line of five or six jeeps waiting for passengers. 'I'm sure another driver will take me for twenty-five.'

The youth smiled. There seemed to Vanessa something insolent about it. He shrugged, very casual and indifferent. 'Does anyone want to take me to Ashagiri for twenty-five?' Vanessa said in a loud voice. But the other drivers simply stared at her and shook their heads. She could tell they were in it together.

'Forty rupees!' said a voice from the furthest jeep. 'I go there for forty.' Vanessa hesitated. Her guide book said twenty. It was still twice as much as she should have to pay. Should she suggest thirty? While she was deliberating, the trio of backpackers swept past her. Before she could gather herself to protest, one of them was shaking the driver's hand and the others were bundling into the back of the cheaper jeep. It took off in a swirl of dust.

'One hundred rupees,' repeated the implacable young man in the bandanna. 'Total, two hundred.' Vanessa wondered if he knew how much she hated him. Her mother was no help. She sat on top of their luggage a few feet away with the untroubled air of someone for whom waiting is an end in itself. 'Okay,' Vanessa said furiously. '*Okay*.'

Now the man was smoking. Not that it made much difference, she thought. What with the mist and the diesel fumes from the traffic on the road, he was hardly adding much to the murkiness.

'Was it always this . . . polluted?'

'We'll see the mountains soon,' Marion said. 'This is a good month for the snows. It was always clear at this time of the year . . .' Her voice trailed off.

'Does *any* of it seem familiar?' Vanessa said gently.

'Oh yes,' Marion said. 'I remember the road. It hasn't changed at all.' The statement wasn't strictly true, thought Marion. The road had never stopped changing. In over fifty years, the tarmac had cracked and been patched and re-patched. Sections had fallen away under the pressure of rain-loosened hillsides. Other parts had been shored up in an attempt to second guess the mysteries of gravity. Bends had grown slightly sharper or straightened out infinitesimally, fences that guarded steep drops been demolished, rebuilt and demolished again as accidents occurred with inevitable regularity. Signs were painted and repainted after every monsoon, the grass verges grew, withered, grew again and the thin waterfalls running down the hillsides and across parts of the road followed a slightly different route each year.

There was probably nothing whatsoever left of the road from fifty years ago. Nothing physical. But the most important thing about it, the way it made you feel – excited, vertiginous, half wondering whether you were going to make it to the top at all – *that* hadn't changed.

'My father used to drive me. At the start of the school year. Around about this time. I sat in the back like this. I had a little case. My mother gave it to me. I think it was blue.'

'What did you keep in there?'

'I don't remember. All I remember is that it was blue with hammered tin corners. There were flowers exactly the same blue. Tiny little ones that grew everywhere. We used to pick them and crush them up. You could make glue out of them.'

'I see you had the sort of childhood where you had to make your own fun.'

'It didn't stick much. Just paper. If you were lucky. We used it in our autograph books. We all had autograph books. All the girls.' Marion rummaged in the depths of her shiny handbag. 'I kept mine all these years. I brought it with me. It's in here somewhere . . .'

'Who on earth did you get autographs from?'

'Each other of course. We didn't know anybody famous so we filled our books up with our own names. It was quite an honour to exchange autographs. Especially if you were the first name in somebody's book. We took quite a lot of trouble with the presentation. Choosing little mottoes and decorating the pages.' She thought of the hours she had spent practising her signature. *Marion Temple, Marion Temple.* Slanting the words, adding experimental curls and flourishes. How easy it had seemed, in those days, to find identity. A sense of self in the crossing of a 't'.

'So *that's* what you kept in your blue case. Your autograph book.'

'I expect so,' Marion said vaguely. It was typical of her daughter to want to find a place for everything. Where had she got this quality from? Certainly not from her mother. Perhaps her grandfather. He had a place for everything too. A routine. In the old Ford, driving up this very road, with her in the back and he in the front. Front seats were for adults. That was the rule. The back of his head, the collar of his tweed sports jacket, his eyes in the rear view mirror looking beyond her, at the road behind. Arrival in Ashagiri in the early afternoon. Pulling up in front of Klein's Restaurant in the main square. And then the customary back to school treat. A knickerbocker glory which he watched her eat. Sipping his single cup of milkless tea as she manoeuvred her long spoon and tried not to make a mess with the cream. Then out again to meet the school driver who would take her and her luggage the last half mile up the hill.

Once, she remembered, the school car was there, but no driver. He was late. Her father told her to get in anyway. He put her luggage in the boot himself and shut the door and stood on the pavement waiting for the driver. She remembered his shoes, brown, highly polished and the way he smiled at her. A small, confirming nod of his head and his hand upraised, palm outwards, like a salute. She waved at him through the window, then looked away. The driver had still not come. He was perhaps two or three minutes late, although it seemed longer. She looked back at her father, still standing there. In the space between farewell and actual departure, it seemed to her that his face had taken on a blankness. As though his mind had moved on to other things. Then the driver came running and he was opening the door and getting in and starting up the engine. The car began to move away and she tapped on the glass to get her father's attention. To say goodbye. He looked back at her. She would never forget that look. Almost of bewilderment. As though wondering what she was still doing there.

As though to say, *I've already said goodbye. I've already said that, haven't I?*

The mist grew thicker, enveloping the jeep with swift, apparent purpose. Somewhere to their left, the women could hear the roar of a waterfall. Fine spray, a few degrees cooler than the rain, flew against Marion's exposed arm. On their right, where the hillside fell away, merely an impression of great, precipitous space where the mist brimmed, deep and unobstructed. Somewhere above and ahead of them rose the unseen mountains, things of the imagination still, despite their closeness.

'Fog!' screamed the driver conversationally. 'You like it? Like London!'

Vanessa tried to ignore him. As the morning wore on, the traffic on the road had increased, slowing their progress. Now they came to a standstill at the tail of a dozen or so vehicles, all honking their horns with ostentatious impatience. A convoy of lorries rumbling slowly downhill had encountered a small landslide that narrowed the road to a single lane. There was no space to get around.

'Gridlock,' said Vanessa. 'I don't believe it.' Men rushed up and down and gesticulated at each other and beat on the metal flanks of their stationary vehicles in frustration, as though they were pack beasts that might, by dint of force, be persuaded to move.

'I think we might be here for some time,' Vanessa said. She pulled a folded piece of paper from her waist pouch. 'We might as well use the time to make plans. I've written down a list of the places we ought to try and visit. The places you've mentioned.'

'That's . . . nice of you.'

'First, obviously there's your school. St Margaret's. Now we should be able to go there. I've read that there's still a lot of schools in Ashagiri. People still send their kids there to be educated. The place must have a lot of cachet left over from the Raj. Then there's Klein's. Maybe still functioning as a restaurant of some description. And the Ashagiri Club of course. Might find some evidence of Grandad there. Old ledgers or whatever. And then that place where you were born. The tea plantation. What was it called? Something bizarrely quaint.'

'Sunny Valley.'

'Yes, that's it. Sunny Valley. It's not actually in Ashagiri. About ten miles further down on the other side, according to my map. We'll have to make a day trip of it.'

Marion wasn't listening. She was staring at the scattering of stones across the road. A small landslide only, easily cleared. Although any vehicle passing that spot while it happened might have been in trouble. Such things occurred all the time.

A memory came to her, seemingly unconnected. The chapel at St Margaret's. Light coming in through the large stained-glass window on the north wall as always, but falling in the wrong place. Golden stripes low down, barring the wooden floor, gathering in a luminous haze about the large feet of Sister Catherine on the dais. A different time of day then, not morning, the usual time for their assemblies. A late afternoon light. The school gathered. Nuns at their seats down the left side of the room. The light all wrong. Sister Catherine all wrong too. No evidence of her customary gripping stare, that finger of hers that jabs the air in front of your eyes as she drives home a point. She makes a short announcement in a level voice. Her eyes have closed. She has finished speaking, but she stands there still. They have never seen her like this.

There is the sound of weeping. All faces turned to the front. Except for Sister Maureen, at the end of the row. She has her head down. Something in that stillness that sets her apart. A terrible solitary quality in the line of her shoulders, her hands clasping the sides of her chair. As though, surrounded as she is by sorrow, she grieves alone . . .

'There was an accident,' Marion said suddenly. 'Not long before I left. A girl got killed. She fell down one of the hillsides. I don't think she was meant to be there, in the place she was killed, I mean. We weren't allowed to ramble off by ourselves.'

'Who was she?' Vanessa said with interest. 'Was she a friend of yours?'

'No. I don't remember her name. I'd have remembered if she'd been a friend.'

Marion gripped the seat in front of her. 'I haven't thought about it in years. There was something else. Something to do with Sister Maureen. She left the school soon after. Very abruptly. I always wondered at that.'

'Oh yes, Sister Maureen. Your favourite. I'm hoping we'll pick up some traces of her too.'

'You know, she was one of the few teachers there who actually looked at you. I mean really *looked*. Not many teachers are like that. Most just want to put you through your paces. But Sister Maureen wanted to get to know you. She had this club. The Four O'Clock Club. After ordinary lessons were over for the day, she encouraged our other interests. Writing, painting, acting. She was very keen on the arts, Sister Maureen. Sometimes she took a few of us on walks. Not around the upper part of town – the safe, British part – but further down, where the Indians lived. To the market and the place where they washed our clothes. All the shirts laid out to dry on the grass. Gymslips hanging over the cosmos flowers. I don't think that she was really meant to do it, but the school must have turned a blind eye. She was a good teacher. Girls loved her. She touched us you know.'

'Touched you?'

'Yes. Nobody ever really touched you at school. She must have known how it was, coming from home, missing your family, how hard it was for many of the girls. She did a lot of hugging. Once she kissed me. It was after a play we put on. *Twelfth Night*. Quite an ambitious project even for the Four O'Clock Club. I was Viola. The main part.'

'I didn't know you were good at acting.'

'I don't know that I was *good*,' Marion said. 'But I used to think I wanted to be an actress.'

Vanessa was silent. What had happened to her mother, she wondered, to make her so tentative? Unable to claim even this most distant childhood ambition. She only *thought* she wanted to be an actress. As if the wanting itself had been somehow wrong, a lie. Vanessa did not wish to be like her mother. Thinking about herself going through her mother's life made her feel cramped, panicky. Where had her mother *been*? What had she thought about, been challenged by, achieved? This was not, would never be, the story of her own life. She was certain of it. But with the certainty came a strange, tugging grief. By rejecting her mother's ways, wasn't she also, in some profound way, forsaking her? The struggle made Vanessa peevish. If only her mother was more organized, took control of her life. But she seemed incapable of doing this, even in the smallest way. Vanessa thought of her trip to Harvey Nichols, three months or so after her father had died. Two hundred and forty pounds she had spent on skin-care products for her mother. 'A new regimen,' she had told her, as she explained how to use the toner, the anti-wrinkle night cream, the under-eye gel.

'It looks so . . . complicated,' her mother had said. Her

strategy for achieving good skin, she said, was simply not wearing her glasses when she looked in the mirror. 'Just *try* it,' Vanessa pleaded. Marion said that she would, but when Vanessa looked in her bathroom a week or so later, the products looked barely touched, apart from a crusty edge on the spout of the moisturizer.

•

The trip to Ashagiri had been Vanessa's idea of course. They were sitting together out on the lawn. It had not been mown for a while and looked deep and very green. All the time she was speaking, Vanessa could see her mother's eyes flickering over the grass in a distracted fashion. She was trying to spot four-leaf clovers. Vanessa wanted to shake her.

'What do you think?' she asked. 'Do you want to do it?'

But her mother seemed unwilling to give a direct answer. Instead she started rambling about going to the seaside when Vanessa had been a child.

'We always knew the way to the beach. It was easy getting there. But we seemed to get muddled on the way back. It only took an hour in the car going, but coming back could take twice that, because we ended up going the wrong way and had to backtrack . . . Your father got so impatient. I was meant to navigate. I didn't do a very good job of it I'm afraid.'

'What has this got to do with Ashagiri?'

'Everything looked different on the way back. The turnings we were meant to take. Everything back to front. I just thought . . .'

'What?'

'That a person's life might be a little bit like that. Easy to get lost on the way back you know.'

'We won't get *lost*, mother! How can we get lost? Not if we plan ahead of time.'

'I suppose not,' Marion said slowly, sounding unsure.

'You'll see. It's just what you need. To get you away from all of this for a while.'

Marion said nothing. It seemed to her suddenly that she had very little to get away *from*. Since Pete's death, the house had lost whatever it was that made it a house. She moved through it without any sense of being sheltered. There must once have been a reason why she had placed a certain vase on a certain table, or hung a particular painting there, on the wall of the dining room, rather than anywhere else. But she could not recall it now. The house was simply a collection of things and those things, in turn, merely collections of atoms that held their shape and meaning only because physical law dictated that they should. Sitting out here on the lawn, with her back to the house, it was easy for Marion to slip into the idea that it was not even there at all. Vanishing the moment her gaze was turned away. The strange thing was that it was precisely the things she could not see or touch – things that existed only in memory – that now seemed far more solid. If she chose to, she could actually be sitting at her old school desk, tracing the outline of every groove and scrape in the wood. She could walk through the dormitory and find her bed with Bucket, her Steiff teddy bear, lying on the pillow, arms stiffly upraised, arranged that way every morning so that he would be greeting her when she returned. On the trees, magnolia flowers close enough to kiss. Huge, milky things that seemed not to have flowered at all, but simply *landed*.

'Maybe not a getting away at all,' said Marion, half to herself.

'October is the best time to go. Think about it. We could be there in two and a half months.'

Her mother gave her a worried look. 'This doesn't have anything to do with . . . Michael leaving you, does it?'

Vanessa sucked in her breath. 'He didn't leave *me*. I left him. How many times do I have to go through this?'

48

'I know that,' Marion said hastily. 'I just thought, with your father gone and now Michael . . .'

Vanessa looked away, thinking suddenly of her father. For many years he had been only a distant presence in her life, so why had his passing left such a void? She had not thought she would feel this way. Grief had ambushed her, taking her before she had a chance to prepare herself. She saw that death's deepest, most secret pain lay not in what it took, but what it gave: love reborn, come crying into a world of silence.

Her father had made her feel safe because she knew he approved of her. Not that her mother disapproved. Such conditions never occurred to her. But her father had expected certain things from his only child and Vanessa had delivered them. Now that he was gone, who would confirm the rightness of her choices? Who was there left to keep score for her?

'Daddy is not the point of this,' Vanessa said tightly. 'It's a completely different thing. What does it matter anyway, what the reason is?'

Marion looked unconvinced. 'It will be good for you,' Vanessa said with great certitude. 'You'll see.'

And now here they were, on the road to Ashagiri.

'Nearly there!' called the driver cheerfully from under the hood of the jeep. He had taken the opportunity of the traffic jam to inspect his vehicle.

'What on earth is he *doing*?' complained Vanessa. The driver cleared his throat and spat twice, with great force, into the engine. He wiped his mouth on the back of his hand and climbed into the driver's seat once more. 'Half an hour,' he said, 'then we will be arriving.'

'I don't think he can be quite right about that,' said Marion. 'It always took much longer than this to get to Ashagiri. And the mist. It hasn't lifted yet. We must be miles away still.' She leaned back in her seat and closed her eyes. 'I'm going to try and get some sleep,' she said firmly.

'Well, good luck.'

It was raining in earnest now, water pouring across the jeep's windshield in a smooth cascade, barely broken by the spindly actions of the wipers which moved to and fro over the glass, helpless and erratic as the limbs of an injured insect. Vanessa tried to calculate how high they were. Ashagiri lay at eight thousand feet above sea level and already she fancied there was a new thinness to the air. She looked again at her list of things to do once they arrived. They would visit each one of these places and find what they were looking for and her mother would be . . . changed. Restored. Quite how this was to be accomplished, Vanessa was still unsure. But she would do it, she knew that she would do it.

The simplicity of this resolve helped her to avoid thinking too hard about what else might have motivated her to take this trip. It was far easier to tell herself she was doing it solely for her mother.

They turned a corner and entered a small village where ramshackle houses, low and dark, seemed tied together by lines of drenched washing. In between were shop fronts with baskets of small, rounded fruits – limes perhaps – arranged on the uneven pavement. Packets of meagre-looking items, strung on long threads, swung without gaiety from door frames. A blonde, wet puppy, curled on a doorstep, raised its head briefly as they passed. There was no other sign of life.

'What is this place?' asked Vanessa. Before the driver could answer, they were already through the village and continuing to rise. Vanessa twisted around to look at her mother. 'Did you see that place? I don't remember that being on the map. Did it look familiar to you? Are you *sure* this is the right road?'

'*I know it's wet, but please don't fret, we have a way to travel yet,*' Marion said, without opening her eyes.

'Oh god, do we have to start this again?'

'*As we climb, we'll try to rhyme . . .*'

'I'm not in the mood.'

'*. . . it will help to pass the time.*'

'What is it with you and rhyming? We did three whole hours of it on the plane. *British Airways, British Airways, hurry up with those food trays.* Everyone must have thought you were demented.'

'I thought that was rather good,' Marion said in an injured voice. 'Come on, Vanessa, don't be a spoilsport.'

'I'm not. Is it too much to ask to have a normal conversation?' She was interrupted by a sudden lurch forward as the jeep driver accelerated sharply around a blind corner. Vanessa gave a cry and clutched at the dashboard. '*Keep your nerve around the curve!*' burst out the driver.

It was the first time since the start of the trip that Vanessa had heard her mother laugh.

•

A short while later, the jeep began to slow down. They were entering a second town, larger than the first. The mist had lifted a fraction, giving them a view of buildings massed against the hillside; a dark confusion of structures strung with telephone wires. There was something odd about the sight but, at first glance, Vanessa could not put her finger on what it was. An impression of incongruity that was small but obscurely disturbing. The jeep turned into what seemed to be the main street, a steep thoroughfare, muddied by traffic, full of potholes and piles of abandoned grit. They passed a large, sprawling bus station, a post office and a row of shops. Then the facade of some kind of temple with doors painted red and gold. An assortment of disparate looking people thronged the pavement. Men in dark green uniforms with crossed knives in their belts, women in saris, Westerners in woollen Indian jackets, beggars, suited businessmen, an old lady in a green ankle-length Tibetan apron, a gaggle of small boys dressed in the maroon robes of monks, jostling together, their flip-flops slapping the mud. Vanessa's eyes moved over the scene in bewilderment.

The jeep travelled through the crowd, climbing up through a residential area, then more shops and finally arrived at a small square full of cars parked closely together around a central pagoda-like structure sporting a washed out, drooping flag, too limp to reveal its emblem. To the left, a view over the bottom half of the town revealed a straggling arrangement of rooftops. There were clothes laid out on the rooftops; T-shirts and trousers and skirts lying flat to dry, somehow, under the pelting rain. Up the hillside to the right, still indistinct in the mist, the shapes of larger buildings, spread out, surrounded by trees. Everything looked grey. The sky, the rooftops, the drenched washing, the ground itself. The jeep stopped with a grinding, tired sound and the driver turned to Vanessa.

'Two hundred rupees,' he said.

Vanessa stared at him. 'Two hundred,' he said again, impatiently.

'I told you before, I'll pay when we get there.'

The driver opened his door and got out and began rummaging in the trunk of the jeep, removing luggage.

'What are you *doing*?'

'Ashagiri,' said the driver. He lifted Marion's suitcase and dumped it unceremoniously on the ground. Vanessa got out of the jeep.

'This is *it*?' Two dirty grey crows cocked their heads and stared sideways down at her from their perch on a telegraph pole, their strong black beaks wet and very shiny. 'This is *Ashagiri*?' The driver continued to unload their luggage without answering.

Vanessa fought to come up with some rational explanation. 'Are there two towns called Ashagiri?' The suggestion was feeble, and, even as she asked it, she knew the answer. Knew too, the source of the oddity that had nagged at her since they had first entered the town. A detail only, but a telling one. That first view of rooftops. Ramshackle concrete walls, buildings crowded together, an impression of muddle and haste. And there, in the middle of it, high up, something extraordinary. The pale shaft of a church spire. An English church spire which might, without incongruity, have found a place across a view of field and sheltered copse, among the tidy barns and warm brick of Kent or the Cotswolds.

This was Ashagiri. They had arrived.

But still Vanessa protested, more out of habit than conviction. 'Where are the mountains then?' she asked the driver, as though he was personally responsible for their location.

He shrugged, clearly considering the question, and by association, his two female passengers, entirely ridiculous. 'Monsoon late leaving this year,' he said shortly.

'This can't be right,' Vanessa insisted. She turned to her mother. 'How can this be right?' Marion was standing perfectly still beside her suitcase. Her khaki linen jacket riding up her back in ugly creases, the bottoms of her too-wide trousers flapping around her feet. Her eyes were fixed on a point in mid-air, somewhere between the ground and her daughter's face, and she held this gaze as though it was something that might break. She bent slightly and plucked at the handle of her case; an ineffectual motion, lacking in purpose, like a person attempting to obey a command whose meaning has been lost somewhere between order and execution.

'The Ashagiri Club,' she whispered.

Still struggling with disbelief, Vanessa stared past her, up a small incline behind the tangle of cars and jeeps. A building emerged out of the gloom like a great ship with curved Deco prow and long balconied deck. Even from a hundred yards away, she could see it was in a considerable state of disrepair. Its pale green walls paint-chipped, its railings rusty and missing struts. Could this really be the same Ashagiri Club her mother had described to her? The place where her grandparents had stayed when they were visiting the town?

There had always been something of a disconnection in Vanessa's mind between the grandparents of her mother's stories and the two old people she had been taken to visit once or twice a year until her grandmother's death and her grandfather's subsequent removal to a nursing home when

Vanessa was twelve. What she remembered of the visits was largely boredom. The clock on the mantelpiece ticking slowly, her grandparents immobile in their armchairs, the house full of objects Vanessa was not permitted to touch. Days spent there seemed always the same. Drives through the Oxfordshire countryside with her mother and father, visits to dull museums and then back to the house for the ritual of dinner.

Her grandfather at the head of the table, with his monogrammed napkin ring resting in its own silvery reflection on the polished wood, her grandmother serving soup from a large tureen. How carefully she filled each of their plates. Tipping the ladle only a fraction to avoid chipping the good china. And how carefully they were required to drink it, the liquid filling their spoons – tilted at the correct angle away from the body – and then the slow, reverential lift to the mouth, their pursed lips kissing the silver, permitting only the smallest of sips. As a child, Vanessa had always been struck on the one hand, by the elaborate nature of this process, and on the other, by the fact that her grandmother's soups never had anything whatsoever in them. Occasionally a lone carrot slice or strand of onion stirred in the depths of the tureen, but these were leached, accidental items. Some days the soup was yellowish, other days it looked more brown. To Vanessa, it seemed about as much point as coloured water.

It was hard to match this with the image of her grandparents in India. There was a glamour to the Indian years of which Vanessa could find little surviving trace. She might not have believed it at all if she hadn't had photographic evidence. In the old black and white pictures, her grandmother, who was not a grandmother then, but a woman called Charlotte, wore wide brimmed hats and python-skin shoes and an expression of satisfied serenity. Her grandfather in a solar topee stood by the side of his horse, one hand on the saddle in a proprietorial fashion. If there had been darkness in their lives, there was no sign of it in the photographs, nor in the descriptions her mother had given her of hunting parties and tennis tournaments and linen shirts forever white, laundered and pressed by other hands.

Now, looking at the old club, Vanessa was struck by the same sense of unreality that she had experienced as a child. Here, in this very building, her grandparents had dressed for dinner and played billiards or borrowed novels by P.G. Wodehouse and Margery Allingham from the club library. After dinner there might have been dancing or a game of bridge. Her grandparents had been noted bridge players, confusing opponents by the combination of steely strategy on her grandfather's part and her grandmother's feigned air of scattiness. In those days, women worked hard at appearing charmingly hopeless. It was considered feminine . . .

Vanessa pulled herself together with an effort. 'Well, come on,' she said, 'we might as well see if it's still operating.' She grasped the handles of both suitcases and strode towards the entrance leaving her mother still paralysed amid the parked jeeps. For a second or two it appeared as though Marion would continue to stand there, dazed and unaware.

'Come *on*,' cried Vanessa. 'These suitcases are killing me.'

They entered a small, neatly swept courtyard crowded in on all sides by urns of flowers. Dahlias and cosmos, marigolds and tiger lilies and a dozen other flowers Vanessa did not recognize, jostled together in extraordinary profusion. On the far side of the courtyard, a single glass vase had been placed on the ground. An ancient-looking man in baggy trousers was bent over it, perfectly still, scissors in one hand, three or four white lilies in the other. Whether lost in some act of profound contemplation, or merely transfixed by the extremities of age, it was impossible to tell.

But the focal point of the scene, what inescapably drew the eye, was far more strange. An antique machine-gun – souvenir of some long-ago conflict – with a long, brass barrel pointing crazily up to the sky dominated the centre of the courtyard. This was bizarre enough, thought Vanessa, but more bizarre still, the fact that three wooden benches had been placed around this relic, facing in, as though inviting guests to perch awhile and admire it at their leisure. Did anyone ever sit here, she wondered. Did anyone ever wake up and think, it's a fine morning, perhaps I'll just go down and spend an hour or two staring at the gun today?

They crossed the courtyard and entered a portico scattered with fraying wicker chairs. High up on the white-washed walls, heads of long, spiral-horned deer butted the air, glassy eyed and blackened by age. An old red oxygen tank hung from a nail between two closed doors. BILLIARD ROOM said a sign on one and LIBRARY on the other, the hand-painted letters faded and marked with dust. At the end of the portico, an opening into the building gave them a glimpse of a dark interior furnished with the dim outlines of desk and chairs.

A man in an immaculate, dark-green suit was sitting behind the desk. In front of him, an arrangement of documents, a brass concierge bell and a neat plaque; MAJOR DAS, CLUB MANAGER.

'Hello,' Vanessa said, a little uncertainly. The Major looked up at them standing in the doorway. He was in his fifties, with a dark, handsome face set in downward lines. On another such features might have suggested a certain discontent, but on the Major they presented the soulful appearance of a man beset by gentle, yet persistent melancholy. This impression was further enhanced by his eyes which were of a dense, surprising green and which seemed to rest now, not on the faces of

Vanessa and Marion, but on a point slightly to their left. Vanessa felt obscurely disconcerted.

'Is this still . . . the Ashagiri Club?' she said. 'Do you have rooms?'

The Major held his peculiar gaze without blinking. 'Are you club members?'

'Well, no,' Vanessa said, 'of course not.'

The Major shook his head with a small, sorrowful motion. 'We are very busy at this time of year but there may be a room or two available. I would need to check –'

'Thank you.'

'. . . although our accommodation is for the use of club members only.'

Vanessa stared at him. 'So you *don't* have any room?'

'Prices are between six and eight hundred rupees a night, depending on size and location. This includes morning tea. Coal for fires is an additional fifty rupees.'

'Are you saying you do have a room for us? I thought only club members could stay here.'

'That is very true,' agreed the Major.

'So . . . either we can stay here or we can't.'

'There is a third option,' said the Major. His gaze roamed sorrowfully over the women's luggage, rested briefly on his own shoes and then fixed itself again on nothing in particular.

'For only a nominal fee,' he said helpfully, 'you can become club members yourself.'

•

A small, kindly faced man in a Nepalese cap led them up a staircase with heavy oak banisters and a threadbare carpet to the second floor. They followed him down a long balcony, flanked on one side by more than a dozen empty rooms and on the other by a sweeping view of the lower half of the town. The wooden railing of the balcony was splintered and frail looking. A mass of electrical cables trailed from the roof and hung in a knot over a pair of wicker chairs that sat vacant, facing into the mist. Their guide stopped at the end of the balcony, at the very last door. He unlocked it and stepped back.

The room was large with a high ceiling and a musty smell; a curious blend of old paper, damp bed sheets, coal dust and something else – difficult to capture, almost intangible – the lonely scent of spaces where objects used to be. For there was hardly anything in the room at all. It was like a room that had been assembled entirely from memory. Those things that were easy to remember – the two lumpy beds, the dressing table, fireplace and pair of tall wicker armchairs – were all in place. But the small things; the pattern of the wallpaper, the ornaments, the colour of the bedspreads, the lampshades, the hooks for clothes, these were all missing, forgotten and the room looked wrong and incomplete.

Marion sat down heavily on the bed nearest the door and stared at the ground.

'Oh look, there's a skylight,' Vanessa said brightly. She crossed the room and went into the small bathroom. 'Plumbing works!' she said, turning on the taps and flushing the toilet.

'The light's a bit dim, but it's *probably* good enough to read by . . .' She stopped and came and sat down next to her mother on the bed.

'What am I talking about? It's awful.'

Marion patted her hand. 'Don't worry.'

'We don't have to stay here. There must be somewhere else that's better. Tomorrow we can have a proper look around the town. There must be somewhere better to stay.'

'No,' Marion said. She took off her glasses and wiped them on the corner of her jacket and looked around her. 'No, I rather . . . like it. It has character. I think that once we've put all our stuff away and got a good fire going, it may seem quite cosy.'

'Tomorrow it might be better weather. Things might look different in the sunshine.'

'Yes,' Marion said, very gently, still patting her hand. 'I'm sure you're right.'

In the early evening, the two women went downstairs for dinner. The club may have seen better days, but it still had an air of ceremony. The large doors of the dark, oak-panelled dining room were opened wide and the tables spread with white cloths. Glass cabinets lined the walls. Inside there were large silver chafing dishes and sporting trophies won by old squadron leaders. A piano stood, lid down, in one corner. In another, an electric heater burned on one bar. It was chilly. Only two of the tables were set for dinner. The Wests', and another, laid for one.

The man in the Nepalese cap appeared again with a tray. He placed two bowls of soup in front of them with careful, formal gestures. They ate in silence. Around the walls, heads of deer and buffalo stared out blankly. Only the eyes of a small brown bear held any expression. The bear was fixed to the furthermost wall and Marion thought it had a sad, bewildered look. It seemed to follow her movements as if to say, *Who did this to me? How did I get here?* She bent her head to her soup but it was impossible to ignore. *Where is the rest of me?* The bear beseeched. *How can you eat at a time like this?*

The bearer whisked their soup bowls away and replaced them with chicken curry. Marion tasted it cautiously. 'It's actually not bad.'

'Why are you whispering?'

'I don't know.'

There was a sound at the door and a young man came hurrying in. 'Sorry I'm late, Prasad!' he called out to the bearer. 'Got a bit carried away again.' His voice, although confident, held a slight catch like the residue of a once bad stammer. A tiny hesitation that gave his words a curious and inexplicably charming pattern of emphasis.

'I completely lost *track* of the *time*.'

His appearance was different too. Most of the Westerners the two women had seen in India fell into one of two sartorial camps. One was the proud scruffiness of the backpacker, adorned with bits and pieces of Indian garb – a stripy woollen jacket here, a pair of baggy cotton trousers there. The other sort, mostly slightly older, and mostly American, in expensive looking fleeces and hiking boots. But the young man before them in a slightly shabby, but perfectly respectable tweed jacket and dark trousers appeared to belong to neither group. As he walked towards his table Vanessa saw, with some surprise, that he was wearing brogues.

He turned and smiled at them. An ordinary sort of face, in Vanessa's opinion. Pale, very English. You could tell what he must have looked like as a small boy. He probably had exactly the same haircut when he was eight years old, she thought.

'John Walcott,' he said, holding out his hand. 'It's nice to have company round here.'

Marion beamed at him. 'You must sit down with us,' she

said, before Vanessa had a chance to prevent her with a look. 'It's so quiet in here, we were actually whispering.'

'Then you can imagine what it's been like here on my own. Recently I've taken to talking to the bear over there.'

'You too!' Marion patted the seat next to her. 'Come, sit down. You've only missed the soup.'

Vanessa felt a little sour. Did her mother have to be quite so . . . enthusiastic? As if this young man was saving them from a completely joyless evening. It was the most animation Marion had shown in hours, she thought with irritation.

John Walcott hesitated. 'May I?' he asked Vanessa.

'Of course. Why not?' she said, summoning up a smile.

The bearer came with a third plate of curry and busied himself transferring knives and forks to the women's table. 'Have you met Prasad?' John asked. 'He does almost everything around here. Lights the fires, serves the tea, gets all the laundry collected . . . He's from Nepal.'

'So far away,' Marion said, giving Prasad a look of sympathy. He smiled a little shyly and nodded. 'Beer? Three?'

'Yes, beer!' John said. He looked at the two women. 'Do you want beer? Good!'

'What were you carried away by?' Marion asked as they ate. 'When you came in, you said you were carried away.'

'Oh, the usual thing,' he smiled at Vanessa. 'Can't seem to help it I'm afraid.'

His eyes were interesting, she thought. Not so much their colour – an unremarkable blue – but in some quality of his gaze. Unambiguous, almost transparent. The look of a man without expectation of misfortune.

'What is the usual thing?' she asked.

'Painting,' John said simply. 'I'm a painter.' He paused, as though considering whether to admit to anything further. 'Well, specifically, a painter of miniatures,' he added in a rush.

'Miniatures? You mean like portrait miniatures?'

'Yes, well . . . no. The same idea, but not portraits. The opposite actually.' As he spoke, he flushed a little, either from shyness or enthusiasm, or perhaps a combination of the two.

'The opposite?' Vanessa wondered whether the man had caught the same disease that strange Major Das suffered from – the inability to speak in anything other than riddles.

'Yes, the opposite. Not people, but landscapes. Mountains actually. The biggest landscapes of all.'

'You paint miniatures of *mountains*?'

Vanessa and Marion did not know what else to say. 'I have completed five,' John Walcott continued with the uncertain pride of the artist. 'And they can all fit into the breast pocket of my jacket at once.'

'How . . . convenient,' Marion said encouragingly. She wasn't quite sure what the young man was talking about, but she was touched by his earnestness.

Vanessa looked down at John's hands. They were overlarge, with blunt, clumsy-looking fingers. But there was a surprising deftness to them. An extreme delicacy of movement. Yes, she could imagine him being able to paint his pictures with those hands, for all their size . . . Vanessa caught herself. The man was clearly an oddball and she was sick of oddballs.

To think, not so long ago, she had almost accepted an invitation to go out for a drink with Martin Sorenson. The fact that she had even considered it for five minutes marked a new low in her life. She had known Martin since school but he had never been one of her friends. Vanessa wasn't sure he had any friends in the true sense of the word. About him hung the unmistakable air of the eternal hanger-on. This fact did not stop him, however, from publishing a newsletter, *The Doomsday Quarterly*, from his home computer which he faithfully mailed to everyone of his acquaintance. 'All the news you need to know about Me!' ran the line beneath the title. Since nobody was particularly interested in regular bulletins about football games he had attended, his receding hairline and inability to get a date – all written in a religiously self-deprecating manner he clearly considered hilarious but which was quite at odds with the massive egocentricity of the news-letter itself – his literary efforts went largely unread.

Scenting opportunity he had called her two weeks after Michael had moved out. 'I don't suppose you'd fancy a drink or anything,' he said hopefully. Vanessa imagined him standing by the phone, in that awful jacket of his – elasticated at the waist and made of such cheap leather that it might just as well be plastic – and was silenced by dismay.

'Stupid idea,' Martin said in the pause. 'Stupid. Of course not.'

'It isn't stupid,' she said at last. 'It's just not the right time . . .'

'No,' he said hastily. 'No of course it isn't. Typical me, putting my foot in it.'

'I'm sorry,' she said. But the truth was that she had con-sidered accepting his invitation. For just a moment or two. She had even got as far as imagining how he would write up their encounter in the *Quarterly*: '*Regular readers will no doubt be familiar with this author's dismal record with the fairer sex, so imagine my surprise when the lovely Vanessa agreed to accompany yours truly to a nearby watering hole . . .*'

What was it about her, wondered Vanessa, that she attracted such men?

She turned to John. 'But why miniatures?' she said sharply. 'What on earth *for*?'

Marion wondered why her daughter had to be so abrupt. She sounded almost scornful. John would be sure to take offence, she thought. He would not want to sit with them any longer. It occurred to Marion that this was perhaps the reason why her daughter had managed to get to almost thirty without finding a man. They were frightened off by her harshness, her habit of challenging everything.

But John Walcott did not seem in the least bit offended. He leaned forward eagerly.

'I like painting small. Detailed. Most people who like doing that choose small things to paint. Insects perhaps, or flowers, things like that. I thought, what's the point of it? Taking a small thing and painting it small. Where's the challenge? But if you could take a big thing, the biggest thing you could think of and put it on a canvas the size of a matchbox cover . . . that seemed a thing worth trying. Actually I got the idea from looking at stamps.'

Vanessa nodded. She might have known he was a stamp collector.

'Lots of stamps show quite big things. Like buildings. Or animals with trees and jungles behind them. I like those the best. Because you look at them and you can see how far your letter has travelled. You can actually see the place it has come from. All in a space no larger than an inch.'

'Like looking through the other end of a telescope,' Marion said.

'Yes, a bit like that.'

'I still don't see why a small picture is better than a big one,' Vanessa protested.

'Not better,' John said a little anxiously. 'But different. You get a different feeling from it, don't you? If you can carry something around, if you can take it out of your pocket every time you want to look at it, it feels as though it really belongs to you. A kind of . . . secret.'

'I can see why people feel that way about pictures of people, but landscapes?'

'Oh, but they do. Maybe more. Places belong to us in a very personal way. Don't you think?' He paused. 'It's hard. I'm not as good at it as I want to be.'

'Do you sell many pictures?' Vanessa asked.

'Not yet,' he said sadly. 'Exhibiting is a bit of a problem. As you might imagine. My whole collection hardly takes up the space of a shoe box.'

Prasad had cleared the main course and was busy wiping crumbs from the tablecloth.

'It's good to know *someone* has seen mountains around here,' Vanessa said. 'I was beginning to wonder whether they were here at all.'

'They're here all right. But most days, you have to get up early to see them. Six in the morning or so is the best time. It starts getting foggy again around nine.' He paused. 'I could knock on your door tomorrow morning if you like . . .'

'That's okay,' Vanessa said quickly. 'I'm sure we'll manage to wake ourselves up.'

'Dessert!' Prasad said, in the tone of someone explaining what it was he was placing in front of them. They looked down and saw three small wedges of a blancmange-type substance. Marion pushed at it with her spoon, frowning.

'I thought so!' she said suddenly. 'It's Shape!'

'Shape?'

'That's what we used to call it. We had this pudding a lot. At school. I'd forgotten all about it!' Her face was bright.

'Why did you call it that?'

'Look at it. No colour to it at all. Now taste it. Go on, take a bite. It doesn't taste of anything, does it? There's no other way of describing it. It's just . . . Shape.'

Vanessa laughed with a sound so loud and unrestrained that it made Prasad almost stumble and drop his tray. She caught John's eye. He was laughing too, openly and with delight, and, for a second, something passed between them before she turned away.

'Shape!' she cried. 'I know people like that!'

But her good mood only lasted a short while. Back in their room, undressing hurriedly in the dim light, Vanessa's anxiety returned. Ashagiri was not as she had imagined. But what on earth, she asked herself, had she been expecting? To find the same town of her mother's stories? Of course it had changed. It was a real place and time moved on here the same as it did everywhere. Besides, it had probably never been as her mother had described. Time had also taken the Ashagiri of her mother's memories and transformed it. Turned it over and over, smoothing and polishing it, until the whole remembered town could be held in the palm of a hand like a pebble, still wet from the sea.

She should have known this, thought Vanessa furiously. Why had she not known this? For all her planning and looking at maps, there had been a blind spot in her thinking about the place. A kind of childishness. She climbed into bed and laid her head down on the thin pillow. It had a sad, yellowy kind of smell as though it had been years since it had last been warmed by human contact. If she was disappointed by Ashagiri, thought Vanessa, how much more unhappy her mother must be.

She watched as Marion prepared for bed. Arranging her shoes carefully side by side, padding from bathroom to her open suitcase to look for her washbag and nightdress. She removed her wristwatch and bracelet and placed them on the bedside table. Vanessa saw suddenly that she wore no wedding or engagement rings. Her hands looked unfamiliar without them. The soft hands of an old woman. When had she removed the symbols of her marriage? Vanessa had not noticed. Had it been the day of her father's funeral, or sometime later when the fact of no longer being anybody's wife finally became a reality? And had she taken them off with grief, wondered Vanessa, or through some sudden impulse of liberation?

She knew nothing about her mother and her mother knew nothing of her. They were like strangers seated together on an empty train. Her mother loved her but this seemed an automatic thing; conferred at her birth and therefore beyond question. Did love without thought, without *choice*, really count?

What was important, Vanessa decided, was not so much to be loved, but to be loved for the right reasons.

She thought of her childhood visits to her grandparents. Her grandmother standing in the kitchen packing a cardboard box of food for Marion to take back home with her. It was a ritual, this packing of food. Enacted on the last day of each visit. Marion stood and watched her fill up the box with tins of baked beans and tomato soup.

'We don't *need* this,' she said. Almost roughly, Vanessa thought.

Her grandmother wedged a loaf of sliced bread in one corner of the box. 'Take it,' she said. 'We can't use it. I bought too much.'

'We have plenty of food at home. You know that.'

'Take it.'

'Oh, *mother* . . .'

As a child, Vanessa had always felt sorry for her grandmother. She was doing her best. It wasn't her fault that all she had to offer was a tin of condensed milk and half a dozen packets of Strawberry Whip. Why did Marion have to be so ungracious about it? Almost as though she was angry at her mother.

It was only years later that the truth came to her. Her grandmother gave boxes of food because it was what she had always done for Marion. Sending her away at the start of each school term with provisions from home. A cake, some bars of chocolate, two mangoes picked by the gardener that morning. It was a sign of love. And the habit had stayed with her. A remnant of the old nurturing instinct, persistent as a facial tic.

Poor Charlotte. She did not have anything else to give. She never had.

Was this why Marion could never take the gift without argument? Without that look of baffled anger that might have been directed at Charlotte or perhaps at herself for feeling sorry for her mother, when it was Charlotte who was to blame. For not loving her enough. Or not loving her for the right reasons.

'I can't believe you brought a bedjacket,' Vanessa said, staring at the pink towelling garment draped around her mother's shoulders.

'It's chilly in here. I thought I might want to sit up in bed and read.'

Vanessa said nothing. She had to admit that the bedjacket, although bulky and somewhat ridiculous, was useful. In her own way, her mother had thought about conditions on the trip more than she had given her credit for. What other strange but appropriate items lurked in the bottom of that suitcase of hers? Vanessa felt suddenly protective. How vulnerable her mother seemed. For all her careful packing, how ill-prepared for this trip. During the entire day, the much imagined day of their arrival in Ashagiri, she had recognized little but the dessert they had been served for dinner. It hardly seemed worth their journey.

'Tomorrow we'll see the mountains,' she said as Marion settled into bed. 'We'll find stuff. I know we will.'

69

She would make sure of it, thought Vanessa fiercely. She would make this trip a success. It would simply be a little harder than she had anticipated.

But as she lay there in the dark, waiting for sleep to come, her resolve was overtaken by a feeling she had not had in years. Not since she had been a child. A kind of helplessness that was not without comfort. Tomorrow will be different, she told herself. Tomorrow will be different. The night would change things. Holding to this thought as a child does, who still finds mystery in sleep, who still believes that we go somewhere different then and are transformed.

On her first day in Ashagiri, the woman from the train found a room at the Paradise Lodge. It was an aptly named establishment, she thought bitterly, as she sat shivering in bed, blankets draped around her shoulders. Prolonged stay at the place would be enough to dispatch even the hardiest guest to their maker. And she was more sensitive to the cold than most. Years spent at her mother's house, where the heating was always set to the highest point on the dial, no matter what the season, had so conditioned her that the smallest draught or touch of damp could bring on a chest infection. She sucked vigilantly on vitamin C lozenges and resolved to search for better accommodation in the morning.

She could have found something better that day but she had been too busy. At first, the town appeared quite different from how she remembered it. There were many more buildings than before and they obscured the old landmarks, forcing her to circle for a while until she found her bearings. But in a little while she saw that the bones of the place had not changed. They had simply become encrusted by the additions of time; barnacled like a sunken ship. Once she realized this, she found her way easily enough, moving steadily uphill until she had left the town behind, her destination clear in her mind.

It had always been an isolated place, out of bounds to the girls at school. And in the more than five decades since she had stood here last, it seemed that few others had visited the spot. The ground was free of litter, the trees grew thick and dark.

Excitement gripped her. It seemed impossible that she should find everything just as she had left it, but then, who would have moved her handiwork? The rocks had been heavy. She had needed both arms to lift them and some she had been forced to roll, squatting close to the ground, her knee socks slipping towards her ankles and her bare legs covered with mud.

If nobody had moved them, only a landslide could have dislodged those rocks. She walked more quickly to where the trees cleared and the hillside, with treacherous lack of warning, terminated in a cliff edge. And there it was, looking just the same as she remembered: the circle complete, each stone in its allotted place. Even the smaller pebbles she had used to fill in the gaps looked untouched.

She stood for a long time on the edge of the cliff staring at the arrangement, seized by an undetermined, yet piercing sense of vindication. The circle unbroken, unchanged. As she had known all along it must be.

The friendship had begun quite suddenly. It was Sports Day. They were seven years old, or maybe eight. Before this, she had never particularly noticed the other girl, apart from registering that she was the kind of hapless child that others instinctively picked on. Too willing to please, too open to taunt, unable to endure homesickness with the required bravado. Her cheeks flushed, her clothes always a little wrong: lumpy socks that looked hand-knitted, the waistband of her skirt hoisted to a comical point just below her chest. She sat in the back of the room during free periods cutting up pieces of paper and stapling them together carefully to make small booklets. Nobody spoke to her.

She had been put into the four hundred metres simply to make up the numbers since she had never shown any previous aptitude for running. Sports Day was always held at a neighbouring school which had a spacious track. There was a large crowd in attendance: pupils from both schools, teachers and those parents who lived nearby and could make the trip. It was a clear day, not too warm. On the roof of one of the buildings lining the track, a weather vane in the shape of a horse and buggy stood quite motionless. The starting gun cracked and the race began.

From the start, it was the fault of those socks of hers. Hand-knitted with insufficient elastic around the top. Another child might have left them to slide, but there she was, bending to pull them back up again. Letting everyone overtake her. Caught between the desire to keep up and the disastrous impulse to tug at her legs. She ran for twenty yards, stopped, ran on a little further. The others were half-way around the track, going fast. A titter began amongst the crowd.

She was running now quite alone. The others had disappeared from sight. And a cheer suddenly rose. For a moment she must have thought they were cheering for her, thought perhaps she was winning. By some miracle, despite all evidence to the contrary. She ploughed on, socks at half mast, a great smile on her face.

It was the smile that did it. The crowd erupted into laughter, standing up in their seats, waving and pointing to some spot behind her. She glanced up, startled. They were gesturing to her. She looked back down the track. There were runners there, a distant line of them, bearing down on her. For a second she appeared bewildered as though wondering how her fellow competitors could have made it back to the start of the race. The crowd roared with enjoyment as the truth dawned.

These were not the runners she had started out with. She had been so slow they had simply started the next race without waiting for her to finish. It was this that the crowd had been cheering. Her own race was long over, won already. Her socks slipped and she reached for them automatically. *Keep going!* someone yelled from the crowd in a shrill, excited voice, *or you'll lose this one too!* And, unbelievable as it was, she had done as she was told.

That was the moment she had recognized something in the girl. She watched her run on, still ridiculously keeping to her assigned lane and she saw that it was not determination that kept her there, labouring towards the mockery of the finish line. She kept to her path simply because she knew of no other direction to take.

They had spoken for the first time that evening, her and the girl. The conversation starting abruptly, without preamble.

'Why is your skirt so high like that?'

The girl said nothing, expecting further torment.

'It would look better not so high. Like mine.'

'I can't.'

'Why not?'

She hung her head. 'It's to cover the holes . . . in my jumper. I think it was moths.'

The other nodded. It was the kind of thing that got one into trouble at their school.

'Can't your mother send you a new one?'

'It was maybe when I got it wet. I was meant to hang it up –'

'I can mend it for you if you want. I've got some brown thread.'

Later, in the night, she heard the girl crying softly. Ten girls shared each dormitory and sorrow had to be kept low. She got out of her own bed and crept in beside her and stroked her hair.

'I didn't get a letter,' the girl whispered. 'I always get a letter.'

'Perhaps they're gone, your parents. I heard that happened once. A girl I know, her parents went away.'

'Where did they go?'

'I don't know. Just away. I suppose they didn't want her any more.'

'My mother and father wouldn't do that.'

'That's probably what the other girl thought too. They took everything out of the house. Even the sink. There was just a hole where the sink used to be.'

'But I *always* get a letter –'

'They could have gone. I think they might have.'

How hard the girl had sobbed. She had listened to her for a long time, stroking and stroking her hair, the pillow wet against her cheek.

'It doesn't matter,' she had said. 'I'll mend your jumper. You'll see.'

●

At first, it seemed as though Vanessa's hope might be realized. She slept deeply and woke in the early morning to the sound of a small knock on the door.

'Mountains,' said Prasad in the tones of someone announcing the arrival of a guest of honour. He was carrying a tray with tea and buttered toast cut up into neat triangles and he set about placing cups and saucers on the table next to their beds and drawing back the curtains. Vanessa went out on to the balcony. The rain had stopped and the sky was a bright, unobstructed blue. Below her, the town straggled, rooftop stacked against rooftop. Now that the air was clear, she could see what a strange mix Ashagiri was. Here a Christian cross, there the gleaming gold dome of a Buddhist temple. Across the square, a string of flags bearing the sign of the Hammer and Sickle. Satellite dishes and advertising hoardings for *Thums Up!* soda. A rooftop café, adorned with yellow umbrellas where a group of boys from the Buddhist school were enjoying breakfast, their maroon robes hitched up over their skinny knees. Beyond the town, the wooded hills were silvered with early morning mist. She turned back into the room.

'Where?' she demanded. 'Where are the mountains?'

He smiled secretively. 'Walk. Higher up.'

They dressed quickly, gulping their tea as they pulled on their clothes. Beyond the square where the jeep had dropped them, the main road continued upwards, curving slightly. At this time of the day there were few pedestrians and the shops lining the road were still shuttered. After a short walk, the road widened into a large, open area, circular in shape. A modest fountain, empty of water with a curling, ornate spout stood at the centre, surrounded by the fronts of shops, clearly more upmarket than those further below, selling curios and books and quality woollens. They knew they must be at the top of the town, for they could see no buildings above them. The road continued on the far side of the circle, but smaller now and more winding, following the contours of the hill. It was darker here, shadowed by great trees. On their left, a mossy stone wall. On their right, a thin metal fence, beyond which the hillside fell away with hidden precipitation.

They were barely a quarter of a mile from the club and the rest of the town below, but they had the sense of entering a new domain. It was very quiet here. A hush not fully explained by the earliness of the hour or the density of the trees. A small breeze brought the distant sound of church bells. Marion took Vanessa's arm. They walked together slowly, saying nothing. They thought they were circling the hill, but then, at last, when the trees cleared and the mountains came into view, they saw instead that it was themselves who were encircled.

The mountains were all about them. Drawing the eye helplessly up. Between the two women and the distant peaks, nothing but cloud that moved in an endless, shifting pattern of revelation and concealment. Like pale oil on water, the mist spread, dispersed, converged again. Low-lying white clouds, bright with the early sun, hung in the valley, making the blue peaks seem to float, forever apart and beyond. In the whole of the world, there was no blue like this. Utterly distilled, beside it all other shades seemed mere dilutions. From time to time, the uppermost clouds lifted and then the snows revealed themselves, clear as dreams are, whiter than hope.

The two women stood quite paralysed, lost for a moment in the sight. For Vanessa, the feeling was almost violent. A stab of success, of strange victory, pierced her. She clenched her fists in triumph, leaning hard against the metal railing that protected them from the drop below. Marion had taken a step back. Yes, she was thinking, yes, this is how it was. The same feeling then as now. As though the mountains, the light on the clouds, were not there at all, but extensions of the mind itself. Too huge for the eye to understand, small enough to be held in a single blink. For one moment it seemed to her that she caught at the edge of something. A wholeness.

'I wish Dad could have seen this,' Vanessa said abruptly. But it wouldn't have been enough for him to simply stand there, admiring the view, she thought. He would have wanted to go hiking. He'd have bought them the right boots, hired guides.

'He had such . . . energy, didn't he?'

'Yes, yes he did. Like his daughter.'

They turned away finally and returned the way they had come.

'Funny to think it was all underwater once,' said Vanessa. 'The Himalayas I mean.'

'Was it?'

'They've found fossils. High up. Of sea creatures . . . ammonites, things like that.'

'I never saw the sea. Not until I was fifteen. I tried to imagine what it was like. I saw pictures of course, but it's not the same.'

'You knew what a seahorse looked like,' Vanessa reminded her.

Marion smiled. 'Yes, I knew what a seahorse was.'

The seahorse lay in one of the drawers of a large chest in the biology lab. Only the older girls in the school were allowed to see and handle the specimens. At the age of six, Marion was considered too young and clumsy. But she knew it was there and her imagination was caught by this strange thing. A seahorse. She had never seen the sea before, but she had seen horses. Her father had three. And Ashagiri was full of them. You could hire them in the main square and take off for long treks into the hills. Marion thought the seahorse might be something like a land horse, only much bigger and possibly blue or green in colour. It would be very wet and sleek and perhaps have foam running off it instead of sweat. It would be very wild of course. Too wild to saddle and ride.

Whenever she got the chance, Marion would stand beside the specimen chest in the biology lab and stare at the drawer containing the seahorse. Sometimes she put her ear up close to it, hoping to hear a wet whinny or the thud of hooves against wood. Although she wanted to look inside more than anything, she didn't open the drawer for two reasons. The first was that she was forbidden and Marion was the kind of little girl who always did what she was told. The second was that she was frightened. She saw herself opening the drawer. She imagined the seahorse, huge and wild, rearing up out of its confinement amidst a wave of seawater, hooves first, nostrils flared, ready to gallop and trample everything – desks, blackboard, little girls – that stood in its way. The vision terrified and entranced her. If she ever wondered how such a creature could have been persuaded to get into the drawer in the first place, or how such a vast animal could fit into that small space, then these questions only made the seahorse even more wondrous and mysterious.

A few years passed and Marion forgot about the seahorse. Then came the day when she, too, was allowed to look at the specimens in the wooden chest of drawers and she remembered again. She was old enough to know that there couldn't possibly be a living, life-sized horse in there, but still, she wondered. What would it look like? When the drawer opened, a small part of her half expected that great wall of water and that great horse riding it out, hooves thrashing and beating it to a froth.

Instead, nothing. She looked down and saw a small bed of cotton wool, slightly yellowed with age. In the middle, something tiny and shrivelled, like an embryo. It was frail, completely dry, the colour of baked mud. A curled brittle tail, a bony little torso all bumps and ribs. There was nothing of the horse about it at all. Except that when she looked closer, she saw that the head had something equestrian about it. The same long face, the same position of the eyes. But this creature had no legs at all. And desiccated as it was, it was hard to imagine it had ever been a living, breathing thing.

Marion was dreadfully disappointed. All this time to imagine a miracle and then to find, after all, nothing but this bony scrap. This tiny dead thing muffled up in cotton wool. And then something unexpected happened. She might have turned away from the drawer in disgust, instead she looked more closely at the creature. She saw that although small, it was nevertheless complete. Its body fitted together with precision and this gave it a kind of beauty. The tail curled so carefully, that little horse's face, so incongruous, yet somehow absolutely right. Staring at the creature, there crept into her mind the thought that there was magic too in this hoarded scrap. Its very shape suggested mystery; the angle of the head, the curve of the back like a tiny question mark.

She had never forgotten it. Returning to the memory many times with an odd feeling of comfort that she could never quite explain. On the first anniversary of their meeting, Pete had given her a brooch in the shape of a seahorse. Its body was made of gold and there was a tiny diamond for an eye. It was before she had told him much about her childhood. Before he knew the significance that the creature held for her. And it was an odd choice of gift for him to make. Surely a little too arty for his normally conventional tastes. She had taken it as a kind of sign.

•

'I'm starving,' Vanessa said with relish as they arrived back at the fountain. 'Let's get a *huge* breakfast somewhere.'

Marion looked around her. The elation of seeing the mountains again was beginning to be replaced by dismay. She had put a brave face on their arrival, but there was nothing about this Ashagiri that she recognized. She could see landmarks that she knew – the outlines of old buildings, the curve of the road, this very fountain they now stood beside – but nothing felt right. The very familiarity of what remained merely adding to the sense of wrongness. Better it had all gone, she thought. Or better that they had never come at all. Perhaps it was not too late. If they left now, before seeing anything more of the town, some part of the Ashagiri of memory might still be preserved. They could catch an evening train, decide on another destination, Nepal perhaps. She had always wanted to see Nepal.

Marion sat down on the edge of the fountain and tried to summon up her courage but she knew it was hopeless. Vanessa would be furious at the change of plans. There would be hours of discussion and argument. And she would not be able to explain.

'Aren't you hungry?' Vanessa said.

The circle was beginning to bustle with people. Shutters rose on the shops with a great clattering. Outside Namgyal's Curio Emporium a man dusted the head of a large bronze antelope, with fussy, proprietorial gestures. The electric sign above the eatery next door crackled into life. PUKKA PIZZA it read, the words flashing on and off. A young man crossed the circle leading two tatty ponies with heads at a weary droop.

'Take a ride?' he called out to the two women. 'Cheap. Very good!'

Marion closed her eyes. There had been a bandstand here. The men in red and gold. The sound of the band and the water splashing in the fountain and the whinny of horses. Real horses. As unlike these unhappy creatures as it was possible to be. The ground swept, the walls kept free of moss, a brightness on everything.

She opened her eyes. A huge stag beetle, the size of a paperweight, lurched over the dusty ground, between the hooves of the ponies and the sniffing, excited noses of two stray dogs. Marion took a handkerchief from her pocket and picked it up carefully. She trotted over to the far side of the circle and placed the insect under a bush, out of harm's way.

'I don't know how you can pick something like that up,' said Vanessa.

'It was stranded,' Marion said.

They walked around the circle a little aimlessly, looking into shop windows.

'There must be somewhere we can have breakfast,' Vanessa said. 'What about Klein's? Wouldn't it be great if Klein's was still here?'

'I don't think it can be,' Marion said quickly. 'I mean, the Kleins were old *then*. They were from Austria. The family probably went home a long time ago.'

'Don't be defeatist. We can look at least.'

As it turned out, Klein's was easy to find, only a short distance away from the main street. It still operated as a bakery with a restaurant upstairs. Vanessa and Marion peered through its window at the display of pastries laid out for sale. Amidst the piles of rather dry-looking buns and garish wedges of sponge, Vanessa suddenly noticed something.

'Look!' she cried. 'Apple strudel!'

Marion nodded, a little sadly. The last time she had stood in this place, the window had been a vision of cream and custard. Chocolate cakes and cheese twists and glazed tartlets worthy of the best patisserie. The Kleins were long gone, strangers had taken over the business, but still the recipe for strudel lingered, like a sweet afterthought.

Upstairs in the long dining room, with its dark, wooden panelling and net-curtained windows, there was an atmosphere of faded style, a whiff of former glory. Marion stood quite still, her hand on her chest. There was the old dresser, with the carved elephants at each corner and the wooden light fixtures hanging from the ceiling. But in the area where a string quartet used to play, a bar had been installed, complete with large advertisement for Marlboro cigarettes, and there were plastic tablecloths instead of linen, and the light, the light was all wrong. How much smaller the place looked! Six or seven waiters in fraying livery stood about chatting and now one was leading them to a table by the window and pulling out chairs for them to sit, and Marion obeyed numbly, heavy with a kind of pain she had never felt before. A scrap of poetry running over and over in her mind, a remnant from the days when memorizing the classics was obligatory. *We will grieve not, rather find, Strength in what remains behind . . .* Wordsworth, she thought mechanically. How meaningless the words seemed. Worse than meaningless, wrong. It was precisely the things left behind that hurt. She remembered seeing a newspaper photograph of somebody's house after a tornado had hit. Out in the Midwest of America, somewhere like that. Nothing left but debris, except a single coat rack, still upright, somehow surviving the devastation. It was the coat rack that made the picture, she thought. It was the coat rack that broke the heart.

'They have bacon and eggs!' Vanessa said greedily, surveying the menu. Marion tried to smile. Somewhere, behind the bar, one of the waiters put on a tape. It was *Bolero*. The music played scratchy and faint, now fast, now slow, as though on a wind-up gramophone placed somewhere far away. Apart from the music and murmur of the waiters, it was very quiet. Then, from the street below, a voice came singing. The song was very short, no more than a line or two and the tune repetitive. But the voice was very sweet. It came from a beggar sitting cross-legged on the ground, with a tin mug beside him. The beggar's eyeballs were as white as eggs, without pupils or irises. He sang his phrase over and over, craning his head upwards as though he could see something in the sky with those blind eyes of his, thought Marion. As though he hoped his song could reach it.

Marion turned back to her menu with a great effort. 'I think, perhaps . . . just the toast,' she told the waiter.

'Are you sure?' Vanessa asked. 'You're not coming down with some awful bug are you?'

'I don't think so.'

Outside, the blue sky of early morning was beginning to cloud over. A brownish haze, rising from the valley far below, crept in tendrils across their view.

'I don't remember that,' Marion said. 'That . . . pollution. Ashagiri was always so clean.'

'Seems hard to imagine now.'

The meal came and they ate in silence. Marion looked at her watch. Soon, in a few minutes, half an hour at the most, she would be standing at the gates of St Margaret's. The moment breakfast was over, Vanessa would suggest it. And how could she refuse to go? When they had travelled all that way for just that purpose? From what she had already seen of Ashagiri, she knew that the St Margaret's she had carried around in her head all of her life was not the same school that now waited for her. But she had always known this. She had known it before the start of the trip and in Calcutta, facing down the ugliness of the Victoria Memorial, and on the train too when the dread of what she was travelling towards had almost overwhelmed her. But then, as now, hope still tugged at her. There were schools still operating in Ashagiri. On the way to Klein's that morning she had seen children going to lessons. Little girls in pleated skirts and boys with shorts and red blazers, the uniforms quaint, a little old fashioned. It was perfectly possible that St Margaret's was one of these schools. Changed of course, how could it *not* have changed? But still there. The netball court, the dorms, the chapel stain-glass golden.

'So how do we get there? Do you remember the way?'

'It was only half a mile or so from Klein's,' Marion said. 'A driver came and picked us up.'

They crossed the street and started uphill once more. 'It's past the church,' Marion said. 'Round past the graveyard and then up a bit. The school is on its own hill. There used to be lots of trees –'

'And Dreaming Rock. Isn't that where Dreaming Rock is?'

'Yes.'

'Who called it that?'

'Everyone did. All the girls. I don't know when it started. Perhaps it was always called that.'

Vanessa frowned, a nervous gesture that made her look a little angry. She had the feeling that she had to keep talking or her mother might stop walking. Simply stop in the middle of the street and refuse to move again.

'You went and sat on it. What did you think about when you sat on it?'

'I don't know what the others thought,' said Marion. 'You weren't meant to tell anybody else.'

'Why not?'

'I don't know,' Marion said. 'I don't remember.'

The graveyard behind the church had been old even when Marion was a child. There had been no new graves dug there for a hundred years. Two cows, the colour of dark chocolate, munched stolidly, their hooves on the tumbled headstones, their eyes deep in the grass.

'Children,' Marion said, as they passed by. 'That place is full of dead children. I used to try and count them, but I always lost track. Children died of everything back then. Dysentery, snake bites, cholera, tetanus . . . there's a grave there of two sisters who fell into an open drain.' Amidst the tangles of wild dahlias and knee-length grass could be seen the scattered words of their epitaphs, making no mention of the violence of their deaths. *Sleeping in the arms of Jesus, laughing with the angels, beloved child of God . . .*

'Amazing how many euphemisms the Victorians had for death,' Vanessa said. 'Euphemisms for everything come to think of it. God, it must have been annoying to live back then.'

But Marion was not to be distracted. She had begun to walk more slowly, taking shorter and shorter steps. Her eyes were fixed on the ground.

'We must be nearly there,' Vanessa said. 'Isn't this the turning up the hill that you were talking about?' They had arrived at a small path framed with a stone arch that was cracked and smeared with moss. A group of chickens pecked busily at the earth. Marion stopped and looked up. She glanced behind her at the way they had come and then back again at the path.

'I think this is it. No . . . it can't be.' She carried on down the road for a few paces and then stopped and returned to the arch once more. 'This *must* be it,' she said. 'But you would have seen the rooftops from here. The school rooftops. And the tennis court. I know you could see that from the turning . . .'

Instead of these, only a long, ugly building was visible between the trees. It was roofed with dirty, brown corrugated iron and its windows were boarded up and quite blank. 'The school is probably behind,' Vanessa said. 'This place must have been built since you were here.'

Marion hovered at the head of the path, looking disoriented. 'It should be . . .' she began. Then, as if noticing them for the first time, 'What are those *chickens* doing?'

'Come on,' Vanessa said, a little roughly. Her mother had a look on her face she had never seen before. A drawing in of her features, a diminishing. 'Come *on*,' she repeated, 'let's get it over with.'

They started up the path, slipping a little on broken stones which scattered the way and soon found themselves passing the tin-roofed building. They turned a corner and saw further buildings above them, half obscured by trees. Vanessa was instantly certain of two things. The first was that this was indeed St Margaret's. It had been invisible from the road below, hidden behind the lower structure. The second was that even at this distance she could tell the school had been abandoned some time ago. What was left of St Margaret's was little more than a shell.

Still visible were the arched windows of the chapel and the long balconies of the dormitories, but everything was listing and hollow. Most of the windows were smashed, the balus-trades crumbling and obviously treacherous. As they came closer, she saw cobwebs trailing over buckled doorways and down old walkways. Creeping greenery had netted the old brick and now spread across window ledges and up drain pipes. Rubbish lay heaped against the walls like the detritus left by some huge, swiftly passing tide.

Vanessa could think of nothing to say. She looked at her mother. Marion's face had taken on a rigid look; the expression of someone who, knowing they are about to be punished and unable to prevent it, takes refuge in a kind of stubborn passivity. The path ended at the old school gates which opened on to a large quadrangle and the entrance to the school itself. And now it was Vanessa who held back and Marion who quickened her pace, entering through the gates almost eagerly as though impelled by a strange, terrible satisfaction.

They crossed the quadrangle where a pale dog lay supine among the weeds and the gallows of a netball post, empty of net, stood rusty and slightly askew. Inside the building it was dark and smelled faintly of urine. A staircase led upwards, rickety and dangerous looking. Upturned desks and piles of rubbish littered the view down long, dim corridors, still decorated with old noticeboards and rows of pegs set at a height for children to reach up and hang their coats.

'What *happened*?' Vanessa said, her voice echoing slightly. The strange thing, she thought, was that the place still felt like a school. The same sense – faint, but unmistakable – of being enclosed in a world of rules and ritual, a place apart, protected by certainties. But everything was broken open. This was not a school that had been tidied up and shut down. No feeling of organized departure, of closure. Instead, this . . . abandonment. As though everyone had got up from their desks and simply left, leaving the school to scavengers, to the violence of neglect.

'What happened?' she said again. Marion's feet crunched through broken glass as she navigated around the debris, one hand against the dark wall for support. Her other hand was deep inside her handbag. She had found her old autograph book and was holding on to it.

All her classmates had signed their names there. It was 1947, the year they had all left India for good. Home was a country they had never been to before and friendship would last for ever. They signed their names and left their messages of goodbye. 'Though I am going far away, I'll think of you every day,' wrote her best friend, Edith Shaw. Where were they all now, wondered Marion. Where were Nancy Smith and Gloria Breeze? Where was the girl who told her to, 'Be a good girl, Lead a good life, Choose a good husband, And be a good wife?' Where was Jill Cobb who wrote 'Chin Up!' next to a small drawing of a bluebird? How forlorn their homilies now seemed. How very short, after all, their eternities of friendship. Had they followed their own advice, given before they knew the meaning of anything?

'This must have been the chapel,' Vanessa said suddenly. 'The glass is still there.' The small room was empty of pews and altar, but an aura of sanctity still lingered about it, product of the stained orange light that bathed its dirty floor and lit the slow moving dust of the air like the floating particles in a snow globe. Marion stood for a moment or two below the window, breathing a little rapidly, as though recovering from exertion. She had removed her hand from her bag and now brought it up to her face in a vague, half-completed gesture which might have been one of protest or merely sorrow. She was thinking that this is what it must feel like to come back a thousand years after one's own death. To come back and see the past uncovered by the present and find nothing more than a collection of artefacts in some archaeological museum. All the toil and texture of it brought down to a broken pot or two. This is why we die, she thought. So we never need to hunt for souvenirs of our own lives, nor witness the way time takes the once familiar and makes it more strange to us than things we have never known or loved.

'At least the stained glass isn't broken,' Vanessa said. 'And Dreaming Rock. We could look for that. Where did you say it was? Is it a long walk away?'

'I don't remember.'

'You must know the vague direction.'

'No,' Marion said. 'No. I don't remember at all.'

•

That night, back in their room at the club, Marion lay for a long time before falling asleep. She was cold. Despite the fact that she had been lying between her sheets for at least an hour, they still felt chilly. As though her body had lost its ability to generate heat. Almost as if she did not exist at all, she thought.

One by one, the pieces of herself had disappeared. First her marriage and then her husband. Her house, her garden. Falling behind her into irrelevance. Then Ashagiri, the old town, all polished and built for pleasure, where you could ride all day through untouched forest. And her school, the rules long broken along with the windows and weeds running heedless now down those corridors.

Last to go, her image itself.

Why had Vanessa insisted on visiting the old photographic studio? And why had she followed? Hanging back and saying nothing as always. The studio was on the way back to the club. It sold postcards now and a small line of groceries along with camera equipment and film. Vanessa had been so eager. Almost desperate, Marion thought. 'Let's just ask,' she had begged. 'You never know. It might still be there. In a drawer somewhere.'

The black and white portrait of Marion aged five years old had sat in the old studio window for years. All through the time she had been at school. The studio owner, Mr Lehkraj must have thought it a good example of his craft although Marion never liked the picture. She had been dressed in an uncomfortably stiff white dress and told to 'look at the birdie'. But there was no birdie and the camera had captured her at the moment of this realization. Her mouth in a small, correct smile, her eyes unhappy, caught between disappointment and the desire to please. Now, in the window of the photographic studio, a large poster of an Indian pop star had taken the place of Marion's image, but Mr Lehkraj's son still ran the place. He was middle-aged himself, with spectacles and a kindly manner.

He hesitated when Vanessa asked about the old portrait. 'My father took many pictures. Hard to keep track of them all now.'

'Maybe you remember this one,' Vanessa persisted. 'It was in the window for a long time.'

Mr Lehkraj the younger smiled. 'It is possible that it is downstairs in our storage . . .' He shrugged. 'But I really don't know.'

Marion tugged at Vanessa's arm. She felt sure that the picture had been thrown away and Mr Lehkraj was too nice to hurt them by telling them so. Why would anyone keep fifty-year-old photographs of people who didn't even live there any longer?

'It doesn't matter,' she said. She turned to the postcard rack and pulled out an image of a red panda sitting on the branch of a tree, its small russet face peering out somewhat disconsolately from the foliage. 'I'll just take this.'

Mr Lehkraj smiled with approval at her choice. 'This is the last red panda left in the Ashagiri area,' he said. 'Although I do believe that even this individual has recently expired. I have some interesting shots of people in traditional dress,' he continued helpfully.

'Thank you,' said Marion. 'But I think this will do for now.'

At the door of the studio she turned back again. 'You've

been very kind.' Somewhere between disappointment and the desire to please, she smiled at him. Correct, unhappy.

Later, in the deepest part of the night, Vanessa awoke and heard her mother crying. Half asleep herself, the sound took on confused shape, the sobs like small, prickly plants bursting into flower one after the other in the dark. Vanessa lay very still without making a sound. She should do something, she thought. Be a daughter, a friend. But unlike her mother, she had never had much of a gift for friendship. She had friends of course, quite a few of them; some she would describe as close if the amount of time spent in each other's company was a measure of closeness. But people rarely seemed to confide in her. Perhaps it was her aura of self-sufficiency or simply that she had never learned that nobody welcomed advice, however earnestly it was meant. That it was enough merely to bear witness to others' lives.

She put her head under the pillow and pressed her face hard against the musty smelling sheet.

After a little while, the crying stopped.

PART TWO

Climbing

•

The woman from the train spent two whole days searching for somewhere better to stay than Paradise Lodge. During this time she made no progress on her research, apart from a mental note to find out what concoctions the locals used to treat respiratory problems. She didn't even bother to unpack her notebooks or ingredients, though she made several forays down to the market to survey the roots and spices on sale. She needed an appropriate environment before she could begin her work. It was to be an important contribution to the field of alternative health. A wide-reaching examination of local remedies in northern India. Her findings would, by necessity, be based mainly on anecdotal evidence and observation. But it would be a valuable work generating a great deal of attention and further investigation.

She found the hotel on the morning of the third day, having visited most of the others in town. She had been to the Claremont and the Fairvue and the brand new Ritzy, built for the Indian market and far too noisy for her taste. She had even been to the Ashagiri Club where the proprietor had insisted on showing her around, babbling about club membership and how very exclusive the place was, although it was clear to her it was nothing but a shambles.

But Glenside was different. Clean and warm and suitably laid out. Her room had plenty of shelf space for bottles, and windows that opened smoothly so that she could regulate the temperature to her liking. The owner was an old woman who seemed to recognize in her a guest of special discernment.

'Please forgive me if I don't get up,' she said, holding out a hand from the sofa where she was lying. 'I'm something of an invalid as you can see. I'm Mrs Macdonald.'

There was a long pause.

'I'm Dorothy.' She came forward to shake the other's hand. 'Dorothy Nichols.'

'It's lovely to see you,' Mrs Macdonald said. 'Have you visited Ashagiri before?'

Again that pause. 'Yes. Yes, I was at school here. A long time ago.'

'Oh wonderful. Which one?'

'St Margaret's,' Dorothy Nichols said.

Mrs Macdonald tilted her head to one side and smiled a little sadly. 'St Margaret's. Such a shame about that place.'

'Yes, a shame,' Dorothy repeated, sitting down on a chair next to the old woman. She leaned forward. 'Is it arthritis?'

Mrs Macdonald smiled again. 'I'm afraid nobody seems to know what it is. Although I'm not sure being able to give it a name would really help. Just a label you know. Of course the truly wonderful thing about not being able to move about is that everyone must come to *you*. I so enjoy meeting all the guests. We have quite a selection here you know.'

'I do have some . . . health experience,' Dorothy persisted. 'I'm here collecting material for a book. Alternative medicine . . .'

Mrs Macdonald's face appeared to light up at this information. 'How wonderful,' she cried. 'A writer! Perhaps I will be able to help. Do you have a background in that kind of medicine?'

'I used to look after my mother. For many years. Twenty-five in fact. During the course of her illness I became interested in the field.'

'A long time to be looking after a sick person. Was it a stroke?'

'A series of them. Over the years.'

'Such a long time,' Mrs Macdonald repeated.

Dorothy Nichols waited for the inevitable questions, the inevitable pitying, incredulous tone that crept into the voices of the questioners. Oh yes, underneath all the professions of admiration at duty borne and self sacrifice endured, always that pity. As though it was she who was the fool and not them, who knew nothing and never would. Behind her back, the muttering. *Such a shame, better to die, asking that of a daughter, doesn't she know there are Homes . . . ?*

But Mrs Macdonald did not seem at all curious.

'You must be a very kind person,' was all she said. 'But you shouldn't worry about me you know. You must put all thoughts of illness behind you now. You will be wanting to get out and about, researching your book and revisiting all the places from your past.'

'Yes. I will be very busy. There is a great deal to be done.'

She went up to her room but it was a while before she began the process of unpacking. She sat on her bed for a long time, almost completely still, moving her forefinger in an exploratory fashion along her lower lip, searching for rough places on the skin. The skin was smooth and a little tight, as it always was when it was healing itself. As her finger travelled, the tip of her thumb followed the bottom edge of her mouth feeling for minute, frayed strands. She found a small crack in the skin and paused, running her finger back and forth over the tiny fissure with speculative pleasure, her mind focused entirely on the movement.

Of late, she had found herself more and more frequently in this state of reverie; a blankness of mind that could last anything from a few minutes to half an hour. The day before, looking at her watch after such a session she was surprised to see that a full forty-five minutes had passed without her being aware of it. It gave her a strange feeling. Such a thing had not happened to her in a long while, since before her mother's death when she had sat night after night in vigil by the bedside and the hours had passed in a trance, her eyes empty, her fingers working and working at her mouth.

She brought her thumb and forefinger together to form a pincer and began attacking the crack in her lip with great concentration. To an observer, it might have looked like mere fumbling, her hand bunched in front of her face, the muscles in her fingers moving spasmodically. But, in fact, there was great delicacy in the action. Two or three patient brushes of the forefinger alternating with the pincer movement. Brush brush pluck, brush brush pluck. Her finger stroking gently over the Braille of the broken skin, then the fierce dart of the pincer pushing the flesh of the lip tightly inwards as it closed in on the almost impossibly tiny ridge of skin exposed for opportunity. And now the brushing abandoned as the pincer moved in for the kill. Pluck pluck pluck *pluck*. The ridge grasped finally between the nails and the motion slow once more, becoming tentative as she tugged experimentally on the scrap, enjoying the way her bottom lip tented out minutely as she pulled, the luxury of expectation delayed.

She ripped the millimetre away with a quick movement, feeling the customary prickle of pain and then the small taste of blood on her tongue. Too deep. The best plucks did not draw blood, but merely grazed the upper levels of the skin, drawing off layers so fine that there were always more underneath. If there was blood, the crude process of healing would be required, the skin swelling a little and then hardening over the area, giving her mouth a raw, ragged look. People would notice.

The old woman had brushed her concern aside but when she lifted her hand, Dorothy had noticed slight bruising on her lower arm. Arnica would help with that. She had brought a small supply of the stuff. Wheatgrass seeds too. Just enough to start a tray or two. She thought of her windowsill back home full of the bright green stalks of the grass, luminous in their youth. It lifted her spirits just to see them. Harvesting the grass had been one of the pleasures of the day. She always took more time than she needed to slice the stalks with her sharp scissors, feeling their slight, almost juicy resistance against the blades of her tool and the snick of metal as they fell into her waiting hand. Later she would pulp them in the small cast-iron grinder, producing an elixir of such astonishing, energetic green that, for a few seconds after she had drunk it, the liquid seemed to vibrate through every tissue in her body.

She was over sixty, though nobody would guess it, she thought. It was not that she wished to look young. Her youth was a distant, inconsequential thing. If she thought of it at all it was only with a prickle of disbelief that she could ever have been other than what she was now. But she was proud of her strength. She looked after herself. With the wheatgrass and all the other remedies. She had nobody to thank for it but herself.

Yes, arnica, she thought. First arnica and then we shall see.

Vanessa was a person who believed that every situation, however difficult, could be resolved by finding the correct key. It could be something as simple as asking the right question, or taking a certain course of action, but once found, it had the power to unlock even the most complicated of problems. This conviction of hers had always stood her in good stead at work where she had been known for whittling down massive reports to a series of pithy bullet points and interrupting wordy meetings with a telling question or two that helped to remind everyone what they were actually discussing.

Now, in the days following their disastrous visit to St Margaret's, she was beset by the conviction that there was still something she could do to set everything right. All she needed to do was to find the key – some meaningful fragment of the past – that would make sense of their journey and rescue her mother from complete disappointment. The trouble was that she didn't know what she was looking for and there was something about Ashagiri itself that seemed to resist even the most determined search.

It seemed to her that the place was neither one thing nor another. A resort town, now enjoyed mainly by Indians and the occasional group of backpackers on their way to somewhere more authentic, more 'Indian'. It was untidy and crowded, clogged with gaudy stalls selling bobble hats and beads and nylon sweaters in acid shades of green and yellow. At night the power failed so regularly it was not even commented upon. Loudspeakers from the cinema down the hill crackled with music and the streets were full of holiday makers promenading up and down, the women in saris that glowed in the dusk, carrying little paper cones of nuts and laughing amongst themselves. But behind all this, another town. Faded, falling into ruin, but still there. A town that came from another time and another place. You turned a corner and there it was. A little lane, flanked by old stone walls, with a view of church spire among the trees. A sudden row of holiday cottages, still intact, their neat gates and wooden porches belonging not here, below the snows, but along some northern seaside front with Bed and Breakfast signs at the door and seagulls wheeling overhead.

Was it here she should look, in the ruins of the Grand Hotel up the hill, with its once broad courtyard obscured by wild rhododendrons? In the Botanical Gardens, within the skeleton of the great glasshouse, faithfully modelled on those at Kew? Or did the solution lie not here, but quite elsewhere, perhaps in the conversation of the three old women who sat in a row at the same time each morning on a bench near the fountain, smoking tiny cigarettes and murmuring to themselves. They smoked and smiled as though amused by what they saw, she thought. Like women with a secret.

For months she had imagined being in this place. Getting her mother and herself to this spot had become another of her projects and Vanessa was good at projects. They had structure; stages to be gone through. Projects made life manageable. They could be focused upon then put aside and once over, there was always the next. Quite separate and full of new possibility.

Her swimming was a project. Fifty lengths three times a week. She always chose the same lane. She went during lunch hours when the pool was usually almost empty. The water was chest deep all the way along because the pool was designed for people who needed physiotherapy. It was open to the general public but most of the other regular bathers she saw there were sick or infirm. A young woman with a limp. A bald man with a soft, blank face who held his hands over the surface of the water as though feeling his way forward. An emaciated youth who looked like Jesus with tattoos all over his chest, walking sideways down the pool with great concentration. The light cast watery reflections on the tiled walls and across the faces of the bathers. They were all different, these people, but in the pool, there was an expression they shared. A dreaming look, inward and intent.

She thought she swam only for the discipline. For the pleasure of counting down the lengths, her breath steady, her eyes on the clock. But what she really loved about the pool was something far more simple. It was the weightlessness. It was the way the water held them all equal, the broken and the whole alike, and silenced the badgering voices of her mind that asked her, what next? What next, Vanessa? As though the present was never quite enough for her and she must always, always be planning for the minute, the hour, the week to come.

For months she had imagined being here in Ashagiri. But where could she imagine herself now?

Each morning Prasad woke them with tea and toast. He pattered into the room and lowered the blinds and enquired whether they wanted a fire set for the evening. He had been working at the club for thirty years. His wife was an invalid so he had to do all the chores at home as well. He had a teenage son who was good for nothing except weightlifting. His son trained every day, said Prasad, and then he came home to eat. He ate and ate. 'Four eggs!' Prasad told them. 'Just for breakfast!' Outside on the furthest balcony, strange

Major Das positioned himself for an hour each day, looking out at the morning. He stood quite still with his head tilted upwards, his nose pointing at the sky at exactly the same angle as the machine gun in the courtyard, his hands clasped behind his back.

'Perhaps he's a poet,' Marion said. She had taken to reading her anthology until late at night. Sitting in one of the wicker chairs beside the fire, while Vanessa did stomach crunches on the floor between the beds. If she would get nothing else out of the trip, thought Vanessa, at least she would have the flattest abs of her life. She put her hands behind her head and forced her shoulders up and down, grimacing with effort.

'How many of those do you plan to do?' Marion asked.

'Don't – make – me – lose – count –'

'Because you're quite slim enough already you know.'

'It's not weight, it's *tone* that's important.'

'You know, you're so pretty –' Marion began.

'I don't want to talk about it.'

'I just don't know why –'

'Just drop it, all right?' Vanessa was not in the mood to hear her mother tell her how she should really be thinking about marriage and starting a family. She was never in the mood. Sometimes, when her mother looked at her in a certain way, almost pityingly, almost, Vanessa thought, as though she felt *sorry* for her daughter, it made her want to grind her teeth. It drove her a little crazy to suspect that her mother persisted in thinking that her life lacked fulfilment despite all the apparent evidence to the contrary.

It was not that she didn't want to be married or have children. Most people wanted these things and she had always assumed they would fit, sooner or later, into her life plan. But this was a generalized conviction, never attached to anything or anyone specific. Not even to Michael. She thought she had been in love with Michael. She had certainly never felt so intensely about anyone else. But clearly she had not loved him enough.

Vanessa paused in the middle of a sit-up. Perhaps, she thought suddenly, she was not capable of real love. Whatever produced it, whatever mechanism of the heart and mind, somehow missing in her. Wasn't everyone born with something lacking? Deficiencies of intelligence or beauty or physical co-ordination. The capacity to love was no different. It could be stunted or even non-existent like anything else. But how did a person know if this was the case? Could they go through life with love like a kind of phantom limb, attached only by the sense that it *should* be there?

Vanessa's stomach ached. She lifted her shoulders and crunched forward savagely.

'Try to understand the concept that I'm doing this for *myself*.'

'I just want you to be happy.'

Vanessa stopped. 'That's funny,' she said, 'I just want *you* to be happy.'

The words came out sounding more flippant than she felt. It struck her that an awfully large part of life was spent wishing other people could be happy. And it was all rather fruitless. At least it was in her case. If only her mother would talk to her. Really talk. Instead, all she seemed to want to do was play rhyming games or describe to Vanessa, in great detail, the life stories of her various friends who all appeared to have met bizarre or unhappy fates.

It wasn't as though Vanessa hadn't tried. 'When did you take off your wedding ring?' she ventured. They were sitting in Klein's Restaurant, their usual lunchtime venue. Marion was picking at a chow mein, her handbag on her lap. She was wondering who to send the postcard of the last red panda to, and how she could phrase the message to make it sound cheerful.

'I noticed the other day that you'd taken it off.'

'I don't know,' Marion said. 'My hands are getting so fat . . . it was getting tight. That's what happens when you get older you know. You eat the same as you always did, but you start piling on the pounds.'

Vanessa looked down at her own pale hands. She was sure this would never happen to her.

'Where is it? The ring, I mean?'

'Remember my friend Tracy Fuller? She used to be quite slender and now she's *huge*. Although that might be because of all those drugs she has to take. Poor thing, just when she thought she'd got over the divorce . . . and that business she started up. It was just beginning to take off when she got the first seizure . . . Some kind of stroke I believe. That reminds me, did I tell you about Ann?'

'Ann? You mean, the woman who lives two doors down?'

'No, no, another Ann. I don't know her terribly well. An acquaintance really. I don't know her last name. I bumped into her in Jaeger the other day. She said she'd been having terrible headaches for months and they did a scan or whatever of her brain and you'll never guess what they found.'

Vanessa sighed. 'A tumour?'

'No! A *twin*.'

'What are you talking about?'

'Her twin. A tiny little thing, a tiny little foetus thing, she said. All her life, there it was, and she never even knew. It must have got incorporated into her body somehow while she was still only a bunch of cells herself.'

'You're making this up.'

'It does happen apparently, although it's very rare. She had an operation and they took it out. Now it's sitting in a jar in the lab at Cornfield Hospital. Can you imagine? Her twin. She didn't seem too bothered about it. She might have been discussing the weather. I couldn't help thinking, what if it was the other way around?'

'The other way around?'

'Yes, what if it was Ann sitting there in the jar and somebody else – who looked exactly like her – buying a cashmere sweater in Jaeger. It could have been. It was only by chance that Ann ended up the . . . big twin. Do you see? And I wouldn't even have known. I would still have been standing there talking to the Ann-twin and I wouldn't even have known. It wouldn't have made any difference whatsoever.'

'I don't think that's *quite* true . . .' said Vanessa, trying to fathom out the logic. 'God, if I hear *Bolero* one more time, I'm going to go mad. I'm going to get up and start doing double axles in the middle of the restaurant.'

'I think it's their only tape,' Marion said tolerantly.

'So where shall we go today?'

Marion bent her head towards her food as though suddenly fascinated by the pattern of shredded cabbage on her plate.

'I thought it might be fun to do a little shopping. That emporium place on Fountain Square –'

'Oh, Mother, we can't just shop. We haven't seen half the town yet. We haven't been to the library at the club. There might be records there. We might find out what happened to St Margaret's. We haven't even tried to look for Dreaming Rock. And there's a natural history museum here. I saw a sign for it this morning. I don't know what state it's in, but Grandad collected bird's eggs, didn't he? It might be worth a look.'

'I wanted to write postcards –'

'What postcards? You only bought one. You can write it here, in five minutes. I've got a pen.'

'I haven't decided who to send it to yet.'

'Send it to one of your desperate friends. Tracy Fuller for example. Send it to her.'

Marion took the pen obediently. 'Dear Tracy,' she wrote. 'Hope you are feeling better. I am having . . .' She stopped.

'What now?'

'Nothing,' said Marion, replacing the postcard in her bag. 'I think I'll finish it later, that's all.'

•

Ashagiri's Museum of Natural History was housed in a small brick building at the end of a winding side street. It cost two rupees to visit. A sleepy-looking man sitting on a chair at the entrance took the women's money and laboriously wrote out a pair of tickets, halting and licking his pencil. They were the only visitors. Inside, the windows were thick with grime and the light dim. Behind rows of glass cases, dark figures loomed.

A dusty black bear whose sagging legs betrayed a slow but inexorable leakage of stuffing reared tiredly in one corner. In another, a crocodile, flattened to the width of a plank, gaped endlessly, its jaws held apart with a stick. A mongoose, whose crossed eyes seemed to be exchanging with one another a long, baffled look of indignation, pressed against the glass, hunched and dull-furred. Unidentified snakes, bleach bellied, embraced themselves in jars.

As her eyes adjusted to the gloom, Vanessa could make out other creatures. Small, snouty rodents, a pair of monkeys. Some had been placed in settings indicative of their natural environment, their paws transfixed among old twigs and sprigs and faded painted backdrops. Others simply leaned, apropos of nothing, against makeshift props, piles of mothballs at their feet. Their squinty glass eyes seemed to follow the two women as they wandered through the small series of rooms.

'Someone should put these things out of their misery,' Vanessa said.

Marion stopped and patted the leg of the black bear. Beneath her fingers, the fur felt very dry. 'Poor thing,' she said. 'Poor old bear.' She thought suddenly of Bucket. His ears had the same nubbly aspect, worn smooth by her habit of rubbing them to and fro against her lips. Such comfort in that small, endlessly repeated gesture.

'I'd be careful if I were you,' Vanessa said. 'You might catch something from that animal.'

It was odd, thought Marion, how even her daughter, never much given to flights of fancy, was referring to the exhibits in the museum as though they were still alive. As if their very decrepitude, the indignity of their situation, had transformed them from mere specimens to individuals once again, fixing them for ever in melancholy half-life.

One of the rooms in the museum was given over to a collection of moths and butterflies. Long glass cases, flush with the wall, held hundreds of the insects, each with its own small, yellowing card with its Latin name handwritten in neat, old-fashioned script. Most of the specimens were ragged, missing wings and parts of thoraxes, or simply faded to a virtual transparency. Some had rotted away entirely, leaving nothing but an empty pin and a name. At the bottom of each case, like drifted sand, the pale crumbs of their bodies lay heaped and undisturbed.

Marion stopped by a case full of butterflies of varying shades of blue. Time had sucked the colour out of most of them, but one, the largest of all, was still a deep, luxurious azure. She tapped the glass as though trying to catch the attention of the pinned creature inside.

'I remember these sort,' she said. 'We used to hunt them with nets.' Her brother had a butterfly collection but Marion couldn't remember what she did with the insects she captured. She lost interest in them once they were dead.

'I just liked to chase them. I suppose it was cruel, but there were so many.'

Vanessa barely heard her. She was bent over a display of birds' eggs in the centre of the room.

'I wonder if Grandad donated any of his collection to the museum. When they lived nearby. On that tea estate where you were born. We must go there by the way. I wonder if he ever gave away any of his eggs. Look, there's a card beside each one saying what it is and where it was found. And names of who found them.'

Marion said nothing. She was thinking of her father's hands as he handled his eggs. He wore white gloves. Each egg had its own special compartment in the wooden storage boxes in his study and there was a tiny key for each box. She did not think it would ever have occurred to him to give even a single specimen away. They had been a family of collectors. Her father with his birds' eggs, her elder brother's butterflies. Now she wondered if there had been anything more to this urge than the simple joy of acquisition. There seemed something peculiarly colonial in the mania to collect and label. She had never collected anything herself. Neither as a child nor as an adult. Perhaps things might have been better for her if she had, she thought. Perhaps a person could find permanence in the gathering of small trophies.

'Egg of Nepal White-Eyed Quaker Babbler,' said Vanessa, reading from one of the cards. 'Taken from the cleft in a tree at 3,000 feet. Donated by W. H. Williams, 1941.'

'They sound as though someone made up the names, don't they?'

She turned around. John Walcott was standing in the entrance to the room, his face with the same expression of general enthusiasm that she remembered from their first meeting at the Ashagiri Club.

'Hello again!' Marion called, sounding delighted to see him.

'Are you looking for something in particular?'

Vanessa hunched a fraction over the case of birds' eggs, as though to guard its contents from any view but her own.

'I'm just looking at the names,' she said.

John crossed the room and stood beside her. 'Any name in particular?'

'She's looking for my father's name,' Marion said. 'Jeffrey Temple. Although I doubt very much she'll find it there.'

'I might,' Vanessa said, her eyes scanning the cards as rapidly as possible. If her grandfather's name was there, she didn't want John Walcott to be the one who spotted it. She was a little surprised at the vehemence of this thought. It was more than mere competitiveness. Although she would never have admitted it, she wanted to be the one who brought the name to her mother, presenting it to her for approval and praise, like the pin cushions and Easter cards she had made at school as a child.

John Walcott rested his hand on the case and gazed inside. 'Such a lot of names,' he said slowly. 'Funny to think all those people are dead now. All labelled on gravestones somewhere, just like these eggs of theirs.' He paused. 'I don't see a Jeffrey Temple.'

'No,' Vanessa said, turning away abruptly. 'No, he's not here.'

'Have you been doing any more painting?' Marion asked.

'A little. I have to get up very early in the morning to catch the light.'

'I'd like to see it, what you're working on. If you don't mind. Perhaps you do. Perhaps you don't like having people look at anything unfinished –'

'I don't mind.' He glanced a little hesitantly at Vanessa. 'In fact, I'd like it very much. I could bring a few of my canvases to show you this evening.'

'Perhaps we could see you actually painting. I've never seen a miniaturist at work. Would it put you off if we came and watched?'

'No, no, of course not. It would be . . . a pleasure. I could come by and knock on your door on my way out. Tomorrow perhaps?'

'That would be lovely,' Marion said firmly.

'It would be very early of course,' he added anxiously. 'Before it was light –'

'Don't worry,' Marion said. 'I have an alarm clock.'

Back at the club, Marion said she wanted to lie down. She had a headache. She fished through her luggage and brought out a large bag of medical supplies. 'I know there's a packet of paracetamol here somewhere,' she said, sorting through jars of rehydration fluid, unused syringes and rolls of bandages.

'Can I get you anything?' asked Vanessa.

'I don't think so. I just need to find the paracetamol.'

'I could ask Prasad to bring you some tea.'

'No,' Marion said. 'All I need is a little quiet.'

Vanessa went and sat outside on the balcony, feeling restless and discontented. Ashagiri was a town of remnants, she thought. Leftovers of one sort or another. So why was it that they had found nothing of her mother's childhood here? Not even as much as a bird's egg. And now it seemed to Vanessa that Marion herself was losing focus in the search. But had she ever been truly committed to it? It occurred to Vanessa that if there had been failure here, it was a failure of the will. Right from the start, her mother had seemed to hang back, full of excuses and evasions. Behind her apparent passivity, a kind of obstructiveness that amounted to sabotage.

The anger Vanessa felt was more than mere annoyance at having her plans disregarded. Her mother had always been elusive, seeming to withhold much of her life from her daughter. But there was one part she had freely shared; her childhood in Ashagiri. And through her stories, endlessly retold, this place had become part of Vanessa's childhood too. At some junction of the mind where memory given makes memory of its own, she and her mother had come together, children both. With sudden, fierce insight, Vanessa saw that the Ashagiri she had always thought belonged solely to Marion was, in some profound sense, hers as well. It was her town too. Her place of childhood certainty, still uncorrupted by self-doubt.

She decided to go down to the club library and look for her grandfather's name among the books there. If Marion was giving up on the search, it only meant that she must do the work for both of them.

●

If the word 'library' implied an area where reading material was contained according to a system – however rudimentary – of categorization, then the library at the Ashagiri Club could lay no claim to the title. It was simply a room full of books piled up without a single discernible shred of order. Most were not even resting on shelves, but lay in great heaps on the floor, their covers curling and pocked with insect holes. There had once been a system here. Opening up volumes at random, Vanessa saw that each book contained a frontispiece that recorded the dates it had been borrowed and returned and by whom. But the last entry appeared to have been made sometime in the late fifties.

What sort of books had her grandfather enjoyed reading? She sat down on the single rickety chair in the centre of the dusty room and started flipping open books around her in a somewhat hopeless fashion. He had liked hunting. And mystery novels. But since the books were not arranged according to subject matter, she had no idea where to look. She found herself scanning volumes of obscure memoirs and novels with titles like *Westward! To The Sea!* written by people she – and probably nobody else alive – had ever heard of. All that labour for immortality, she thought, reduced to little more than food for paper mites.

She was startled by the sound of somebody clearing their throat. There was something about the way Major Das was standing in the doorway looking at her that suggested he had been there for some time. Vanessa gave a guilty start.

'I was just looking through some books,' she said.

He nodded. 'I have many . . . curiosities.'

Well, that's certainly true, thought Vanessa.

'Items you may find of some interest.' His gaze swept distractedly around the room. 'I can see you are . . . concerned with the past.'

'Yes,' said Vanessa eagerly. 'Yes, that's exactly what I'm concerned with.'

There was a pause. Major Das brushed at the sleeve of his coat as though to remove an invisible speck of dust. He cleared his throat again. 'These items,' he began, 'are not for general viewing you understand. They are strictly for –'

'Club members?'

'Precisely.'

'I'd very much like to see them.'

'Please follow me,' the Major said importantly.

Outside the library, in the portico facing the club's court-yard, he paused beside the old oxygen canister hanging from the wall.

'First man on Everest,' he said, tapping the metal. 'Tenzing Norgay. He used this very tank on that historic climb.'

'Really?'

'It is empty of course,' Major Das said, a little dismissively. 'Come, I have other things.'

He ushered her through a door into the old billiard room. It was entirely empty apart from a small chest of drawers at the far end. Major Das crossed the room and stopped in front of it.

'It is necessary to keep my items locked up at all times,' he said, as he withdrew a single, ornate key from the depths of his waistcoat pocket. 'They have a certain . . . value.'

'Very wise,' Vanessa said, peering into the drawer opened ceremoniously in front of her. Resting on a scrap of chamois leather she saw a glass disc about the size of a large coin, encircled by a thin band of gold. 'What is it?' She reached in to touch the object, but Major Das brushed her hand away, with a small hiss of caution.

'Hitler's monocle,' he said in a breathy, reverential whisper.

'His *monocle*?'

'Yes. He gave it to the Rajah of Peshwarighat. As a token of thanks. How it fell into my hands is another story.'

'I didn't think Hitler wore a monocle.'

'It is a little known fact.'

'I'm not even sure he wore glasses.'

'That is what he wished the world to believe,' Major Das said with great satisfaction.

'I see,' Vanessa said carefully. What else had the man got stashed away, she wondered. Winston Churchill's ear plugs?

'Thanks for showing me,' she said hastily, 'but I have to . . . go and see how my mother is doing. She's a little under the weather. Nothing serious, but I've left her alone too long you see, and . . . I really must get back.'

The Major's attention was still riveted on his prize. 'Of course,' he said, vaguely. 'Of course you must.'

Back in the room Vanessa found her mother sitting upright on the bed, combing her hair.

'Where've you been?' Marion asked, smiling.

'Nowhere. Another wild-goose chase. How are you feeling by the way?'

'Better. I had a nap and when I woke up, the headache was gone.'

'That's good. You look better.'

'I had the strangest dream,' Marion said.

The dream had begun with a feeling. The feeling had great force but it was also elusive. It was like a scent that had the power to call up a certain memory but the more you breathed it in, the fainter the thought became. Except that in the dream, what she scented was not a memory, but something even more elusive. A way of thinking, almost a way of being, that seemed to hint at great truth and joy. While still struggling to find and hold it, she found herself suddenly on the road to Ashagiri: the steep, rocky hillside to her right, fog in the valley to her left and the road curving away from her in a long bend.

Two girls stood a hundred yards away, holding hands and looking at her. She saw them both very clearly but when she awoke, she found she could not describe any detail of their appearance. What she remembered was only the piercing certainty that she knew the girl on the right. The sense of recognition was overwhelming. Marion opened her mouth to call out but no words came. Only the paralysing realization that she could give no name to that face which seemed so extraordinarily familiar. She was filled with a strange, uncomprehending distress. As though in failing to identify the child she had missed something terribly important. An answer to a question, an opportunity.

'That girl who was killed –'

'Which girl?'

'In the accident. I told you about her. She'd been out sketching. She wasn't meant to be there at all.'

'So why was she?'

'Sister Maureen gave her permission to go,' Marion said slowly. 'She was a member of her Four O'Clock Club.'

'So it was Sister Maureen's fault?'

'Yes. That was why she left. It must have been. She had to leave the school because she was . . . responsible. I never realized that until now. How terrible it must have been for her.'

'More terrible for the girl I would have thought,' Vanessa said.

'Yes, of course.' Marion thought for an instant of how it might have been. The sudden lurch forward as the ground shifted and then the sky darkened by tumbling stone. Arms raised to shield her head, instinctive, helpless.

'I can't even remember who she was,' she said.

●

When the alarm went off there was silence for a short while, then Marion turned over in bed. Vanessa could tell by the changed quality of her mother's breathing that she was awake.

'What time is it?' she said.

Marion half lifted her head from the pillow and then let it thud back down. 'We have to get up,' she said weakly.

'What time is it?'

'Five-thirty.'

'It's the middle of the night!'

'We have to get up. John will be coming round for us soon.'

'You can do what you like,' Vanessa said. 'I'm staying right where I am.'

'We can't, Vanessa. We said we'd go.'

'No. You said. You're the one who wanted to see his painting. You go.'

'I don't feel very well,' Marion said in a small, babyish voice. 'It's my head again. My headache's come back.'

'Tough.'

'You go. You can go without me, can't you?'

Vanessa sat up in bed in outrage. 'You made the arrangements! Take another paracetamol or something. Leave me out of it.'

'John will think us so rude –' Marion began.

'No!'

'One of us has to go. He'll think we have no manners at all.'

'Who cares?' Vanessa said bitterly. But she was already

reaching for the light switch by the side of her bed. 'Who the hell cares?'

Marion peeped at her from under the covers as Vanessa thumped around the room, pulling on sweat pants and her North Face jacket.

'These headaches of yours seem to come on at very convenient moments, I must say,' observed Vanessa.

'Don't forget to take your camera. You'll want to take plenty of shots of the sunrise.'

'The only thing I want to shoot right now,' Vanessa said, 'is lying six feet away.'

'You'll be glad you rose . . . to see the snows.'

'Don't push it, Mother. God, I look awful,' Vanessa said, catching sight of herself in the mirror. 'I look like I'm about to die.'

'You look fine. Just run a comb through that knot in the back of your head.'

'If you think,' Vanessa said furiously, 'that I'm going to doll myself up at this time of the night –' She was interrupted by a knock at the door.

'Have fun,' Marion said, settling herself comfortably into the pillows. 'Don't worry about me.'

Outside it was very cold and so dark that Vanessa could barely make out the shape of the wooden balcony supports. John Walcott stood a few feet away, with his face discreetly averted. He turned with a smile as she emerged.

'Mother isn't coming,' Vanessa announced grumpily. 'She says she has a headache.'

He looked worried. 'Perhaps we should make it another day. Would that be better?'

'I'm up now,' Vanessa said ungraciously, 'so we might as well go.' She stared at him. He had buttoned up his sports jacket, but apart from this one measure against the cold, his outfit was unchanged.

'Is that all you're wearing?'

'Oh, I'm used to the chill. I'm hardy.' He cast a somewhat envious eye at her jacket. 'That looks very snug. Just the thing.'

'Don't you have anything to cover your head?'

'Don't need it.' He thought of the yellow bobble hat stuffed into the pocket of his jacket. He had bought it at a stall in town. It was very warm but – he suspected – made him look somewhat ridiculous. 'It's not so bad once you get walking.'

'Let's go then, I'm freezing.'

Instead of turning right as she had expected, John led her left, down the hill towards the main town. The street was deserted. He walked easily with long strides and she had to pick up her pace to keep up with him.

'Isn't that heavy?' She pointed to the pack on his back.

'I'm so used to it, I hardly notice.' He smiled at her and for a moment there seemed to Vanessa to be something almost intriguing about his expression of perpetual good humour. It made her wonder fleetingly what his face might look like in the grip of other, very different emotions.

'Are you always this cheerful in the middle of the night?'

He looked at her as though about to respond, then seemed to change his mind.

'Once the sun comes up, it'll get much warmer,' he said, turning abruptly down a narrow alley between a shoe shop on one side and a tea house on the other. Without the dim light from the occasional street lamps on the main road, the alley was pitch dark. John reached into his pocket and produced a torch. 'Mind your feet,' he said, aiming the beam at the ground before her. They walked for several hundred yards in silence between dark walls. The ground was muddy here and once, when she reached out a hand to steady herself, Vanessa touched brick that felt wet with something other than mere water.

After a little while, the buildings thinned out, replaced by what seemed to be plots of land, haphazard and scrubby. John stopped and swung the torch away, leaving her in darkness.

'There's a bit of fence to climb I'm afraid,' he said. 'But it's pretty easy.'

'How on earth did you find this route anyway?' Vanessa asked, brushing aside his proffered arm. The fence was little more than a low wire strung between two posts and she managed to lift her legs over it with only a small moment of awkwardness. 'I don't remember reading about this in any of my guidebooks.'

'Prasad actually. He knows everything about this place.'

'Are we outside the town yet?'

'Not quite. There's a bit of a scramble until we get to the path. It's not for long. Then we'll start going uphill. It's about a forty-five minute walk from there to the top.' He swung the torch at her face, making her blink. 'Are you all right?'

'I'm fine,' she said, a little sharply.

It was lighter now, the dark seeping by slow degrees from the hillside above them, but Vanessa could still barely see where she was going. The ground was very steep and covered with loose stones that made her stumble with each step. At several points in the climb she was forced to use both hands to steady herself, her fingers clutching at the earth, her feet threatening to slide out from beneath her. John was making swift progress ahead. Every so often, a large rock, dislodged by his feet, tumbled past, narrowly missing her head.

'Sorry,' came his muffled voice.

Vanessa, bottom in the air, hands clutching the puny branches of a shrub, gritted her teeth.

'Here we are!' John called, disappearing over the top of a small ridge. 'Do you need a hand?'

She scrambled up the last few feet. 'Sorry about that,' he said anxiously. 'No other way to get to the path, I'm afraid.' Vanessa spent a moment or two brushing at her jacket in an attempt to hide the fact that she was panting heavily. All those lengths at the pool, she thought bitterly, and I'm still a wreck.

'It's easier from here.'

'I'm okay,' Vanessa said, annoyed by his concern. 'But I don't think my mother would have made it up there.'

'I never thought of that.'

The path they were on led towards an opening between two small hillocks, dipped briefly and then continued up a long, slender ridge that broke the darkness around it like the great spine of some sea creature slowly rising to the surface. At the foot of this ridge, John stopped and turned to her.

'The first time I went up here . . . well, you never get used to it, not really, but the first time –'

'What about it?'

He hesitated. 'Promise you won't look up? Not even once. Just keep your eyes on the ground.'

'Why?'

'Just promise.'

'All right. I can't see anything very much anyway.'

'It'll be hard,' he said earnestly. 'You'll want to look up, but you really mustn't.'

'All right,' she said again. 'I'll try.'

It was easier than she thought to keep her word. The path, though clear, was steep and Vanessa found that she needed to walk with her head down just to keep up with John's long strides.

'I've never seen anyone else up here,' he said as he walked. 'I don't know why other people don't come up this route.

There's another path on the other side of town that all the tourists take. You can get good views at the top of it, but nothing like this.'

'What do you do when you're not travelling? Back home I mean.'

'Bicycle courier,' John said. 'In London. I do it for as long as it takes to save up money to go away again and paint. The next trip I want to take is to Japan. To Mount Fuji.'

'Why there in particular?'

'You know Hokusai?'

'Not really.' Vanessa had a vague recollection of blue curving water. 'Oh, didn't he do those wave pictures?'

'Yes, that's right. Huge waves. You look at them and all you see is water and then you see, in the background, painted very, very small, always the same thing. Mount Fuji. It's the smallest part of the picture but the most important.'

Vanessa lifted her eyes from the ground slightly to look at him as he walked ahead of her.

'Why?' she asked. 'Why is it the most important thing?'

'I'm not sure,' he said simply. 'That's why I want to go. To find out.'

She was silent.

'Japan is very expensive,' John continued, a little sadly. 'It will take me months to save up. At least a year. Perhaps not even then. What do you do back home?'

'I work in the sort of place which employs bicycle couriers. A corporate imaging company which is basically a grand way of saying we tell other companies what their logos should look like and where to stick them on their letterheads.'

'You're a designer.'

'Oh no. I manage a couple of the accounts. I tell the designers what to do.' She paused waiting for him either to question the validity of an occupation that existed solely to

126

make rich companies even richer, or worse, to feign interest in a field he clearly knew nothing about. But John did neither.

'I wouldn't mind it so much,' she said impulsively, 'if it was ever acknowledged that all we really do is charge hundreds of thousands of pounds to take an existing logo, slant it, turn it red and tell clients what size it should appear on billboards. I mean, it's not as though it doesn't work. We can literally make millions for companies by changing the way they present themselves. But it's not like that. It's all got to be . . . elevated into some big self-justifying enterprise. Our chairman, Terry Pryce, gives whole lectures on the archetypal significance of the Shell symbol. And the swastika. He talks about the swastika almost with envy. No, not almost, with *total* envy. Because it has such enormous "brand recognition" as he puts it.'

'You make it sound . . . dishonest.'

'Yes, I suppose I do. But not dishonest in the ordinary sense, dishonest to itself somehow. It's hard to explain.'

She paused. 'I say I work there, but actually I don't. Not any more. I gave my notice.'

'Something better came along?'

'No. I just suddenly decided.'

'Why?'

Vanessa was silent. How could she explain the disturbance of the last few months? Something had happened when her father died. Something had happened to her. To the sorrow of her father's passing was added a new sense of her mother's vulnerability. Of a life spent in the shadow of someone else. It seemed to her a kind of . . . nothingness. And, wrapped up in the pity of this thought, came the whispered suggestion that there were other ways in which existence could be empty. That a life of activity and movement without any true goal – her life perhaps – was also a kind of nothingness.

Her mother had faced limited choices but she could hardly say the same for herself. The world had been laid before her, fringed with the expectation of success. She could go anywhere, do anything.

She looked up at John walking ahead of her. How could she complain of being good at almost everything she had ever tried? How could she say that the only thing that had not come easy was satisfaction that lasted beyond a week or two? That her life since her father's death had been lit by a kind of slow-burning panic that came from a sense of having too many choices and no clear direction to take.

'I suppose I just didn't like it any more,' she said at last.

'But you used to like it, didn't you?'

'Yes. I was good at it at any rate. Which is the same thing, isn't it?' She paused. 'My father thought it was a great job. Right on track. Being on track was a big thing for my dad.'

'Was?'

'Yeah. He died last year.'

John looked back at her. 'God, I'm sorry. He must have been quite young still.'

'Late fifties. Went to the gym four times a week. Golf at the weekends. Never smoked.' She shook her head. 'Nothing else to say, really. Nothing useful anyway.'

They had been climbing for half an hour or so and the dawn was approaching fast. Vanessa could now see that the ridge was covered with patches of pale, wiry grass and low juniper bushes that gave off a sweet, almost heady, scent.

'When can I look?' she asked. 'Can I look now?'

He stopped. 'Please don't,' he said urgently. 'You'll understand why. It won't be long.'

'How high up are we going?'

'It's a little over a thousand feet above Ashagiri. Beyond the tree line. You might notice the change in altitude just a little.'

'Yes,' she said, seizing on this explanation for her new breathlessness. 'Yes, I think that I am noticing it all of a sudden.'

They continued to tramp upwards in silence. As the sky lightened further, Vanessa had to struggle against a feeling of precariousness. It was not that the ridge was too narrow – turning her head very slightly from right to left she could see that it stretched for a good fifty yards across – but rather that she sensed the space on either side of the ridge had deepened immeasurably so that, despite the fact that she was placing her feet as sturdily as ever, she felt obliged to check her balance with every step. Her breath was coming faster now and she had quite forgotten that her hands were cold.

'Not too far now,' John called. 'We're nearly there.'

The path began to level out gradually. He had picked up his pace a little, forcing her into almost a trot. 'Stop going so fast,' she gasped. 'I can't keep up.'

'Sorry.'

During the whole of the walk up, Vanessa had been grateful that the morning was almost completely still, with only a light breeze at their back. Now, in the silence, she heard a new sound. A light and multitudinous flapping, as though made by a great number of objects, each insignificant by itself but together forming a strange kind of music. She almost raised her head then but John had stopped in front of her and placed a hand on her shoulder.

'It gets a little narrow here. You mustn't look up quite yet. You'd better take my arm.'

She stiffened automatically as he took her by the elbow, suddenly wondering whether she was being made a fool of. 'This had better be good,' she said, shuffling forward.

'You can look now.'

He took his hand away and stepped back.

She lifted her head and the sight struck her like a blow. All around her, completely encircling the ridge apart from a small opening in the direction they had come, rose the mountains. Closer than they had appeared down in Ashagiri. Far closer. Snow-topped, massive, each rocky point, each arctic ledge and sheer cliff drop outlined against the pale sky with the sharpness of blades that cut deep and are gone, even before pain. Below her, where the ridge ended and fell steeply away, she could see the tiny silver thread of a river. By her side, strung out on four or five long lines supported by wooden posts, hundreds of Buddhist prayer flags, the size of large handkerchiefs, fluttered in the breeze. It was this that was making the flapping sound she had heard on her approach. The flags, once vividly coloured, were faded to different shades, some still bright, others blown to transparency; mere scraps of mist held together by a cobweb of threads.

'The sun will be up in a minute,' John said. He had his back to the mountains and was looking instead at her face as though what he saw there was, for a brief moment, more compelling than the peaks themselves.

The second he spoke, the sun, still hidden behind the mountains to their right, hit the tallest summit in the range. A sudden band of gold appeared against the snow, striking with such swiftness and authority it seemed as though it should be accompanied by some great, ringing noise, although quite what this would sound like was impossible to imagine. The light held still for a moment as though in deference to the ascendancy of the mountain and then spread down. Vanessa closed her eyes for an instant. She was aware of her hand in her jacket pocket, holding on to something; a sliver of gum wrapped in foil and for a second this tiny object seemed perfectly strange to her. As though she had lost some connection to her own fingers, the details of her own person and could not regain it without an effort of concentration. She saw that John had sunk down on to his knees beside her as though engaged in some obscure worship. And for a confused moment, this behaviour did not seem odd or out of place. But he was simply showing her something.

'See the incense sticks?' he said, pointing to the base of a small cairn on the very edge of the ridge. 'People bring them up here and light them. It's considered a holy place.'

'Yes,' she said slowly. 'Yes, I can see that.'

He slipped the pack off his back and unbuckled it. 'Are you hungry? I've got a couple of chapattis in here somewhere. I saved them from supper last night. They're surprisingly good when they're cold.'

'You really are on a budget, aren't you?'

He shrugged cheerfully. 'I don't like wasting things.'

'So this is where you come to paint,' she said, still staring around her.

'I'm lucky. I don't need an easel or anything like that. I just sit on that rock over there with my work on my lap.' He reached into his bag and brought out a small board with a square magnifying glass attached above it.

'See, you can adjust the glass to the height you need,' he said, demonstrating the action. 'I put the canvas in here and then look through the glass at what I'm working on. It folds up pretty smoothly although this hinge needs a bit of oiling –'

'Where did you find such a thing?'

'I had to invent it actually. It took me ages to get the angle right.'

As he talked, Vanessa nibbled on the edge of her chapatti. The dough was flabby but still tasty and she found herself taking larger and larger bites, suddenly ravenous after the rigours of her climb.

'Well, aren't you going to set it up and get to work? That's why we came up here after all.'

He shook his head. 'Not today,' he said, carefully repacking his equipment.

'Why not?'

'Just not the right time.' It seemed to her that his face had changed, become secretive.

'It's me, isn't it?' she said abruptly. 'I'd put you off.'

'Oh *no*,' he said with great vehemence. 'Please don't think that. It's not true at all.'

'It *is* true,' she insisted, wondering why it suddenly mattered so much.

'I didn't come up here this morning with any idea of working, if you must know,' he said in a rush. 'I didn't have any intention of it, to be honest.'

'Then why did you bring all your stuff?' Vanessa asked relentlessly.

'Habit probably,' he said lightly. He looked at her in that way of his; openly, without bravado. 'Or perhaps I just needed a pretext to spend time with you.'

His directness made her smile. 'I'm flattered,' she said, and was surprised to find she meant it.

The sun had reached their ridge at last, finding their cold hands and drying the almost imperceptible film of dew – only one or two degrees finer than the cloth itself – on the prayer flags around them.

'Can't I even see what you've been working on?'

'Maybe later . . . when we get back.'

'Why? Why can't I see it now?'

'Because –' He swept his arm out towards the view. 'Because of all this, I suppose. Seeing . . . the real thing and then seeing my work right next to it . . . you can't help making the comparison. You can't help thinking –'

'Oh, come on,' Vanessa said briskly. 'Hand it over.'

'Well . . . .' He reached unwillingly into the breast pocket of his jacket and took out a small plastic bag.

'It's not quite finished,' he added anxiously, passing her a canvas rectangle slightly larger than a playing card cut in half. She took it carefully by its edges.

The painting showed the highest mountain at first light, caught in its moment of sudden, sourceless gold and it was like a jewel between her fingers. John was right, she thought, it was not like the real mountain. The proportions were changed, made broader, slightly foreshortened, and the whole surface given a thin sheen, as though covered in some clear liquid, thicker than water and very bright. It took her a little while to realize what she was looking at. Not an image of the actual mountain at all but a painting of its reflection, floating minutely in the wet curve of a wide open eye.

'It's . . . extraordinary,' she said, fascinated.

'It's not finished,' John said again, even more hastily. 'It needs more work.'

'It's beautiful. I really mean that. I'm not just saying it to be nice.'

'Well . . .' He took it from her quickly and replaced it in the plastic bag. 'I like doing it, you know.' Vanessa watched him wrap it up and tuck it in his pocket once more.

'How do you know?' she said suddenly.

'What?'

'That you like doing it? I mean, how do you really *know*?'

John did not seem to find the question peculiar. He paused for a while, considering.

'It's not like you said before, about liking what you do just because you're good at it because most of the time I don't think I'm much good at this at all. I don't really know the answer. It's not as though I ever had any kind of plan for it. It just turned out this way.'

'Oh.'

'You sound . . . disappointed.'

'No,' she said quickly, 'no, I just wondered, that's all.'

By the time they got back to the Ashagiri Club it was mid-morning and Vanessa was tired. She found her mother having a cup of tea on the balcony, her legs comfortably resting on a foot stool. In front of her on the table were a multitude of brown paper packages. She looked up excitedly at Vanessa's approach.

'There you are! Did you have a good time?'

'Yes I did, as a matter of fact.'

'I've been shopping,' Marion said in the tones of one confessing to some crime. 'I meant to go exploring. I was actually on my way to the taxi stand to find out how much it would cost us to go to Sunny Valley when I saw the shop and got . . . distracted.'

•

In fact, Marion had had no intention of going anywhere in Ashagiri where she might be disappointed by memory. Since that excluded most of the town, it had crossed her mind not even to get out of bed at all. For a long time after Vanessa left she lay and examined the cracks and stains on the ceiling with the pointless absorption of a prisoner holed up for years in the same cell. At last hunger drove her out from beneath the covers. She dressed carefully, applied her lipstick and then gave herself her customary mirror-smile; artificial, a touch placatory, as though to reassure herself that the face she presented to the world could cause no offence. Downstairs, in the club dining room, Prasad brought her pancakes with small slices of banana embedded in the batter. The meal lifted her spirits slightly.

'Where's the best place to buy gifts?' she asked him. 'The Curio Emporium?'

He shook his head quickly. 'Too expensive. Not real. It's better you go to Avari's.'

He gave her directions and she set off, handbag clutched under one arm, trying not to look around her more than she needed to find her way. She told herself she might be walking anywhere and the people and the buildings around her were merely creations of her own imagination that could be banished by an effort of will, but the noise in the street and a hundred intriguing details of shape and colour so tugged at her attention that from time to time she was forced to stop and close her eyes for a second before she could proceed. She was relieved that Avari's shop, though tucked away in a side-street, was easy enough to find. She opened the door and paused for an instant on the threshold with a feeling of sudden anticipation that was close to joy.

Whatever architectural proportions Avari's shop once had were now entirely blurred, obscured by the sheer multitude of his wares. Items of all different shapes, sizes and colours crowded the corners and hung in a dizzying array from the ceiling. Hats, rugs, stools, statuettes, ornate weaponry, brass cups and bowls, carvings, dolls, flags, masks, marble paper-weights, embroidered waistcoats, cushions, paintings, wall hangings and what seemed like thousands of pieces of jewel-lery that sparkled temptingly in the soft light. In the centre of this horde, behind a glass case full of enamelled boxes, sat Avari himself, plump-faced and bewildered looking, as though half mystified by the evidence of his own prosperity. A tiny ruby glimmered in his ear. At Marion's entrance he looked up with a smile of great charm.

'Can I help you find something?'

'Not really. I'm just . . . browsing.'

He smiled again. 'Browsing . . . such a nice word. Like sheep in the field.'

'I think that's grazing,' Marion said timidly.

'Yes. Browsing and grazing. Both nice things to do.'

'You have such a lot of things . . . I don't know where to start.' She moved over to a pile of rugs and brushed the top one with her hand. 'Everything is so beautiful.'

'Please take your time. You cannot browse in a hurry. It must be done slowly. Perhaps with some tea?'

'That would be nice,' Marion said, her hands flickering over an array of brass Buddhas. 'These are so lovely. I think I shall have to have at least one.'

She moved around the shop, returning from time to time

to the counter to place a chosen item and take a sip of Avari's tea. It was warm and very quiet and after a while she began to lose sense of how long she had been there. Avari watched her purchases pile up without comment, making no effort to draw her attention to any item in particular.

'You live in England?' he asked at last.

'Yes,' Marion said. 'Although I used to live here.' She smiled at him uncertainly. 'A long time ago.'

'And what do you think of it now?'

'I . . . don't know.'

Avari sighed. 'They have let everything go to rack and ruin.'

She shook her head politely. 'No –'

'Yes, it is true. Rack and ruin. Everything used to be so different. The people were different. Poorer of course. Very poor, but everyone was compassionate. They were a class apart. Money did not matter then. Love and understanding was the currency in Ashagiri.'

'I'm not sure that's *quite* true,' murmured Marion.

'You used to be able to see the mountains from all over town. Now there is no view. All these concrete boxes going up. Quick, quick. No time to browse and graze. No time at all.'

'It's not that bad,' protested Marion.

He shook his head.

'Change has brought good things too,' persisted Marion, more out of a desire to cheer the man up rather than be argumentative. 'All this development, people on holiday. It's good business.' She swept her arm around the room. 'Your lovely shop . . .'

He glanced around him and it seemed to her again that he looked bewildered. As though he was seeing the place for the first time.

'Well,' she said brightly, 'I suppose I should pay for all this.'

It crossed her mind that she should make some attempt to bargain. She knew that was what she was supposed to do and Vanessa was bound to ask about it and would think her spineless if she hadn't. 'Is it possible – ' she began.

'I can give you a ten per cent discount,' interrupted Avari. 'And two for the price of one on the bangles of course.'

'That's very kind of you.'

'Plus, the earrings I shall give you for nothing,' he continued, putting them into a little silk drawstring bag.

'Are you sure?' asked Marion before she remembered that she was meant to be persuading him rather than the other way around.

Avari smiled and shrugged. 'Would you like for these to be delivered to Glenside?'

'Glenside?'

'Where you are staying – '

'But I'm not. I'm at the Ashagiri Club.'

He looked surprised. 'But why? Why are you not staying at Glenside?'

By the time she left the shop, Marion was in high spirits. She spread out her purchases on the balcony table at the club and examined each one with enjoyment. Shopping was a great comfort, she thought. The pleasure was not so much in the acquisition, but in the choosing of each item. It was a kind of self expression.

'I got a good price for this stuff,' she told Vanessa.

'Really?' Vanessa said sceptically.

'Two for the price of one!' Marion said, holding up the bangles for inspection. 'Look at these cushion covers. Such detailed embroidery.'

'What's this?' Vanessa held up a small brass bell with a handle. 'It looks like something you memsahibs used to summon the servants.'

'I'm not exactly sure,' confessed Marion. 'I just liked the pattern on it. It came with a little wooden stick . . .'

Prasad had arrived with a fresh pot of tea and an extra cup. After he had finished arranging them on the table he hesitated for a moment. 'Please,' he said, holding out his hand. 'I will show you.'

He held up the bell in one hand and began to rub around the rim with the wooden stick, his face solemn with concentration. For a moment, Vanessa was tempted to laugh but then something unexpected happened. The bell began to hum. It started as a low vibration and grew steadily louder and clearer until it was a single, singing note that seemed to come from everywhere at once. Round and round went the stick on the bell and the noise rose until it seemed it could go no further. Marion had never heard anything like it. It was the sound light might make, she thought. Glistening, unbearably pure. Prasad stopped moving the stick and the sound hung in the air for a second and then drew away, like something melting slowly on the tongue.

'Buddhist prayer bell,' he said politely, replacing it on the table.

The two women stared at the object in astonishment.

'Do you think I could do that?' Marion said at last. She picked up the bell and started rubbing the rim, but the stick slipped in her fingers. No sound emerged except the slight scratch of wood against metal. She tried again. 'I'm doing what you did, aren't I?' she asked Prasad. 'You just rubbed it, didn't you?'

'You must practise,' he said.

Marion put the bell down. 'I forgot to tell you. I think we should move.'

'Where to?'

'Glenside. It's a hotel. Up above Fountain Square. They have hot-water bottles at night.'

'How do you know?' Vanessa was irked that her mother appeared to have discovered something that she had missed. 'Have you been there?'

'Avari told me. The man in the shop. He thought we were staying there because apparently it's the best hotel in town.'

'It's probably got the highest prices too. He must have taken one look at that handbag of yours and rubbed his hands together in glee. He must know someone at the hotel. They're probably in it together.'

'He wasn't like that at all,' Marion protested.

Vanessa looked unconvinced. 'It has *hot-water bottles*,' pleaded her mother.

'I suppose we could take a look.'

'They do a proper dinner every night. You don't have to be a guest to go. Four courses. Avari says they have piano music –'

'I suppose anything's got to be better than the evening entertainment in this place,' Vanessa said rather grudgingly.

'We'll have to dress up a bit,' Marion said excitedly. 'I just *knew* my silver shoes would come in useful!'

When the white-turbaned bearer ushered them through the door of Glenside's main drawing room, Vanessa assumed the man had made a mistake. The dozen or so occupants, seated on generous armchairs drawn up to the fire, had the relaxed and intimate air of a private party. The room itself seemed designed for just such a purpose. The formality of high ceiling and crystal chandelier offset by a comforting, haphazard chintziness. Dark-green velvet drapes – only slightly worn around the edges – were closed fast against the evening. Needlepoint cushions scattered the sofa and a clock ticked quietly on the broad mantelpiece. But there was something irrepressibly exotic about the room, despite all the homely touches. Perhaps it was the pair of black-lacquered coffee tables or the vase of huge, tropical blooms above the fire, or the green silk gown of a middle-aged Englishwoman reclining on a sofa in the centre of the room. She was gesturing as she spoke, lifting her arms to reveal draped sleeves embroidered with a pattern of blue, entangled dragons.

Vanessa turned to the bearer. 'We were looking for the *restaurant.*' But he seemed not to hear and now the woman in the green gown had noticed their presence in the doorway and was smiling and holding one hand out in greeting.

'There you are! I'm so glad you could join us,' she said, as though everything up until then had simply been a prelude to the Wests' arrival.

Marion stepped forward. 'You'll have to forgive me for not getting up,' continued the woman. 'Please come in and have a drink. We're having the most interesting discussion.'

Now that Vanessa was closer she could see that the woman was older than she had first thought. A good deal older. Her face had the transparency of extreme age, a glowing quality of the skin that comes only at the start and very end of life. Her hair and eyes were grey, a pale silvery shade that complemented the green of her robe. Around her neck she wore a necklace of jade beads strung on a scarlet thread. It was her smile that made her look younger than she was, thought Vanessa. Most old people had lost that joyful lift, that swift connection between lips and eyes. Perhaps, with age, one's face itself simply got in the way.

She knew at once that this must be Mrs Macdonald.

Her mother had talked about Mrs Macdonald on their approach to the hotel. 'She's run this place for years and years Avari said. Her husband was something or other in the army. When he died she pretty much took over.' Marion was wearing her new pink shawl purchased that morning and picking her way carefully through the grime of the street in an effort to protect her shoes.

'They stayed on you see. After Independence. That's when they bought Glenside.'

The hotel was hidden from the road in a thick surrounding of trees. A driveway – just wide enough for a car – led steeply up to a sloping front garden, bordered by a white-washed fence. Vanessa was struck by how orderly, how very *clean* everything looked. They crossed a small, impeccably swept courtyard, past terracotta pots of orange and pink geraniums and entered the visitors' lodge where a large, gold-trimmed guest book lay open on the desk.

'Do we need to sign even if we're just having dinner?' Marion asked the receptionist, an efficient-looking young woman with a pencil behind her ear.

'Oh yes, everybody signs.' She offered a pen. 'For the last fifty years all visitors to Glenside have signed the book.'

At first, the hotel reminded Vanessa of the kind of country house seen only in films in which everyone spent the time swishing tennis racquets around and getting telegrams from the war office. But the Victorian furniture, the collection of walking sticks by the door, the slightly scuffed oriental rugs, had the quality of things accumulated rather than placed, no more designed than a scattering of fossils exposed by the searcher's pick. For the first time since arriving in Ashagiri, Vanessa realized she was in an environment virtually un-changed since her mother's childhood.

'You must be Mrs Macdonald,' Marion said, shaking the woman's hand. 'It's really very kind of you –'

'Please take a seat.' The old woman gestured rather grandly to the chair beside her. 'Is this your daughter?'

'Yes. We've been staying at the club, but then a man in a shop told us about your place –'

'Ah, the club. You have met Major Das then. A strange man. But then, he was a strange little boy. It was probably because of his mother. She had such a temper. She used to get so cross with her husband she'd run up and pour ink into his bath. And he was such a frail man.' She smiled. 'What would you like to drink?'

She was looking at Marion as she spoke and Vanessa took the opportunity to examine the other guests in the room. Her eye passed quickly over three or four men in business suits talking quietly in one corner and a dazed-looking girl perched on the edge of one of the sofas who held her skinny arms tightly crossed at the elbows as though fighting the impulse to clutch at herself. Next to the girl was a young Indian in a startlingly blue sports jacket, and a backpacker type, with ginger goatee, who was shovelling peanuts into his mouth and ignoring both of them. But it was the solitary man leaning against the mantelpiece who held her attention.

Dark, beautifully cut trousers. A collarless tunic buttoned up to the neck. Thick, over-long black hair. The face a little too broad perhaps to be conventionally good looking, but arresting all the same. A touch authoritarian, she thought. Something intense about him only reinforced by the restraint of his clothes, the still way he held himself.

Vanessa glanced around her quickly as though in disbelief that she was the only person staring at the man. He seemed positioned there precisely for others' regard. The light above him, the room's furniture, the mantelpiece itself against which he leaned, given context only by his presence. He lifted his glass to his lips and turning slightly caught her gaze. She saw, with astonishment, that his eyes were dark blue.

She looked away quickly. Mrs Macdonald was saying something to her.

'. . . lucky you've come at a time when we have plenty of younger guests. I can keep your mother all to myself. Such a treat for me to chat about old times.'

'Yes, that is lucky,' Vanessa said automatically, wondering what she was talking about. Her mother's face wore a look of bewildered pleasure at all the attention.

'I was just telling Mrs Macdonald about our trip. About coming back. She says lots of other people do it too. Come back, I mean. They all find it terribly changed. I'm not the only one apparently.'

'No, you're not,' Mrs Macdonald said firmly. 'I once entertained a woman who simply refused to leave without a bag of stones she took from the wall behind Fountain Square. She had to prise them out with a pair of scissors. Mementoes, she called them. She'd come all this way and she wasn't leaving without bringing something back. I often wonder what she felt when she got home and unpacked them and saw they were just stones after all.'

'Maybe she made them into a rockery,' Marion said, thinking suddenly of her garden at home.

'What school did you go to? I wasn't educated here myself, but several of the old schools in Ashagiri are still going from strength to strength.'

'I've already thought of that,' Marion said sadly. 'St Margaret's. It's completely gone.'

'St Margaret's! But we have a guest from St Margaret's.' Mrs Macdonald clapped her hands together in delight. 'Right here at Glenside!' She gestured eagerly to the bearer. 'Where is Miss Nichols? Is she still in her room?'

The bearer nodded towards the door.

'Ah, there you are!' cried Mrs Macdonald. 'Right on cue. I have someone you are going to be so excited to meet.'

Marion and Vanessa turned to look at the new arrival.

It was the woman from the train. The one who had made such a fuss about her seat.

She was dressed for dinner in a soft wool skirt and sweater. Her extraordinary hair was the same as they remembered except that here, too, there had been an attempt at formality; a green plastic hairslide in the shape of a bow had been clipped above the right ear. Vanessa stared at it, unsure why such an innocuous item should rivet her attention. Perhaps it was the way it had simply been stuck there, apparently serving no function, as though the wearer had positioned it merely in the hope of looking the part without really knowing what it was for. The shape was all wrong, too girlish somehow for Miss Nichols' dour countenance and, for a second, Vanessa felt a sudden, inexplicable unease.

'Someone from your old gang,' Mrs Macdonald said. 'From St Margaret's. Marion West. Do you remember her?' She turned to Marion. 'But I'm forgetting. West wasn't your name then, was it?'

'It was Temple,' Marion said in a nervous, hopeful voice. She smiled at the newcomer. 'Marion Temple. When were you at St Margaret's? I'm so sorry I didn't recognize you on the train but it's been such a long time, hasn't it? I must look completely different too –'

Something briefly crossed the woman's face. A flicker of alarm, or perhaps simply surprise. Then she smiled. Her eyes had the appearance of wet stone.

'What's your full name?' Marion asked. 'Maybe it will jog my memory –'

'Dorothy,' the woman said. 'Dorothy Nichols.'

'Dorothy . . . the name *does* ring a faint bell. Perhaps you were a year or two below me. That would explain why I don't remember better. Little girls are so cliquey, aren't they?'

'No doubt that is the explanation.' She turned to Mrs Macdonald abruptly. 'I have some matters to discuss with you. I think you will find them of great interest.'

'Wonderful,' Mrs Macdonald said. 'Then we can all sit down to dinner together.' She glanced at Vanessa as though belatedly remembering her presence. 'Somebody else for the table . . .' Her eyes swept the room, lighting finally on the figure of the young man in the sky-blue sports jacket. 'And Bharani! Bharani must join us too.'

At the sound of his name, the man seemed to bound out of his seat. He came forward and presented a large hand. 'A pleasure to meet you!' he said with great vigour. 'A true pleasure.'

'Bharani has become quite a feature at Glenside,' Mrs Macdonald said fondly. 'I cannot quite imagine life without him.'

'This lady is so good,' Bharani told Vanessa. 'This lady is

like my own mother. But everyone loves her. I am just one of very many.'

A gong sounded from some distance away. 'And now it is dinner!' Bharani said, rubbing his hands together as though all the elements that could make his life complete had come miraculously together. 'I will escort you.' He took Vanessa's arm.

'Shouldn't we wait for Mrs Macdonald?'

Bharani shook his head. 'Such a very brave lady. It is her back I believe,' he whispered. 'For the last ten years she has been obliged to lie down, never to rise. The bearers will take her. It is all arranged.'

'What's wrong with her?'

'Nobody knows. It is one of the great mysteries. She has consulted everyone of note in the medical field to no avail.' His cheerful expression dimmed slightly. 'I know that she is often in great pain. Great pain. And recently, in the last day or so, she has suffered a new setback. She has been fainting clean away. We are all very concerned.'

He smiled again. 'But she is always so full of joy. It is a truly humbling thing.'

'I see –'

'Tonight I believe Chicken Maryland is on the menu,' Bharani continued enthusiastically. 'It is quite delicious.'

They were passing down a long corridor flanked on both sides by black and white photographs. Views of the hotel, sports teams, portraits of men and women on horseback, sweeping vistas of the mountains with trees rather than buildings in the foreground. Vanessa's attention was caught by a number of shots of the same woman. A small, rather stout figure with a piercing, resolute expression. In one picture she was dressed in Tibetan garb, a conical hat crammed low over her eyes. In another, she was posed next to several men –

clearly dignitaries of one sort or another. In a third, she was bent over a desk of the old-fashioned folding kind that explorers from another era obliged their porters to carry through all terrains.

Vanessa stopped and tapped one of the pictures. 'Do you know who this is?' she asked Bharani.

'But of course,' he said, with some surprise. 'Everyone knows who that is. It is Alexandra David Neel.'

'Who's she?'

'Who is Alexandra David Neel?' Bharani repeated, as though he could barely believe his ears. 'She was the first European to set foot inside the city of Lhasa.' He shook his head. 'It is a very well-known story.'

'I didn't know that,' Vanessa said, somewhat mortified. 'Why are there so many pictures of her?'

'Alexandra David Neel and Mrs Macdonald were great friends. You must get her to tell you about it. It is a truly entertaining narrative.'

'How long have you been staying at Glenside?' Vanessa asked as they entered the dining room. 'You seem to know a lot about it.'

'Tomorrow it will be precisely ten and a half months. This is Mrs Macdonald's table here.' The dining room was smaller than Vanessa had expected and seemed to be lit entirely by candlelight. The tall windows that dominated two sides of the room were bare; against their panes, the reflections of glass and silver, softened with the milky sheen of age, seemed to dart and swim like fish in a dark ocean. Eight or nine tables were covered with pale pink cloths, each decorated with a small vase of nasturtiums. In the far corner stood a piano, behind which the top of a woman's hat could just be seen: a turquoise, knitted cloche with a curiously off-centre look about it, as though it was on back to front. At Vanessa and Bharani's entrance, the hat bobbed from sight and the piano began to play with a halting, but cheerful tune.

'We are the first!' Bharani said, a little triumphantly.

'Over ten months! What have you been doing here all this time?' asked Vanessa as she took her seat. She noticed that the table was larger than the others in the room, probably to make space for the chaise longue drawn up to her left.

'I'm a student.'

'At one of the schools here?'

'Oh no.' He made a dismissive gesture. 'They are just for children. I am enrolled in a number of correspondence courses. I am studying French and physics and currently I am also learning ballroom dancing.'

'Dancing? By correspondence course?'

'Of course. It is very simple. They send you little drawings where all the feet must go. Pages and pages of feet all turned in the right direction –'

He was interrupted by the arrival of Marion and Mrs Macdonald, the latter carried in the arms of the bearer. With the voluminous folds of her dress pinned against the man's body, Vanessa could see how small she was, how little effort to lift. He placed her down carefully on the chaise longue and adjusted cushions until she was comfortable, propped up on her left elbow at the level of the table. She gestured for Marion to sit beside her. Dorothy Nichols, bringing up the rear of the party, saw the gesture and paused, hovering by Mrs Macdonald's seat.

'I'm perfectly comfortable, Dorothy,' Mrs Macdonald said. She turned to Marion. 'Dorothy has been so very kind. She's been looking after me you know. All her lotions and potions have been most comforting. It is miraculous what she concocts in that room of hers. She is quite the alchemist.'

Dorothy Nichols permitted herself a small smile. 'It is an

apt analogy perhaps. Mainstream medicine regards anything alternative with the same hostility that alchemists once suffered. The same suspicion.'

'Well, in that particular case, the suspicion was right, wasn't it?' Vanessa said.

'I was using the example as an *analogy*,' Nichols said, without looking at her. 'The idea of taking base elements and turning them into something as valuable as gold is a very fitting one. You could say the same for many alternative remedies.'

'Dorothy has had many successes,' Mrs Macdonald said. 'I'm a bit woolly on the details, but I believe she once cured herself of a terrible rash when the doctors couldn't help her at all. What was the name of that rash again, Dorothy?'

'It was uticaria,' Dorothy said, somewhat unwillingly. 'More commonly known as hives.'

The others stared at her expectantly.

'Of course according to *mainstream* doctors,' she continued, drawing out the words with sarcastic emphasis, 'it was all in my head. Psychosomatic.'

'Dorothy used baking powder,' Mrs Macdonald said admiringly. 'She covered herself in the stuff and stood in the bathtub all night. In the morning, the rash was quite gone.'

'*Baking powder?*' Vanessa repeated.

'It was a paste of which baking powder was merely one of the ingredients,' Nichols corrected. 'To be effective it needed to be applied over every square inch of the body.'

There was a short silence around the table.

'I should tell you a little something about our other guests,' Mrs Macdonald said to the Wests. 'We have quite a distinguished gathering at Glenside at the moment. Over there, at that table, we have the high-altitude convention from Southern India. Scientists from different fields studying the effects of oxygen deficiency on the body. They are using the hotel as a conference centre.'

She paused. 'Then there are Greg and Tish.' She pointed to the man with the ginger goatee and the thin woman Vanessa had noticed in the drawing room earlier. They were sitting at a table with the dark-haired man she had noticed before. He looked bored, she thought. He was smiling at his companions but she could tell he was bored. There was something about his face that made him incapable of hiding such an emotion. Or perhaps he simply did not care to. 'Poor Tish,' Mrs Macdonald continued. 'She is so very thin. We have been trying to build her up for a whole week now.'

'Greg looks healthy enough,' Vanessa said.

'Yes Greg. He is so . . . enthusiastic.'

'It is Greg who makes Tish sick,' interjected Bharani. 'Always making her go this way and that. He must always visit the most run-down areas and spend the smallest amount of money. And then one Buddhist monastery after another. But they are all alike. Once you have been to one, you have been to all, and the food is so very second-rate. As soon as Tish is well, they will be off again. It is a great shame.'

'It is because Greg is in love with exploration,' Mrs Macdonald said. 'He doesn't mean to be cruel. Tish has had dysentery twice. And the flu as well. And yesterday I saw her in the corner breathing most strangely into a brown paper bag. We simply can't let her go again until she has more strength.'

'Who's the man they're sitting with?' Vanessa asked casually.

'That is the Prince.'

'The Prince?' For an instant, Vanessa thought that the old woman had picked up on her admiration and was making sly reference to it. She flushed slightly. But there was no trace of mockery in Mrs Macdonald's words.

'Yes, Alex Khusam, the Prince of Rupkhand. It's a small region to our north. His grandfather was king there before the area was annexed by India some time ago. The family was forced into exile for a number of years. Alex was educated in America. His mother is American, you know. She's never been back to this part of the world, but Alex spends most of the year here now. The old palace in Rupkhand is still there. Maintaining it has become his passion.' She smiled. 'I have seen a photograph of his mother. Such a beautiful woman.'

'So if Rupkhand was annexed by India, then it's not an independent kingdom any more,' Vanessa said. 'And he's not actually a real prince.'

'Not *technically*. But everyone still calls him that. And it suits him rather well, don't you think?'

'Yes,' Vanessa said slowly, 'yes, it does rather.'

'Have you been . . . to St Margaret's yet?' Marion said rather timidly to Dorothy. 'I went there a few days ago and it was quite a shock.'

Dorothy nodded. 'It was to be expected. It was the only school in Ashagiri that had a policy of not allowing Indians to enrol. An example of the kind of bigotry that the town would be only too happy to forget.'

'Yes. Yes, I see what you mean.'

'I have few happy memories of the place myself,' Dorothy continued. 'Even at that young age, I was aware of the injustice of the system. Even then, I knew we had no right to be there. No right at all.'

'I'm afraid all that never occurred to me,' confessed Marion. 'I just accepted it, I suppose. In the way children do. It was only later, when I was older . . .'

She wanted to say that later, when she was older, she too had fought against the whole premise of her upbringing. But it was hardly true. Oh, she had believed in the rightness of

Indian independence. How could she not? The idea of a handful of Europeans trying to rule a whole sub-continent that didn't belong to them in the first place had quickly come to seem quite absurd to her. Absurd and shameful. But this was a general belief, not applied to her everyday life. She had never challenged her parents, never questioned her father's conservative politics, his ingrained racism, his resentment of the world, nor wondered at her mother's compliance and her inability to adapt to a life where nobody called her memsahib any longer. Hadn't she instead always done exactly what they expected of her? Even down to marrying the 'right' sort of man? Her gaze wandered over the table to the vase of flowers in the centre. Nasturtiums. Pete in the Adirondack chair.

There's something I have to tell you . . .

Marion was beset by the feeling that she should remember something. Something important. But she had no idea what it was. Trying to reach this memory was like peering into a long, narrow tube and not finding daylight at the other end. A bit like her upright Hoover, she thought. It had a long pole for reaching into corners, but, right at the top, the pole curved slightly, blocking your vision when you needed to look down it to check for dust clots. You were never sure whether the darkness you saw was a clot or simply the angle of the pole.

She had the same sensation now. A mental craning without any sense of what she was looking at.

'Do you remember a teacher, an older woman, Sister Maureen?'

Dorothy Nichols hesitated a fraction before answering. 'I do have some recall of that name, yes.'

'Do you know what happened to her?' Marion asked eagerly. 'I've always wondered. Did she go back to England do you think? She left so suddenly –'

'I really don't know.'

'Did she teach you? She was different from the others, I thought you might remember her.'

'I'm afraid I don't.'

'I think you would have done if she had taught you. Who were your teachers? Perhaps I'll recognize the names.'

Dorothy cut her off. 'It was a part of my life I don't choose to remember,' she said dismissively. 'An unhappy time. A repressive environment to spend one's childhood. Most repressive.'

'It can't have been that bad,' Vanessa said, leaping to her mother's defence. 'I mean, you weren't *abused* or anything –'

'No,' Marion said, 'I think I know what Dorothy means.' She smiled at the other woman. 'I understand if you don't want to talk about it.'

'What do you think of this food?' Mrs Macdonald asked. 'I think the cook has outdone himself tonight. He seems to go from strength to strength.' Despite her enthusiasm, Vanessa noticed that she had barely touched her plate, transferring only a scant morsel or two from fork to mouth with her right hand. Bharani, however, was already reaching for a second helping. He seemed to have temporarily dropped out of the conversation the better to concentrate on his meal.

'It's delicious,' Marion said. 'Everything is so good. The meal, this place . . .'

Mrs Macdonald smiled. 'There have been times when it was a struggle keeping it going you know, but I like to think of it as a kind of refuge.' She paused. 'Oh dear,' she said, looking over at the piano in the far corner of the room. 'Poor Lily. She's playing "The Blue Danube" *again*. I think it's the only one she still knows all the way through. But I simply don't have the heart to tell her to stop.'

'She has a new hat,' commented Bharani, a little indistinctly through his mouthful of food.

'Yes. She *will* insist on knitting, you know. She made Bharani a most peculiar tank top the other day. I don't believe she ever buys new wool. She simply unravels things she's made before. I keep seeing the same shades in different reincarnations.'

'How very Buddhist of her,' Marion said.

'Yes, isn't it?' She leaned over and patted Marion's hand.

'I can tell that you and I are going to be friends,' she said. 'You will come and stay here, won't you?'

As soon as dessert was over, Dorothy Nichols rose abruptly from her chair.

'It is time for your treatment,' she told Mrs Macdonald.

'Must I really go? I'm having such a wonderful time.' But the old woman's face looked weary.

The bearer came and she raised her arms to be lifted. And in the motion was none of the stoicism of those long habituated to helplessness, but instead a kind of alacrity, for all her evident fatigue. As though she had chosen to be carried and was glad of it. Marion, who noticed such things, thought it must make the bearer's task an easy, almost a joyful thing.

'Please stay on and have coffee,' Mrs Macdonald said as they left. 'We serve very good coffee, you know.'

As the bearer settled her on the broad sofa in the private sitting room, Dorothy Nichols rubbed her hands together briskly to warm them.

'I believe these treatments of yours are doing me a great deal of good,' Mrs Macdonald said, resting her head back against the sofa's cushions, with the care of a person returning an item of great fragility to a bed of velvet. 'I can't imagine what I'd do without you.'

'There is no great mystery to massage,' Nichols said. 'It simply requires a great deal of practice.' She rolled up her sleeves. 'I will need to turn you. Like this.'

She had decided that tonight's session would be a longer one than usual. She would spend half an hour on the feet alone. It would help steady her mind. The meeting with

Marion West had thrown her into something close to panic, although she had managed to hold on to her poise during dinner. What did the woman know? She seemed benign enough, but Dorothy Nichols wasn't fooled by an air of amiability. It was what people usually adopted when they wanted to interfere.

'If I could slip your gown away from your shoulders. Yes, that is right.'

She looked at the pale, slack skin beneath her hands. These first few seconds of contact were always the same. The instant of disgust like the shudder of entry into cold water. Then this passing as she found her rhythm, concentrating on the aromatic scent of the oil, devotedly working without pause over the body beneath her until her arms ached. Strong as she was, there were nights recently when she had found it hard to sleep for the pain in her shoulders and wrists. But she grudged none of it.

'You have very dry elbows. I must give you some of my new balm. It is almost ready for use.' Vaseline would help, of course, but for several days now she had been experimenting with her own brand of salve; a concoction made from oils she had found locally. At present, the mixture was still useless for her purposes since it had refused to gel adequately. Several shallow dishes of the stuff in different states of lubricity lay on the windowsill in her room. The combination of ghee and tallow was a particular failure, she thought. It was far too liquid, and worse, seemed to attract flies.

'I feel very selfish taking up so much of your time,' murmured Mrs Macdonald. 'You must be neglecting your research because of me.'

'Not at all,' Dorothy Nichols said soothingly, although she hadn't made a single entry into her notebooks for several days now. Her work, which had been so long in the planning, had retreated in importance since her arrival at Glenside. She felt little regret. After all, she could return to her research at any time. The old woman's trust had been established quicker than she had imagined that first day. But then, thought Dorothy, didn't she always make the mistake of assuming that others maintained the same rigorous level of thought that she did herself?

She held one of Mrs Macdonald's small bony feet in each hand, thumbs resting on the instep. The skin here was so fine that it was possible to see through quite clearly, to the blue tangle of sinews and veins beneath. Someone had painted the old woman's toenails red. The varnish was carefully applied, very bright.

There was no way she could have anticipated the appearance of Marion West. It was the worst stroke of bad luck. The question was, what could she do about it? Her grip tightened on the old woman's feet. The soles were as dry and as yellow as old newspaper left out in the sun. Perhaps she was worrying without cause. After all, if the West woman had had anything to say, wouldn't she have made her objections then, at the moment of their introduction? Beneath her hands, the old woman's feet squirmed slightly.

'Did you do this for your mother?' Mrs Macdonald said, her words muffled slightly by cushions.

'Yes, of course. Many times.'

That and other things too, thought Dorothy Nichols. She knelt at her mother's knee and lifted her feet one by one to clip the toenails. Her mother's legs were fat, but spongy. She had her skirt hoisted up over her knees so that if Dorothy raised her eyes she could see right up it between her legs. There was no sound in the room. Only the sharp *tack tack* of the nails being cut and then the rasp of the nail file as she worked to smooth the rough edges. Her mother had embarked on one of her silences again. Having lost almost all power of movement, silence had become her preferred form of punishment.

But then it had always been a weapon. When Dorothy was a child her mother called it being sent to Coventry. It was years before Dorothy realized that Coventry was a real place and not just a word for helpless exclusion. 'We're going to have to send her to Coventry again,' her mother said, and then Dorothy would hear them talking about her. Her mother and father. Quite openly as though by forcing muteness on her, they had also made her deaf. 'Have you looked at her face?' her mother said. 'She does nothing but pick at her lips. Pick pick pick. You can get lip cancer that way.'

She was always careful to file her mother's nails in the same direction. If you changed direction it could split the top layer. The powdered nail, fine as talcum rose in a tiny cloud around her fingers. It had a dry, sickly smell. Later, she would wash her hands, using the little brush resting on the bathroom sink to remove the powder that had found its way beneath her own fingernails. But the smell lingered on for a while, despite all her efforts. Whenever she brought her hand up to her face she caught it again, the smell of her mother's helplessness, her will.

Those silences of hers could last for days. It was her way of maintaining the upper hand, no matter what indignities her body had brought her to. So when, in the last year of life, her mother was robbed of the power of speech altogether, Dorothy found the lack of conversation quite normal. Besides, this was a different kind of silence than before, one in which she stepped with relief. For the first time in her life, silence was a thing she owned.

'Are you getting tired?' Mrs Macdonald asked. 'You should stop if you're tired.'

Dorothy massaged her ankles. They were so thin her thumb and finger could meet around them. The calf muscles above were quite wasted away. The old woman was close to death, she thought. Great care was required.

'You must have loved your mother such a lot.'

'Yes,' Dorothy said and felt a rush of unexpected grief. She let it pass like a person turning their face out of the wind. She had no language for needing and being needed. Within her, love and rage, like conjoined twins, beat with a single heart.

'I think that will do for tonight,' she said, drawing the old woman's robe around her body once more.

Mrs Macdonald sighed. 'Thank you. I can't tell you how much better I feel for that.'

She raised herself once more on one elbow and looked at Dorothy. 'It's almost time for my little jaunt outside. To look at the stars, you know.'

'I will call for the bearer.'

'No, not yet. Come, sit down here with me.' She patted the seat beside her.

Dorothy hesitated. The green fabric of Mrs Macdonald's robe was spread out in a great pool over the sofa, slippery and slightly shimmering. It would be impossible to avoid all contact with it. Just a minute before she had been touching the woman's naked flesh, but that had been professional contact, whereas this seemed a different thing altogether. A kind of intimacy Dorothy Nichols found strange, almost disturbing.

'Come,' Mrs Macdonald said again.

Dorothy perched herself on the edge of the seat.

'I have to look for the stars every night,' Mrs Macdonald said. 'It has become a habit.' She laughed. 'Being like this, one's viewpoint is rather limited to upwards, you know.'

Dorothy kept her gaze fixed ahead. The room they were in was smaller than the main drawing room. A private parlour kept exclusively for the old woman's use. Not many guests were allowed entry to this sanctum, she thought. It was a mark of special privilege.

'I see you are looking at the thangkas.'

In fact, she had not been looking at them at all. They merely occupied the space on which her eyes had been resting; two rather dark pictures painted on some sort of fabric. She made out a pattern of grimacing faces, surrounded by circles and swirling shapes that might have been clouds or lotuses.

'Yes, quite wonderful. Wonderful examples of Buddhist tradition.'

'I've had them a long time. Nearly all my life. Since I was thirteen. I was given them, you know.'

'A generous gift.'

'Yes, wasn't it? They're from Tibet. The explorer Alexandra David Neel gave them to me on her way back from Lhasa in the twenties. Can you imagine? I was just a little girl but she must have taken to me. I thought she was just the most wonderful woman in the world. We were living in Darjeeling then, of course. She didn't stay long. I never saw her again after that, although I kept track of her travels.'

Dorothy Nichols smiled politely. She had the feeling that she should say something, that conversation should be maintained, but, for the moment, nothing occurred to her. It didn't seem to matter. Mrs Macdonald continued to talk, despite her silence.

'It's funny, but I've always counted her as one of my true friends even though we were together for such a short time. She lived to be over one hundred years old. Such a life of adventure.' Mrs Macdonald laughed. 'I thought I would become an explorer like her one day, but as you see, I didn't get very far at all.'

'But Glenside is so beautiful . . .'

Mrs Macdonald laughed again. Almost everything seemed to make her laugh. 'Oh, I've never regretted staying. Not for a moment. I had five children. And that's an adventure in itself. They all live quite a long way away now, but they come back for Christmas. With my grandchildren. I have eighteen, you know. Christmas at Glenside is wonderful.'

She paused and Dorothy could feel her looking at her in that intent way of hers, head slightly to one side. 'Destiny is a strange sort of thing, isn't it? It always sounds as though there should be something rather *far flung* about it. But sometimes, well, it's right there all along. Underneath your own doormat, if you know what I mean.'

Dorothy Nichols wasn't sure she did know. Again she had the feeling that it was important she add to the conversation. Mrs Macdonald was talking about something which seemed rather private. Was it an invitation of some kind? She racked her mind for an appropriate response. Perhaps she was meant to tell the old woman something about herself. Something private. But whatever small ability she might have had for exchanging confidences was quite beyond her that evening, swamped by other preoccupations. It was Marion West's fault. The woman was interfering already. Dorothy's hands clenched savagely on her lap.

'You are looking tired again,' she said at last. 'Shall I call the bearer now?'

•

'So what do you think of Mrs Macdonald?' Marion asked as the Wests were preparing for bed that evening. 'Do you think we should take her up on her offer?'

'She made it sound as though she was inviting us to her home instead of trying to get us to stay at the hotel.'

'Well, it *is* her home,' Marion said. 'I thought she was lovely.'

Vanessa said nothing. Despite herself, she too had been impressed by Mrs Macdonald. During the course of the evening, a growing sense of well-being had overtaken her. Perhaps it was the excellence of the food, or the candlelight or the satisfied murmur of conversation filling the room or the size of her gin and tonic. Or perhaps none of these, but simply the sight of Mrs Macdonald in the arms of her bearer being carried out into the hotel courtyard to look at the stars. It was the last thing they saw as they left. On the driveway, walking down to the street below, they had both looked back in the same instant. As though, for a moment, they shared the same sense of disbelief in the existence of Glenside itself and needed to turn to see it once again. And there she was. Her long dress trailing to the ground, her head tilted up to the sky. Quite still, simply looking. Vanessa could not quite explain to herself why she had felt so privileged, nor why, despite the fact that they had paid for their meal – easily the most expensive they had come across in India – she should feel as though she had been given a gift.

'It was a nice evening, wasn't it?' Marion said.

'Yes. Yes it was.'

After Dorothy and Mrs Macdonald had left, Bharani called to Greg and Tish to join them at the table for coffee. Vanessa noticed that Alex Khusam was excluded from the invitation. Bharani appeared to stare straight through the man. Despite this, however, Khusam looked over at them as though considering. Then he pushed back his seat and approached the table. While the others bustled to find spaces, he stood very still to one side, waiting.

'Alex Khusam,' he said at last, holding out his hand to Vanessa. His hand felt cool and very confident.

'Would you like to sit down? I'm sure we can make space for another chair.'

'There's no need,' he said. 'I never drink coffee.' His voice held the trace of an American accent. 'Is this your mother?'

Marion smiled at him uncertainly. 'There really *is* space for another chair,' she said. 'We can all squash up a bit.'

He smiled with great politeness as though the idea of squashing up was something he was not in the habit of doing, but that he was too well-mannered to point it out.

'Thank you, but perhaps another time.' He looked again at Vanessa. 'Are you staying at Glenside?'

'Not at the moment, but something tells me that's going to change.' She smiled. 'Mrs Macdonald seems quite keen that we should.'

'She's hard to resist.'

'Yes, isn't she?' She was distracted by the sound of Bharani stirring sugar in his coffee, rattling spoon against china with some agitation.

'This is such excellent coffee,' he chattered. 'A wonderful brew. Mrs Macdonald has it brought all the way from Southern India.'

Vanessa turned back to Khusam, but he was gone.

On the other side of the table, Tish was looking up entreatingly at the waiter hovering over her. 'I can't drink coffee. It keeps me up.' She put one hand over the top of her cup as though, despite her plea, she might be forced to receive a helping anyway. Vanessa didn't think insomnia had anything to do with her refusal. Tish had eating disorder written all over her, thought Vanessa. She had seen that look before. The old age behind the eyes.

'I don't have that problem myself,' Greg said, wiping a drop from his goatee with the back of his hand. 'I can sleep through everything. Or anywhere, come to that. In the middle of Delhi railway station, in roach-infested boarding houses, in a completely rank trekking hut at Yuksom. You name it, we've slept there. Haven't we, Tish?'

'The bathroom in the hut had . . . crap . . . on the ceiling. I kept thinking how it got there. All night. Wondering how it got on to the ceiling.'

'This trip has been a bit of a culture shock for Tish,' Greg said happily. 'But we're working on that.'

'Well, I'd have thought crap is crap, wherever you are in the world,' commented Vanessa.

'You must have seen some wonderful things,' Marion interrupted hastily. 'Mrs Macdonald was telling me you are particularly interested in Buddhism. In the monasteries.'

'Yes,' Greg said eagerly. 'Mrs Macdonald has some very interesting connections.'

'Alexandra David Neel!' Bharani said. He turned to Vanessa. 'You see, everyone knows of her. She is very famous.'

'In a past life, she thought she had been one of Genghis Khan's Mongols,' said Greg. 'She spent her whole life studying Buddhism. Nothing stopped her. Nothing. She lived in *caves*.'

Tish seemed to shudder a little. 'Greg's been reading her autobiography. It's given him a lot of . . . ideas.'

'She had this guru, this teacher,' he continued. 'He was a hermit. He taught her telepathy and tumo.'

'Tumo?'

'It's a discipline. A practice of breathing that enables you to stay warm even in sub-zero temperatures. The usual test for a disciple was to stay out all night during winter, with no clothes on, wrapped in wet sheets. You had to dry the sheets one by one, by meditating on the fire within.'

'David Neel didn't do the sheet test,' Greg continued, 'but she bathed in a stream and sat out all night completely naked.' He paused. 'She gave two thangkas to Mrs Macdonald. They're Tibetan religious paintings. She's got them hung up in her private room. She took me in there to show them to me.'

'I too have seen them,' Bharani said importantly. 'They are worth a great deal of money. A very great deal. Many museums and institutes around the world would be thrilled to include them in their collections. But Mrs Macdonald will never be parted from them.'

Their room at the club seemed sparser than ever by comparison. It was late, but neither she nor her mother were ready for bed. Marion sat in the wicker armchair by the empty fire in her pyjamas and pulled her shawl tightly around her. She was thinking of Dorothy Nichols.

'It's so familiar. Her name, I mean. The more I think about it, the more familiar it seems.'

Vanessa rolled her eyes. 'Horrible woman. She sat there, glowering at me all night. Whenever I said anything to her she looked away to the side. Did you notice? As though she'd catch something just from eye contact. As if I was going to give her another outbreak of hives. Can you imagine her standing in the bathtub with nothing on but baking soda? That's one image I wish I didn't have in my head. It's going to keep me up all night.'

Marion ignored her daughter. She was looking through her autograph book, carefully reading each name.

'I *knew* I'd seen it before! It's right here, nearly at the end. She's got a whole page to herself. Look, Vanessa, isn't it pretty?'

The small page was almost entirely taken up with an elaborately crayoned border of flowers. The drawing was extraordinarily detailed. Each petal shaded and distinct, each leaf carefully outlined. Butterflies with bright, veined wings hovered amongst the blooms. In the very centre, two tiny bluebirds had been drawn, their beaks grasping the curling letters of the name written there. As though they were carrying it aloft as they flew.

Dorothy Nichols.

'I'm going to show this to her,' Marion said excitedly. 'I bet she never thought she'd see it again.'

'I wouldn't if I were you. She made it very clear the topic was off limits. I thought she was mean about it. A mean person.'

'You shouldn't say that. You don't know what a person's been through in their life.'

'I don't care. I think she's a beast.'

'But look at how beautifully she did this page. She must have taken hours over it.'

'Being able to draw doesn't mean you're not a beast.'

Marion shut the book regretfully. 'There's a lot about people you don't understand.'

'I understand enough.'

Her mother sighed. Vanessa was so implacable, she thought. So very full of certainty. Everything was either one thing or another with her. Had there ever been a time when she too had been this way? Marion didn't think so. Her whole life seemed to have been spent in the quiet, empty spaces between the convictions of other people.

'I think we should definitely move there,' Marion said. 'Don't you think so? What about tomorrow?'

'All right,' Vanessa said. 'I suppose we could.'

'I shall miss Prasad. And John of course. I don't suppose there's any chance we could persuade John to move too, is there?'

'I doubt it. He can barely afford this place.'

'Poor John. Perhaps we can invite him to dinner at Glenside once we get settled there.'

'While we're on the subject of making plans, perhaps we can also think about going to Sunny Valley. I don't know why you've been putting it off.'

'I haven't been putting it off,' Marion said. She picked up her book of poems. 'I think I'll read for a bit before turning in. You don't mind if the light stays on for a while do you?'

Vanessa peered up at the bulb hanging from the ceiling. 'You mean the light is on?' she said sarcastically. 'I didn't realize. So it's settled then? We'll go to Sunny Valley as soon as possible. Perhaps the day after tomorrow.'

'I don't know', Marion said, turning the pages of her book, 'why so many of these poems are about some place called Yarrow. There's "Yarrow Visited" and "Yarrow Unvisited" and "The Braes of Yarrow" whatever *they* are. They're all really sad for some reason. The saddest one of all is called "Willie, Drowned in Yarrow".'

'We should be settled in by the day after tomorrow,' continued Vanessa. 'We can get a taxi from the stand down town or perhaps Glenside has drivers we can use for the day. I'll have to find out. I'd rather use a hotel driver. The man who brought us up here had a deathwish.'

But Marion was not paying attention. 'It's not as though Yarrow even rhymes very well with anything,' she said. 'Although *barrow* and *marrow* do spring to mind.'

'What are you talking about?'

'*Why should Yarrow, inspire such sarrow?*' Marion looked hopefully at her daughter.

'Oh, Mother, that's lame. That's really lame.'

For the first time since arriving in Ashagiri, Marion opened her eyes the next morning without the small drag of disappointment she usually felt upon waking up. The day was bright with none of the fog that so often crept over the town by mid-morning and she took this as an omen of good luck. She packed quickly and then sat out on the balcony with her tea waiting for Vanessa to be ready. Below her in the garden, the marigolds were coming into full bloom; great bushes of burnt orange, exotic and at the same time utterly familiar. There had been marigolds like this at Dreaming Rock. She remembered the smell of them, the way the plants spread down the hillside. They did not bloom year round. There must have been many times she had sat there without seeing them. But her memory – catching, as memory does, at an episode or two and making them a perpetuity – was only of the rock at marigold time. As though the place was immune from the year's changes and knew no other season.

She thought of how it had been then. Her knees drawn up, her eyes scanning the view, seeing not what lay before her, but a different place. Still unvisited, imagined only, but no less real for that. Her life to come. The trees disappearing into the distance, the burning flowers, the sky alive. An intensity of feeling more certain than hope, too strong for words. She remembered it still, this vision of hers. Looking at the marigolds brought it back for a moment, as clearly as though she still sat there on Dreaming Rock and the years in between nothing after all. Where then, thought Marion, was the division that separated that vision from the memory of itself? Was there a point where the two things joined? Time to come meeting time past along some equatorial line scored through a person's life. If so, there must have been a day, a moment, when she had crossed it. Some ordinary afternoon, spent in the usual way, when she had, without knowing it, passed from one continent to another.

She sipped her tea and smiled a little to herself. Lines and maps and territories to be marked out. It was the colonial in her, she supposed. She was thinking like her father. She stared at the marigolds, absorbing their colour, watching as the club gardener, ancient and dogged, crept slowly among the bushes, deep in the endless labour of tending to growing things.

Perhaps, she thought, there was no line after all. Nothing to separate dream and memory. Could it really be as simple as that? All the borders between then and now torn down just by thinking it was so? After all, the two things were very similar if you looked at them from a distance. Both places in the mind, she thought. Both places of safety.

She was interrupted by Vanessa's voice sounding peevish. 'Have you seen my fountain pen? I can't find it anywhere.'

'Have you looked on the table?'

'Of course I have! That's the first place I looked. It's not anywhere.'

She emerged from the room carrying both their suitcases. 'It will probably turn up when we're gone,' she said grumpily. 'Major Das will have something else to add to his collection. He'll put it in a box and tell people Rudyard Kipling used it to write *The Jungle Book*.'

'It's just a pen, Vanessa.'

'Daddy gave it to me. For my graduation.' Her father always gave appropriate gifts, she thought. He believed in the usefulness of things. She remembered a restaurant. The pair of them sitting there, looking out of the window at an old man in the street beyond. She was perhaps ten or eleven. The old man was carrying a rolled-up umbrella in one hand and a dangling rosary in the other. 'See that?' her father had said, tapping on the glass and smiling. 'Everything he needs right there. Fully equipped, do you see?' She had not really understood the joke, only later understanding that her father had not meant any mockery by the comment, but only a kind of admiration at the demonstration of a principle.

'He'd *hate* me losing that pen.'

'I was just looking at the marigolds,' Marion said to distract her. 'They're such tidy things at home, but here they seem to go quite crazy.'

'Yes, well. I can see why. Do you think Prasad will help us carry this lot up to Glenside?'

'He's already waiting downstairs.'

It was a short walk to the hotel. At the entrance, Prasad lowered Marion's suitcase which he had been carrying over his shoulders and shook both of their hands with a small, polite movement of his elbow. Marion dug in her handbag for money to give him.

'I also have a present for you,' she said, presenting him with one of her cardigans, a black cashmere embroidered with small beads. 'It's for your wife,' she added, a little anxiously. 'I hope she likes it.'

'That was nice of you,' Vanessa said, when Prasad had gone.

'Don't you remember him telling us about her? How she's an invalid? I thought it might cheer her up a bit.'

'I'd forgotten.' Vanessa looked at her mother. 'You don't forget about things like that. You're such a nice person . . .'

The Wests' room at Glenside faced north, away from the town, towards the mountains. Vanessa went quickly to the window and looked out.

'We can actually see the snows from here,' she said with excitement. If it wasn't for the view she might have imagined herself in the bedroom of an old-fashioned English cottage complete with primrose chenille bed covers and yellow sprigged wallpaper. A bathroom with claw-foot tub adjoined the room, the door discreetly covered with a heavy drape. The room seemed full of those domestic items that two generations ago must have seemed indispensable, but had now passed into quaintness. A china washbasin and matching jug, a pair of embroidered handkerchief sachets on the bedside table, three long hatpins with beaded tips stuck in a faded pincushion by the mirror. Marion unpacked her bedjacket and laid it out carefully on her pillow.

'It looks as though it comes with the room,' Vanessa said. 'My stuff on the other hand . . .' She looked for a place to stow her North Face anorak. 'I think I'd better keep this in a drawer. Red nylon doesn't seem to go with the decor somehow.'

'Do you think they serve afternoon tea?' Marion said rather eagerly.

'I'd be very surprised if they didn't.'

'You don't mind if I go down and look, do you? I can finish my unpacking later.'

'You don't have to ask my permission for everything, you know. Why on earth would I mind?'

After her mother had gone, Vanessa continued putting her possessions in order. It was very quiet. Every so often she stopped what she was doing and returned to the window to look out at the view. The sky was full of clouds, huge dark-bellied things, their edges lightening to white where they met blue. She didn't think she had ever seen clouds like them. So full of shining substance, so monumental. Perhaps she had simply not looked up often enough. The sight brought a rush of optimism. They had given up too easily on their search, she thought. Been too easily discouraged. There were things to be found here if they only looked in the right places. The man in the photographic shop, for example. Mr Lehkraj. He didn't have her mother's picture any longer, but he must surely have others. Things of more general interest. Pictures of St Margaret's perhaps, before it fell into ruin. The Ashagiri Club in its heyday, pictures of hunting trophies and old sports teams. He couldn't have thrown them *all* away.

She found her mother in the dining room sharing a table with Tish. The pink tablecloths of the night before had been replaced with white ones, liberally strewn with plates of scones and cucumber sandwiches. Perhaps emboldened by the fact that the latter had had their crusts removed, Tish had ventured to take one on to her plate and was deep in the task of extracting the thin green slices. She lifted her head and smiled suddenly at something Marion said and it seemed to Vanessa that she looked less nervy than before, almost happy.

'What are you two talking about?'

Marion looked up. 'It's so funny. I was just telling Tish about some of the things I've seen here. The way people try to get you to buy things. There's a stall down near Klein's where they sell woollens. They've got these little labels on all their shawls. To try and convince customers that they're buying quality. Do you know what they say?'

'One Hundred Percent Shawl!' Tish said in a rush. 'Isn't that funny?'

'The funniest thing of all,' added Marion, 'is that it's perfectly true.'

Vanessa laughed. 'Have you finished eating? Because I thought it might be a good idea to go back to that photographic shop. I've been thinking Mr Lehkraj might have some interesting stuff in archive. It's worth a try.'

Marion made a little face. 'Oh, but I can't. I promised Tish I'd take her on a little shopping trip. We thought we'd walk up to Lookout Point and then pop in to Avari's. She hasn't been shopping once since she got here. Have you, Tish?'

She shook her head timidly. 'If you had other plans –'

'No,' Marion said. 'We hadn't made plans.'

'I suppose it can wait,' Vanessa said, surprised and a little indignant. 'Perhaps I'll go by myself.'

'Or you could come with us.'

'No,' Vanessa said, 'I think I'll go by myself.'

•

Outside, she found herself walking faster than usual, fuelled by the uncomfortable sense of having been thwarted. It crossed her mind that there was something perhaps a touch obsessive about her insistence on digging up clues to Marion's past. Was it possible she was using the project as a kind of . . . distraction? Vanessa was interrupted from this train of thought by a jeep that had slowed to a crawl beside her.

'Do you want to go for a drive?' Alex Khusam said.

Vanessa looked up in astonishment. He was gazing at her, one elbow resting on the open window of the jeep, his eyes disconcertingly steady. Almost as though he hadn't just drawn up beside her, but had been watching her for some time. His invitation too seemed oddly lacking in spontaneity. As if he didn't really mind whether she came or not, thought Vanessa. Or as if he already knew what the answer would be. She was struck again by the remarkableness of his looks, the sheer strangeness of those high, flattened cheekbones and incongruous eyes.

'All right,' she said. It was not until she had crossed to the other side of the jeep, opened the door and hoisted herself up into the passenger seat beside him that it occurred to her to ask where he was going.

'You'll see.' He smiled a little, his eyes fixed ahead as he manoeuvred back into the traffic.

They passed through the town without further talk. Khusam drove fast, one hand on the wheel, guiding it almost idly with the flat of his palm. Vanessa could think of nothing to say.

There was something about the man that made chit-chat irrelevant. Or perhaps it was simply the surprise of finding herself there with him; the sense somehow, against all expectation, of being *selected*.

He glanced at her briefly, with an amused look. 'You can put your coat in the back if you like,' he said. 'There's no need to keep so bundled up.' She took it off, a little embarrassed by the rustling of the nylon. Khusam was in shirt sleeves, the fabric rolled up to his elbows, his collar undone. She felt certain he thought her uptight.

'It *is* a little warm today,' she said, trying to sound light. She looked out of the window. Once out of the town, she had assumed Khusam would take the road downhill, back towards the smaller village below. But he had turned off while she had been busy with her anorak and they seemed to be curling around the hill in a completely different direction. This road was far narrower than the other and even more in need of repair. Large boulders and scatterings of smaller stones littered the verges and the tarmac was broken and rough. Khusam seemed quite unperturbed by these obstacles, however, and continued to drive at speed, hardly tightening his grip on the wheel at each blind curve and bend. Although it made Vanessa nervous, she said nothing, ashamed of her fear. It seemed to belong with her newly despised anorak, lying balled up in the back of the jeep. Besides, she was far from certain that Khusam would slow down, even if she asked him to.

'This road needs . . . work,' she said, unable to quite refrain from comment.

He took another sharp bend, swinging out a little wide until the jeep was at the furthermost verge, with nothing but a few bushes and a foot or two of loose rock between the vehicle and the steep drop below. Vanessa couldn't help noticing, with the unwelcome clarity that seems to come at such moments, that the tarmac around the bend had been eaten away in great chunks. Just for a second, the two left-side wheels on the jeep must have been travelling over nothing but air.

'Three months ago, my cousin took a dive off this road,' Khusam said casually. 'It took them a long time to find his jeep. The trees are very thick down there.'

Vanessa wasn't sure that right now she wanted to know where his cousin had ended up. 'That's terrible.'

'Don't worry. It happened at night. He was probably drunk.'

'You mean you drive this road *at night*?'

'A little slower,' Khusam said, looking at her quickly and smiling. 'He was only a very distant cousin,' he added.

'Oh.'

They turned another bend. A man was crouched by the side of the road. At this distance, it was hard to tell whether he was tying a shoelace or rummaging for something among the stones.

'There's John!' cried Vanessa. 'I know him.' At the jeep's approach he stood up and turned towards them. He was carrying his box of paints. She noticed that the strap had broken and been clumsily tied back together. He raised one arm, as though in greeting, or perhaps simply in the hope of a lift. But there was no time to ask Khusam to stop. As the jeep swept passed him, Vanessa saw his face, turned towards her in sudden, surprised recognition. Then he was gone.

'I know him,' she said again. 'I think he might have wanted a lift.'

'We can stop and go back if you like,' Khusam said, making no effort to slow down. He looked at her and raised his eyebrows, half mocking, half conspiratorial.

'Maybe not,' she found herself saying. 'I'm sure he can find his own way home.'

She thought of John standing on the roadside watching them disappear and felt a little sorry. What was he doing there? Had he walked all the way and was he now about to walk all the way back? At the same time, she couldn't help feeling a touch superior. How startled he had been to see them. Almost foolishly so. It was hard to imagine that expression ever appearing on Khusam's face. Khusam looked as though he *belonged*. Like an insider. And for a moment or two, it seemed to her that this was a quality that might be shared, if only by association. She put John Walcott out of her mind.

'Are you going to tell me where we're going yet? Are we going to Rupkhand?'

He shook his head. 'That's a two-hour drive. We're just going part of the way.'

'Is your palace very beautiful?'

He paused. 'It was.'

'You're restoring it, aren't you?'

'It's slow work,' he said, suddenly intense. 'But it will be done.'

'Where are you getting the money?'

'My family is rich,' he said indifferently. 'After we left, my mother . . .' There was a short, distasteful pause. 'My mother married again. A rich American.'

'Oh.'

'The work will be done,' Khusam repeated. 'Down to the last detail. Everything except for the palace gates. They must stay the same. Untouched.'

'The gates?'

'When the Indian army came, the guards died defending the gates. Two of them. The soldiers took us out and we walked over their bodies. My father bent down and wet his hands with their blood and marked the gates with it. He made me watch this. He said I must remember these men died for us. I must always remember this.'

'How old were you?' asked Vanessa, shocked.

'Seven.'

Vanessa was confused. 'But I thought . . . Mrs Macdonald said, the takeover was peaceful. That almost everyone . . . wanted the Indian government to come in. It made good sense, she said, for military and economic reasons.'

Khusam's face tightened. 'They were butchered. Both of them.'

'But why?'

'They had been told to hold the gates.'

'By your father?'

'It was what they had been told,' he repeated. 'Their family had been with us for generations.'

It was odd, thought Vanessa, how people with servants seemed to describe them in the same way they might talk about the family silver. But it was a fleeting thought. Khusam was smiling at her, light-hearted again.

'You must come to the palace one day and see it for yourself.'

'I'd like that.' She leaned forward and hugged her knees. He was still looking at her and smiling.

'Get out,' he said suddenly.

'What do you mean?' The jeep was travelling at high speed.

He laughed. 'What I said. Get out.'

'But why?' Had she said something wrong?

'Just do it.'

'I can't.'

'Stand on the dashboard. You haven't experienced this road until you've ridden it on the outside.'

It took a few seconds before she realized what he was telling her to do. To leave her seat and climb out on to the side of the jeep and hold on as he drove, completing this manoeuvre while they were still in motion since he showed no sign of stopping or even slowing down.

'I can't,' she said again.

He looked at her mockingly. 'Are you too frightened?'

'You want me to open the door, while we're still *going*?'

'You can get out through the window,' he said carelessly. 'I've done it a hundred times.'

She looked out at the verge rushing passed and the steep drop to her left. The idea of actually doing what he said was preposterous, but the alternative of feebly saying 'I can't' again seemed suddenly even more impossible. Even cowardice takes strength, she thought miserably, gripping the edges of the window with both hands. She raised herself up half out of her seat and levered her head and shoulders out of the window. The wind in her face took her breath almost completely away.

'I really don't think I can do this.'

'The dashboard,' Khusam ordered. 'Get your feet on the dashboard.'

She managed to turn her head and twist the upper part of her body, reaching up with a desperate grab at a handhold on the top of the vehicle. Her bottom was now resting on the open window and it was only the thought of the ridiculous picture she must make, half in, half out, with her legs dangling foolishly inside that gave her the impetus to continue. She looked down and swung one leg out, finding the narrow perch of the board. The wind whipped at her hair, blinding her. She found a grip for her other hand on the side of the door and twisted her body again, so that her stomach was flush with the jeep and she could pull the rest of her body clear.

'There! You see, there's nothing to it,' Khusam said. Her head was level with his and she saw that he was grinning. 'Things look different from out there, don't they?'

She nodded, still gripping on to the door with both hands, not daring to remove her gaze from the inside of the vehicle. He turned a corner suddenly and her body swung out for a moment, making her almost shriek.

'One hand!' he laughed. 'Ride with one hand.'

She shook her head desperately, looking up ahead at the road rushing to meet them, the trees blurring, the air warm and wild in her face, a roaring in her ears. In a little while, she was able to glance left at the hillside dropping below, at the rocks from previous landslides interspersed with bushes, and, further down, the tiny fold of the valley itself, sunlit and calm, clean as a parting through hair. She relaxed her grip slightly.

'This isn't bad.'

'What's that?'

'I said, this isn't bad!' she shouted. He laughed again, without looking at her. 'I can see *everything*,' she said. She closed her eyes for a second. 'Even when I shut my eyes!'

Khusam crunched the gears, speeding up still further.

'Hold on now,' he called, 'or you'll find yourself meeting that cousin of mine.'

They drove for several miles before Khusam stopped to turn around. Vanessa slid back into the seat beside him gratefully, hoping that the return trip would be free of further ordeals. There had been a touch of cruelty in that last reference to his dead cousin. He had been tormenting her, she thought. The surprising thing was that she didn't resent it. Instead she was flattered, almost gratified by the attention. And there was something alarming about this response, something dangerous, although Vanessa, still recovering from her wind-battering ride, was not sure what it was. They spoke little on the return journey. Vanessa possessed by her thoughts and Khusam increasingly sombre as though each turn of the wheel carrying them away from Rupkhand robbed him of energy.

By the time they arrived back in Ashagiri they were both quite silent. Khusam parked the jeep and Vanessa turned to look in the back seat.

'Oh Christ,' she said furiously, 'I've lost my coat.'

It had been three days since Mrs Macdonald's last massage treatment. Each evening, when the customary time approached and Dorothy Nichols asked if she was ready, she had refused. Smiling all the time of course, but still refusing. She had been too busy talking to Marion West. The two of them after dinner, with their heads together. And last night, disappearing into the private parlour to continue their talk alone. And what were they discussing that was so very interesting? Dorothy asked herself. What could it be that was more important than the care, the vital ministrations she could provide? Nothing. They talked about nothing. Gardening mostly. Roses and herb gardens, the endless pros and cons of propagation techniques. Or the pair of them would start a discussion on some pointless topic to which Dorothy could contribute nothing, and even had difficulty following. Last night, for example, the West woman had begun talking about her memories. A dull enough subject to start with, but then she had gone on, in that rambling way of hers, to talk about memory itself. Something about travelling, Dorothy thought. Although what that had to do with memory quite escaped her.

'. . . already half into it you see,' she had said. 'When you're travelling. Already half way into memory. The need to remember part of every moment. Buying souvenirs, taking pictures . . .' She had stopped, a little breathlessly. 'I'm not making much sense, am I?'

It was the only thing she had said that Dorothy could agree

with. But there was Mrs Macdonald, nodding and smiling as though the woman wasn't talking rubbish, but instead had said something rather profound.

'I can see that,' she said, 'the way nostalgia gets woven into the present. As though the moment had already passed, even as you live it . . . I've never travelled much so I've never felt that, but I can see what you mean.'

'I know what you mean too,' Tish had piped up, looking at Marion with a fawning expression. The girl had always been quite silent before the Wests' arrival but now, here she was, imagining she could add to the conversation. 'Being here, away from home . . . it's all a bit surreal.'

'Being transitory you can't help thinking about the complete impermanence of totally everything,' Greg had interrupted, seemingly apropos of nothing. 'It's a Buddhist thing. Going Forth it's called. All the yoga masters got into it. That's the first thing they did.'

It was inexplicable. Thinking about it today, over lunch, Dorothy had found herself working at her mouth again in full view of the rest of the diners. Her mind revolving around the whole subject with such intensity that it was a while before she realized that she was attacking the inside of her cheek, twisting the bottom half of her face out of shape as she manoeuvred her jaws so that her teeth could grab a scrap of tearable skin. She had been forced to excuse herself from the table and find refuge in her room where she sat on the bed, her mouth moving furiously, without restraint.

Dorothy closed her eyes and tried to visualize the circle of rocks up on the hill. She had been to the spot twice more since her initial visit; each time the need to return rising in her with great urgency. But now the summoned image failed to materialize. What else was Marion West telling Mrs Macdonald? It seemed the pair of them looked at her differently from before. Like people with a secret. She had told herself that Marion knew nothing, but now she wondered. Perhaps the woman was simply . . . waiting.

She was interrupted by a soft knock on the door of her room. Dorothy glanced automatically at the small row of medicine bottles on the table by the window and half stood up. The knock came again. It could be one of the servants, she thought, although she had given them specific instructions not to disturb her. But perhaps there was an emergency that required her presence. Mrs Macdonald might have taken a turn for the worse. She stood up again and went to the door.

'I'm sorry to disturb you,' Marion said. 'Is this a bad time?'

Dorothy's heart thudded violently. To be thinking about the woman and then to see her standing there seemed too extraordinary to be mere coincidence. She automatically moved into a blocking position as though to protect the rest of the room from the intruder's eyes.

'I was resting,' she said tightly.

'Oh. I'm sorry. Perhaps I should come back another time . . .'

She said nothing. The questions would begin now. The accusations. But Marion seemed on a different mission altogether. She was holding something in front of her and was now proffering it with a kind of awful, tentative persistence. A small book. Old by the look of it.

'I wanted to show you this,' she was saying. 'I thought you'd be so interested. I've kept it all this time.'

Dorothy took the book from Marion and glanced down at it without comprehension. Perhaps if she did what the woman wanted she might contain the encounter within the small space of the doorway and the hall beyond. But Marion, seeming to take this exchange as some kind of licence to enter, had already moved past her.

'How beautiful your room is!' she cried. Dorothy could see her eyes travelling over everything. 'Glenside is such a lovely hotel, isn't it? We were so lucky to find it. What are those plants growing on your windowsill? Some kind of grass? I don't think I've come across that sort before.'

'Wheat. Wheatgrass.'

'Wheatgrass? What a lovely green it is. Is it part of your research? Mrs Macdonald told me about your writing –'

'What is this book?' Dorothy said hastily, moving into the woman's line of view.

'My old autograph book. Don't you remember? We all had them. You probably lost yours ages ago.'

'Yes. I must have done.'

'Look towards the back,' Marion said eagerly. 'About three or four pages from the end.'

She flipped through unwillingly.

'Have you found it? It's right there. Your page. When I saw that I thought I simply must show it to you. It's so pretty, isn't it?'

Dorothy stared at the name and the two bluebirds. She was unsure how to proceed.

'Thank you,' she said at last, closing the book. 'It was very kind of you to show me.'

There was a short silence which she again hoped would put an end to the conversation. But the woman seemed oblivious. She was now pattering around and peering at everything. Dorothy thought that in a minute or two she might actually start fingering her possessions.

'It was very kind of you to show me,' she said again, trying to inject her words with as much finality as possible.

'I hope you don't mind me looking at all your remedies,' Marion said. 'You know so much about all this. Did it take you a long time to learn it?'

'Many years.'

'You're so good with sick people,' Marion continued admiringly. 'I wish I had that gift.' She thought of Pete in his last days. The little suck and hiss of the machine injecting morphine into his body every hour. Her own hands frozen, it seemed, on her lap as she watched him sink.

'Most people are so frightened of illness, aren't they? Of other people's almost more than their own. Yesterday afternoon, when Mrs Macdonald fainted, nobody knew what to do. We all just stood there. Except for you.'

'It was a simple matter.'

'She's lucky to have you around.'

Dorothy inclined her head slightly as if in modest assent.

'It was a little while before I realized she *had* fainted,' Marion continued. 'But she was quite unconscious. How did you know what to do?'

Dorothy's discomfort at the other's presence took second place in her mind for a moment or two as she thought back to the scene. Of the two Wests and Tish and Bharani standing like shop-window dummies staring at the old woman. A long helpless pause during which time it seemed she was the only person in the whole room able to think and act. Moving swiftly to Mrs Macdonald's side, lifting her head gently, restoring her to consciousness.

'It was a simple matter,' she said again with a trace of grandiosity. She handed the autograph book back to Marion.

'Well . . . I suppose I should leave you in peace,' Marion said.

'Yes.'

Marion moved towards the door, disconcerted at last by the other's abrupt manner. Perhaps it was simply shyness, she thought, that made Dorothy Nichols so obviously uncomfortable. Or maybe she was feeling ill herself. She glanced at the

187

bottles of medicine on the table by the bed. It occurred to her that few people considered the well-being of caregivers. They were simply expected to keep going, endlessly attentive and full of energy. But Dorothy was not a young woman and her efforts were surely draining.

'I hope you're feeling more rested by dinner,' she said gently. 'I'll see you there.'

After she had gone, Dorothy returned to her bed and sat down again but it was impossible for her to find calm. The woman's recent presence seemed to hang about the room like a smell. She should have felt nothing but relief over the nature of Marion's errand, but instead she gnawed at her cheek with increasing disquiet, her eyes fixed on the carpet, her mind turning over the woman's words, her looks, the way she had stared around her. A nosy parker, a nosing, poking parker. Imagining everyone was fascinated by that little book of hers. Dorothy almost laughed, but her hands were in the way.

What did Marion West imagine that autograph book was? Some kind of proof that she had had friends? As if it mattered how many had signed their names there.

From the moment she had first approached the girl on the evening of that long ago Sports Day, the two of them had no need of anybody else. She had become the girl's protector. A champion of sorts. All taunting and bullying came to an end. The other girls could see that an alliance had been formed and it made them cautious. The pair drew curious looks for a while and then they were simply ignored. It was better like that.

They were the Roundheads and the others, the others were the Cavaliers. Roundheads were unpopular and they wore the wrong sort of clothes but they won in the end.

'Because they were in the right,' she told the girl.

The girl made badges for the two of them. Circles of

cardboard, intricately coloured, with a large 'R' in the centre and safety pins stuck on the back. For months they wore them pinned to their woollen vests beneath their school shirts.

The Cavaliers wanted to destroy the Roundheads, she told the girl. They were the enemy.

The girl listened and nodded.

'I won't tell,' she said. 'I won't ever tell.'

At night they lay side by side in bed and she talked to the girl. Stories of vengeance and escape. Of the school burning and landslides in the night and the two of them together in a world without teachers or parents.

'But where would we go? Wouldn't we thtarve?' the girl said. In the night they spoke like that, without pronouncing their S's. It was an old Roundhead trick to avoid eavesdroppers. When you were whispering, S's sounded particularly loud.

'I think my parentth would come looking for me,' the girl said.

'They couldn't if you changed your name.'

They had no need of the others whose cliques shifted week from week, who filled their little autograph books with each other's names and thought it counted for something. For over two years it had been like this. A long time in the life of a child.

But despite the reassurance of these thoughts, Dorothy Nichols still found herself dwelling on Marion's last words. Not so much what had been said, but the way in which they had been uttered. As though the woman had been sorry about something. No, as though she felt sorry for *her*. Rage grew inside her and in the luxury of her solitude she allowed it room, feeling it uncurl and stretch within her. It was always cramped, this rage, even now. It pressed against the inside of her like something trying to get out. Sometimes it felt as though her skin itself would split.

The woman had been trying to be kind to her. *Kind*. Was that what she was: an object of others' pity? She thought of Mrs Macdonald who never had anything but good things to say of everyone. Even Bharani. 'I can't imagine Glenside without him,' she had said. Making him feel wanted when everyone could see the man was a chuntering idiot. Was there really any difference in her mind when she told Dorothy that she could not do without *her* as well? Repeating it over and over simply to make her feel needed, useful?

Dorothy closed her eyes, her hands momentarily stilled by the horror of this thought. After all her care and attention, not to be the giver of charity after all, but just the reverse. An object of others' pity. An object of *kindness*.

It was impossible. She pushed the idea away. She had known what to do when Mrs Macdonald had fainted. And she would know what to do again.

The stomach pains began in the early afternoon and with them came the dizziness. The sky took on a grainy look, speckled like a dirty windscreen. Beneath Vanessa's fingers, the walls of the bedroom seemed to shift very slightly, recoiling infinitesimally as she made her way to the bathroom to be sick. She knelt on the floor and gaped at the lavatory bowl. On the underside of the lid there was a small picture of a bird and the single word CUCKOO printed in neat, black letters.

Vanessa heaved and spat.

'Cuckoo,' said the bird.

She rose to a squatting position, hands resting on the sides of the bowl. Then vomited again.

'Cuckoo, cuckoo,' sang the bird in a scratchy voice.

Vanessa wiped her mouth. 'Fuck you, bird.'

'Who are you talking to in there?' her mother called. 'Are you all right?'

'Fucking bird won't shut up.'

Her hands had grown to twice, three times their normal size, but when she brought them up to her eyes to see, they looked the same as ever.

'Cuckoo,' the bird said again. Her mother's face appeared, frighteningly close.

'I think you'd better lie down.'

She was sitting on the bed and her mother was kneeling to take off her shoes. And it was dark suddenly. Night-time already. Marion was dressed in pyjamas, wiping at her with a wet cloth.

'Get off. Get off me,' Vanessa said. Her mother pulled down the sheet and rubbed her arms and chest with the cloth.

'Keep still, Vanessa,' she said. 'I have to bring it down.'

'What down?'

'Keep still.'

Each minute was a hill she must climb, though the hours swung past. Neither awake nor asleep, buried alive inside her body, rock piled on rock. And then the spades coming to dig her out. Dark earth and terrible pain in her stomach as the blades thrust down.

'Make it stop,' she told her mother. Marion put a thermometer under her arm and held her hand tight against her chest.

'One hundred and five,' she whispered. The numbers like a prayer. 'One oh oh oh oh five. Jesus. Jesus.'

It was morning perhaps, or perhaps only ten minutes later. 'This is Doctor Kaskusthan,' her mother said. Someone looking down at her. A man. Dark eyes, cool hands.

'I'm sorry to wake you,' her mother was saying.

'That's okay,' Vanessa said. 'I wasn't asleep you know. I thought I was, but when I woke up, I realized I hadn't been at all.'

'I didn't know what else to do.'

Doctor Kaskusthan was wearing a dressing gown. 'Does it hurt here?' he asked. 'And the vomiting. Any blood in the vomiting? In the diarrhoea?'

'I'm sosorrysorry,' Vanessa said.

He was gone then and it was morning at last. Her mother drinking a cup of tea at the table across the room and the light clear and sweet.

'You have dysentery,' her mother said. 'Doctor Kaskusthan has given me antibiotics for you.'

She slipped back again. Into the sleep that wasn't sleep but a quiet waiting for unburial. Tea appeared, black with a little sugar. In the bathroom, the cuckoo sang. Her mother came and went. It was dark and then light again. Somebody knocked at the door and she heard Marion saying thank you and the door closing.

She slept and dreamed of being watched. Beady eyes in small faces. A whole row of them, quite still, looking at her. Then woke, in her first afternoon of real recovery, to find it had not been a dream at all. At least, only a partial one. At the foot of her bed, someone – surely her mother – had placed a dozen dolls. Avari's finest. All lined up in traditional Tibetan and Nepalese costumes with painted cloth faces. Vanessa sat up in bed and stared at them. Of course it was her mother's doing. She had put them there while Vanessa slept, hoping to cheer her up.

She had never really liked dolls, even as a child. But that hadn't stopped her mother from buying them for her. Large pasty-faced things with frills around the neck and cords coming out of their backs that you pulled to make them say things. *Will you be my mama? I need a weewee.*

Vanessa lay back down against the pillow. She had been in bed for over three days and her sickness had been overtaken by a new feeling of disgust at her unwashed state. Beneath the blankets, her legs felt papery, insubstantial. How like her mother it was to leave the dolls there. A sideways kind of giving, as though she suspected – through long experience – that her gifts to her daughter were never quite right. Disappointing.

Her mother had so wanted her to be a girlie girl, thought Vanessa. The kind who would jump with joy at a doll who went weewee. She thought suddenly of that trip they had all made when she was twelve. Her mother and father and her, driving across America. They had an itinerary. New York, Niagara Falls, Chicago, Yosemite National Park. Two weeks of sightseeing in a rented Lincoln. Her father driving and her mother with the map on her lap and Vanessa in the back picking at the leather seat.

Her father had his itinerary and she had hers. A chain bracelet to which she was adding silver charms, buying one at each place they visited. All the gift shops had them. A minute Empire State Building from New York, a leaping fish from Niagara Falls. Even the Hoover Dam had a charm – far more attractive than the real thing in Vanessa's opinion. They had tiny pennants attached to them with the name of the spot they came from. She had collected eight and they clinked satisfyingly against her wrist whenever she moved her arm. When the bracelet was complete, it would chart every single spot they'd been to, recording the entire trip.

And then they arrived in Arizona and her mother read the map wrong. It was hard to understand how she had done this, since the roads were few. They were meant to be going to the Grand Canyon. Instead they found themselves driving blind across desert. A hill, brown and smooth as a pudding, slap in the middle of the horizon, thin clouds scratching the vast sky and the road so long and straight it was impossible to tell at what speed they were travelling.

Her father stopped at a small town to ask directions. It was very windy. The wind had made a scarecrow out of the boy pumping gas. He walked bent, clothes blown against him, all shoulderblades and knees. The wind made his eyes small and his mouth very wide. 'Call this windy?' he said. 'You ain't bin here when it's windy.'

'Are we heading in the right direction for the Grand Canyon?' her father shouted. Behind the gas station a group of trailers had boarded up windows and keep out signs nailed to the doors.

'Grand Canyon?' said the boy. 'Nearest place is Tuba City. Straight on down the road.'

'That's where we're going then,' her father said as he got back into the car. Her mother sighed.

'I don't know how I lost it,' she said plaintively. 'The Grand Canyon. I mean, it's so big. You'd think there'd be signs . . .'

Tuba City wasn't a city at all. Just another small town in the middle of nothing. Vanessa could tell the instant they arrived that it had no gift shops. They stopped at the Tuba City Truck Stop. It was late. The small restaurant was almost empty. A hugely fat man in a broad purple tie was sitting at the back under a framed photograph of Bruce Springsteen.

'I think the best plan would be to stay in town tonight and press on in the morning,' her father said.

'Why?' asked Vanessa. 'We have time to get to the Grand Canyon. I know we do.'

But now her parents were talking to the man in the purple tie. Asking about motels in the area. He pointed to the picture above him. 'Bruce Springsteen,' he said proudly. 'He came here, you know. Had coffee in that very seat you're sitting in. Eggs. Wanted them over-easy. He was sitting there for an hour before someone recognized him. You should have seen the number of trucks in the parking lot when word got round.'

'Why do we have to stay here?' Vanessa persisted. 'Why can't we go to the Grand Canyon?'

'Cheer up, Vanessa,' her father said. 'Make the best of it.'

'It's an adventure!' her mother said.

She sat in the booth with her parents, furiously picking at a plate of chips.

'What's the matter with you?'

'Nothing.'

'So stop behaving like a baby.'

'There isn't a charm for this place,' she burst out finally. 'What's the point of being here when there isn't a charm?'

'Oh, so that's it,' her father said with exasperation.

'I'll get you two at the next place,' Marion said kindly. 'Your bracelet will be so pretty . . .'

She had bent her head to her plate. What was the use of telling her mother she'd missed the whole point? Just as she'd missed the road they had meant to take. The bracelet was meaningless now. It was meant to be a record of where she'd been and now it was ruined.

'Don't bother,' she said bitterly.

No, her mother had never really known what she wanted and why. Vanessa sat up in bed again and fingered one of the dolls. It was odd what one remembered from childhood. Petty grievances. At least her mother had always tried, which was more than you could say for many people's mothers.

There was a knock at the door.

'Come in,' Vanessa said and immediately regretted it. She must look dreadful, she thought. But it was too late. John was standing there with a packet of biscuits in one hand.

'I'm *sorry*,' he said, glancing around the room. 'I thought your mother –'

'She's gone off somewhere. It's okay. I've been awake for ages.'

He hovered uncertainly by the door. 'I've brought you something.'

'What is it?'

'Hobnobs. They're a bit crushed I'm afraid.' He placed the packet down carefully on the bedside table. 'I've been saving them for a special occasion.'

Vanessa knew John's dwindling funds had reduced him to a diet of lentils and rice and was touched by the generosity of the gift. 'Please,' she said, 'sit down. Stay and talk.'

'Are you feeling better?'

Vanessa was glad she couldn't see how greasy her hair must be. 'Much better, thanks.'

'Your mother has been giving me regular bulletins. I was worried about you.'

She rolled her eyes. 'I think she's been enjoying it in a funny sort of way. She doesn't get much of a chance to fuss over me.' She paused. 'I don't normally give her much of a chance.'

He looked at her, smiling a little. 'I like your mother,' he said. 'You can talk to her.'

'Do you think so?' Vanessa frowned. 'Sometimes it seems as though –' She broke off. Marion had come into the room carrying a tray.

'Hello, John,' she said. 'I was hoping you'd drop by.'

'Thanks for the dolls,' Vanessa said quickly.

Her mother's face brightened. 'Oh, do you like them? They're lovely, aren't they? I was going to buy just one, but I couldn't decide which because they're all so nice. Avari gave a discount –'

'They cheered me up. And John's brought me some Hobnobs. All the way from home.'

'You can't eat them yet,' Marion said. 'You can't eat anything except perhaps a little rice water.'

Vanessa looked at her mother. 'You really *are* enjoying this, aren't you? Me being sick.'

'Don't be silly, Vanessa. I've been terribly worried.'

'What have you been doing with yourself? Apart from looking after me and buying dolls.'

Marion shrugged. 'Nothing really. Shopping with Tish. I've got her into beads.'

'Beads?'

'There are some lovely ones here. Lapis and amber. She's going to make necklaces to take home for her family. She seems quite cheered up by the idea.'

'What does Greg think of it?'

'Not much. According to him it's a gender thing. He said

197

there was no more pitiful sight than a man trapped in a beadshop. He'd rather be dispatched with a single shot to the head.'

'Supportive as ever, I see.'

'I've also been talking to Dr Kaskusthan,' Marion said. 'He really is the nicest person.'

Marion called him Doctor, but he was really a professor. One of the delegation from Southern India who were staying at Glenside. He was a neuroscientist he told her, although he was qualified in medicine and had practised it in his youth before he turned his attention to research.

She had sought him out at breakfast the morning after Vanessa's night of fever to thank him for his help.

'I was glad to,' he said simply. He was an elderly man, a few years older than her with one of those faces that seem brought to life not by any particularly pleasing arrangement of features or animated temperament, but by an unmistakable and transforming intelligence. She felt strangely relaxed with him, as though they were old friends.

'I was so worried. I didn't know what to do.'

He smiled. 'But you did exactly the right thing.' He gestured a little shyly to the empty seat beside him. 'Please. Sit down.'

'Oh, I can't. I have to go back and check on Vanessa. She was asleep when I left, but I need to be there.'

'She will be fine,' Kaskusthan told her. 'She is in good hands.'

'Perhaps later?'

'I'd like that. Yes.'

The truth was, he missed his wife. This conference and others like them took him away from home for weeks at a time. He had been married for thirty-five years, he said. They sat out in the hotel garden and talked until the lights came on in the dining room behind them and it was time to go inside.

'Your husband?' he asked.

'He's dead,' Marion said. 'Cancer. Last year.'

'I'm so very sorry.'

'We were married for a long time too.'

'I think,' Professor Kaskusthan said, 'that being with some-one for many years . . . it takes on a life of its own. But at the end, where does it go, this life? We hold no funeral for it. It passes quite unrecorded.' He paused. 'Perhaps that's the greatest loss of all.'

'I think you have to be our age to understand that,' Marion said sadly.

'Maybe.'

They were silent for a moment or two.

'You said you were a neuroscientist,' Marion said. 'But what exactly do you do?'

'I study memory.'

She stared at him. 'I didn't know you could do that. As a science, I mean.'

'Oh yes.' He leaned forward eagerly. 'Memory is a *huge* field.'

She had an image suddenly of a broad meadow. The grass knee-deep, full of flowers.

'How lucky I met you,' Marion said. 'Perhaps you could help me remember something.'

Kaskusthan laughed out loud. 'If only I could. But all I study is the mechanism. The nuts and bolts. Memories themselves . . . well, they're still as elusive as they ever were, I'm afraid.'

'But I've been trying so hard,' Marion persisted. 'The trouble is, I don't know what I'm supposed to be remembering. It's difficult to describe. A sense of . . . wrongness, I suppose, which remembering this thing – whatever it is – would explain.'

'Perhaps you're trying *too* hard,' Kaskusthan said. 'You know it's impossible to forget something on purpose. It just can't be done, although we can certainly suppress memory. And the reverse is true too. Sometimes it's impossible to remember by a conscious act of will. It seems the effort of remembering something actually blocks recall. It gets in the way of it. Which is why things come to you when you're not actually thinking about them any longer. You have to let memory find its moment.'

'I know it's there somewhere,' Marion said stubbornly.

'Perhaps, but we forget more than we think,' Kaskusthan said gently. 'We believe we have pretty good recall of our lives, but really, we don't remember much at all.'

'So why do we remember some things and not others? It seems so random.'

Kaskusthan smiled a little ruefully. 'We don't know. Not fully. It is a terribly complicated thing.' He stopped. 'I could give you the long answer and be talking all night and still not explain it properly.'

'How about the short answer then?'

He paused to think. 'People, most people, think of memories as discrete, unchanging portions of the past. But they are not like this at all. In fact, memories have as much to do with what is happening in the present as the past.'

He spoke very seriously. As though it really mattered to him, thought Marion, that she should understand. It was rare to find such passion in a person of his age. A man still in love with his subject. And his wife too. That was perhaps rarer still.

'I'm not sure I understand –'

'The act of remembering involves both the meaning we gave to an event in the past and also the circumstances we find ourselves in years, even decades, later,' Kaskusthan said. 'Two things you see. An event in the past and a trigger – a landscape, a person, a state of mind – in the present. It's in the relationship between them that we find memory. Usually faulty, sometimes even quite incorrect. Always subjective.' He stopped. 'I think I'm giving you the long answer after all. I'm sorry if I'm boring you. I do have a tendency to take the lecturing approach.'

'So what you're saying,' Marion said, 'is that conditions have to be right for some memories to resurface. Which means that there must be whole *chunks* that never see the light of day again. Because we don't find or simply don't encounter the right . . . triggers.'

'Yes. And they can come back again quite suddenly. Like Proust and his famous madeleine.'

'I still don't know why I can't remember this thing. It feels as though I should. That coming here . . . should have brought it back.'

'Perhaps it was something that didn't seem very important at the time,' Kaskusthan suggested. 'Research has shown that we encode memories more efficiently – far more efficiently – when our emotions are involved. Especially negative emotions. Trauma, sorrow, fear –'

'Yes, maybe that's it. It didn't seem important then, but now it does.' She smiled a little sadly. 'I wish we knew at the time what it was we were going to need to remember. What was going to *become* important.'

'But that would mean all memory would have a known purpose. But if there's one thing I've found in my work, it's that memory – large parts of it – has no apparent purpose. Or if it does, it's beyond our understanding.'

He paused. 'There's a boy living in Bombay. When he was twelve, he was diagnosed with a brain tumour. They had to operate to save his life. The boy survived, but his ability to form memories did not. All the things he remembered before his illness stayed with him, but from the day of his operation onwards he was unable to remember anything new. To talk to this boy, you might, for a few moments, assume that all is well. He can converse fairly brightly about a number of things, appears cheerful enough. But after a while, he falters, he loses the thread. It is clear that he has no idea what he is talking about, nor what he *has* been talking about, nor who you are nor why you are there.

'But there's one way that this boy can retrieve memory. By writing. It's an extraordinarily rare phenomenon. He can put pen to paper and write down things that have happened to him although at the time of writing, he has no idea what the words mean or what he is writing about.'

'At least that's something,' Marion said. 'To be able to write down memory. It isn't completely lost then, is it?'

'But here's the catch,' Kaskusthan continued. 'The boy cannot read. He cannot read what he has written. And when others read his words back to him, they make no sense. So who do they belong to, his memories? And what is the point of him writing them? He fills notebooks. Every day writing, writing. But for what purpose?'

'I don't know,' Marion said slowly. 'Perhaps another boy . . . The boy he would have been without the illness.'

He smiled and said nothing.

'You don't agree.'

'Who knows what the truth is?'

'That's the thing about science,' Marion said. 'The thing I find comforting in an odd sort of way. It's so very . . . unsentimental.'

'But not without its own kind of poetry.'

She looked at him searchingly. 'It's that, isn't it? For you –'

He smiled and shook his head. 'I don't know. It's certainly true that the more one studies what is known and what *may* be known, the more one comes up against . . . the unknowable. Perhaps that is the attraction of it.'

'It must be wonderful, your job,' she said with a touch of envy.

'Well, sometimes. Amid all the dull conferences,' Kaskusthan said. 'The field of memory may be large but one sees all the same old faces time after time. One hears the same old arguments. Still, it's nice to be here in the mountains.'

'Yes, the mountains. I never needed any . . . madeleines to remember those. When you grow up with these mountains, they never really leave you.' She thought suddenly of Pete. How maddening he would have found this place and how beautiful. They should have come here together a long time ago. Before it had changed so much. While they had still been young.

'Next time you come, you must bring your wife,' she told Kaskusthan very earnestly. 'You must stay at Glenside together. I feel sure it would make her happy.'

For several days following her illness, Vanessa was too weak to go anywhere except for short forays outside, leaning heavily on her mother's arm. She had eaten almost nothing for over a week and her jeans needed a belt to hold them up.

'I must have lost at least a stone,' she said, with some satisfaction. 'People should come out here and do this instead of spending a fortune at health spas. The Dysentery Diet. I could market that.'

'You're far too thin,' Marion protested. 'It's not healthy.'

They were walking very slowly up the road towards the Anglican church, stopping frequently for Vanessa to rest. Marion rummaged in her bag and produced a small banana.

'Eat it.'

'I was only *joking*, Mother –'

'Just eat it.'

A young man in a striped tank top approached them. He was carrying a plastic bag in which three chapattis lay curled.

'Hello,' he said. 'Where are you from?' His English was fluent, almost without accent.

He took Marion's hand and shook it, keeping it held in both of his own as he talked. His manner seemed calm but Marion could sense agitation in the pressure of his fingers, a compulsive edge to his confidence.

'Do you know anything about concussion?'

'Why? Is someone hurt?'

'Please,' the young man said, 'tell me what you think. When

my brother was a child he fell and hit his head. For many years he was fine. But now he has fallen sick. He lies in his bed staring at the ceiling. He says strange things and yells and shakes for no reason.'

'It sounds like some kind of brain damage,' Vanessa said.

The young man waved her words away. 'Yes, yes, of course. We know this. I think it is too late to save his life. I want to know something else.'

Marion glanced at Vanessa helplessly. 'We can *try* I suppose –'

'My brother does bad things,' the young man said. He looked down at the ground. 'Forgive me for my impoliteness, but he masturbates fifty times a day. He blasphemes. He does not know himself.'

'I'm sorry,' Marion said uncertainly. 'That does sound rather awful . . .' She looked around her a touch nervously. There were no other people in sight. The young man's face had taken on a pinched, anxious look and it occurred to her that perhaps, in the coded language of the mad, it was himself he was talking about.

'It must be very hard for you,' she said cautiously.

'What I want to know is this,' the young man said. He leaned forward intently, obliging her to take a small step back. 'Do you think God will punish him?'

Marion and Vanessa were silent.

'He was not a bad man before . . .' the young man said.

Marion looked at him and saw, not the confusion of madness, but only a deep, unendurable misery. He loves his brother, she thought, perhaps more than anything else in life.

'No,' she said gently, but with great authority. 'No. God does not punish the sick.'

The young man nodded as though it was the answer he had been expecting, but one which failed to reassure him. He opened his plastic bag to show the two women the charcoal-speckled chapattis that lay inside.

'It is my brother's breakfast,' he said simply. 'I am taking it to give to the beggars. He would do it but he does not know himself any longer.'

He closed up the bag. 'I will give it in his name.'

Marion stared after him as he walked away.

'God,' Vanessa was saying, 'what a weird conversation. Only in this place would a complete stranger wander up to you to have a discussion about masturbating relatives –' She broke off. 'What's the matter? You look upset.'

Marion shook her head. 'No. No, I'm fine. It's just something he said –'

'I wonder how many other people he's asked. About God I mean. I get the feeling we're not the first. Or the last.'

But Marion wasn't listening. She was thinking about Professor Kaskusthan and triggers. The way something comes back to a person when they least expect it. A young man in a striped tank top talking about forgiveness. Quite unconnected, it would seem. And yet connection was there. And was this further proof of the complete randomness of all experience, wondered Marion, or quite the opposite? A sign that there was an order to things, that nothing was separate from anything else . . .

Vanessa was flapping the banana at her. 'Do I have to finish this thing? It's making me feel a bit sick.'

'Yes,' she said automatically. 'I don't want to see any of it left.'

'You've become a complete and utter tyrant,' Vanessa complained.

'So where did it happen, the great theft?' Vanessa asked. 'Show me exactly where it happened.' It was two days later and some of her old eagerness had returned. She could walk unassisted now and was anxious to resume her search.

They were visiting Ashagiri's Botanical Gardens. Despite the ravaged aspect of the park's central glasshouse, the grounds were well tended, the beds full of flowers and the lawns tidy. A row of women moved together up a small incline, clearing the pathways of twigs and leaves. They bent slowly, heads turned towards each other, hands easy at their task. The sound of their voices came faintly to the two woman on the light breeze.

'I don't know,' Marion said, looking around her. 'It could have been anywhere really. It wasn't such a big thing, you know, Vanessa. It wasn't such a terrible thing.'

They arrived at a small bench in the shade of a great, nameless tree that spread its branches low and dark, almost to the ground. Marion sat down with a sigh. 'It was something any little girl might have done.'

'But not you. You were always so *good*. It's the only time you were ever remotely naughty.'

'I couldn't resist.'

The Gerber daisies had been so very pretty, she thought. No, more than pretty, almost eatable. She could still remember the colour of them, a deep, saturated pink. As a child it seemed to her that every colour in the world had a responding body part. You felt red in your throat and yellow on the tips of your fingers and green against your temples and blue deep within your heart. When she looked at the daisies she could feel their colour on the inside of her eyelids. She blinked rapidly, enjoying the novelty of the sensation. But the group of girls she was with were already moving on. Dawdling was always discouraged on school walks.

They were not permitted to pick the flowers in the Botanical Gardens. It was not just a school rule, but a park rule too. Everyone knew that. And she was a good child who never broke the rules. But there she was, on her knees suddenly, pulling at the stems. She still didn't know quite what had possessed her. Except that the daisies were so very pink and she wanted them. Not only in her eyes and her hands, but all the way through her. Knowing even as she reached for each flower that picking them would not be enough, would bring her no nearer to real possession, but still unable to stop herself reaching for one and then another and then a third, her movements hasty with greed and guilty panic.

'How did you think you'd get away with it?' Vanessa asked. It was her favourite story. She loved to think of her mother's moment of defiance. And yet what a small rebellion it had been. A little girl picking forbidden flowers.

'I didn't think. When the teacher turned around I just stuffed them in my knickers. She saw them straightaway of course. You can't fit a bunch of Gerber daisies in anybody's knickers, however large.'

'And then you got punished.'

'Yes. I had to learn a psalm. Every time you did something wrong you had to learn a psalm. Some of the girls were always memorizing one of them or another. One girl, I remember, knew all of them. She was the naughtiest. I always liked her, you know. She had the most spirit of almost anyone I've ever met.'

'I wonder where she is now,' Vanessa said idly.

'Still not doing what she's told I expect. There were daisy petals in my knickers all day. They all fell out when I undressed for bed.'

'So where did you pick them from? Show me the bed. Perhaps there are still some growing there. We could pick one if nobody was looking. Just one.'

'Oh, it's all changed, the layout. I don't know. Anyway, why spoil the gardens?'

'I hardly think picking one flower would make much difference.'

Marion got up from her seat. 'If everyone had that attitude, there wouldn't be much left, would there?'

They walked further down the hill to the old hothouse. The building was beautifully constructed, the ironwork arching and delicate but there was hardly a pane of glass that was not shattered or showing creeping black spots of neglect. This hothouse kept nothing at bay. It let in the rain and wind along with the burning sun. The two women wandered through the massed pots of flowers and ferns, pausing beside an old, algae-encrusted stone basin where fish flickered briefly in the murky water.

'The funny thing is, it doesn't seem to matter,' murmured Marion.

'What doesn't?'

She tilted her face up to the broken roof of the hothouse and watched the clouds pass between the empty panes. 'The fact that this place is so . . . wrecked. Look at everything. It's doing wonderfully anyway. I've never seen such huge begonias and those fish are positively fat.'

Vanessa kicked at some loose gravel on the path. 'Why keep it here then? It's such a mess. None of the plants are even labelled. What's the point of a botanical garden where you don't know what anything is?'

'I think it's rather lovely. A bit like a folly.'

'Yes, but follies were *designed* to be that way. This is just . . . abandoned.'

'Why are you always so *rigid*?' Marion said abruptly.

Vanessa looked at her in surprise. Her mother was normally never critical. The last few days had wrought a change in her. She seemed preoccupied, almost impatient.

'I am not,' she said tightly. She kicked at the stones again. This trip to the Botanical Gardens was turning out to be as pointless as all their other jaunts. Her sickness had wasted days and days of their time. And her mother had used it as an excuse to simply potter about. Frittering hours away in the hotel garden peering at plants or perched on her bed rubbing at that bell of hers, trying to make it ring, or taking long meals in the dining room, dawdling over cups of tea while she chatted with everyone . . .

'What makes you think I'm rigid? I'm not rigid.'

'Come on. We should be getting to the police station before it closes for the afternoon.'

The office of the Superintendent of Police was located towards the bottom of the town, in one of the narrow alleys that led off from the market and the grinding mêlée of Ashagiri's bus station. The two women were obliged to wait for half an hour before the Chief of Police found time to see them.

Vanessa glanced at the group of half a dozen uniformed officers in the small room. They didn't seem to be doing anything very much, she thought impatiently. They leaned against the walls and smoked and chatted with each other. Every so often, one or other of them looked the two women over casually, holding his gaze until it became a stare. Vanessa pursed her lips and kept her eyes on the ceiling. Beside her, Marion had pulled out her book of poetry, seemingly indifferent to the delay.

The Superintendent of Police had a great many stamps on his desk. They were all resting on their own little ink pads and his fingers flickered over them constantly as though he could hardly restrain himself from marking everything that came within sight. When he turned his attention to the Wests, however, his hands stilled, fingers together, to form a steeple. 'How can I help you?' he asked, looking at them very penetratingly.

'I want to report something stolen,' Vanessa said. 'My jacket. I need you to sign a form that I can use to claim the loss on my travel insurance. It was an expensive jacket.'

He held up one hand to slow her down. 'You wish to report a theft?'

'Yes, my jacket.'

'Are you certain it was stolen?'

'It was in the back of a jeep. When we stopped the jeep it was gone. It couldn't have fallen out. It must have been taken while we were driving through town. Perhaps when we stopped in a traffic jam.'

The man nodded. 'Perhaps when you stopped in a jam . . .' He paused for a long moment. 'You were driving this vehicle?'

'No. All I need is for you to sign a form for the insurance people.'

The Superintendent pushed a piece of paper and a pen across his desk towards her. 'I will need a full statement,' he said. 'Passengers in the jeep, duration of journey, purpose of said journey. Please leave nothing out. I cannot give authorization without a full statement.'

Vanessa took the paper with a small sigh and bent her head to the task. While she worked, the Superintendent turned his attention to Marion.

'Poetry,' he said, glancing down at the book in her lap. 'A

fine thing to read.' He smiled pleasantly. 'Tell me, are you familiar with one of our greatest poets, Tagore?'

'Not really,' admitted Marion.

'A very fine poet, Tagore,' he continued, raising his voice slightly. The other officers in the room nodded enthusiastically and a murmur went around the office. 'Yes, Tagore, Tagore.'

'Very fine, very spiritual,' the Superintendent said, 'well worth a read.'

'I'll have to look out for his work,' Marion said with great interest. 'Thanks for the recommendation.'

Vanessa finished her statement and handed it back to him. 'Will there be a long wait for the paperwork?'

He scrutinized the page in front of him for several long moments without answering.

'Is there anything wrong?'

He put the paper down and stared rather sternly into space for a second or two.

'I think this is the wrong word,' he said at last. 'You say here that your jacket was stolen. I think' – he paused, eyes narrowed in concentration – 'I think . . . *disappeared* is a better word.' He paused again, as though turning the word over in his mind, examining the meaning of it from every angle. 'After all, we do not know for sure that it was stolen, but it has, undoubtedly, *disappeared*.' He looked at the statement again.

'Also, you have missed a comma out. Here.'

Vanessa glanced over at her mother in exasperation. But Marion was smiling.

'Everyone here seems to be a poet of one sort or another,' she said.

Alex Khusam was sitting on one of the sofas in the main lobby reading a newspaper, holding the pages with the tips of his fingers. On anyone else, it might have looked fussy, as though he was worried about keeping his hands clean. But instead the Prince appeared . . . well, rather *lordly*, thought Vanessa and was immediately ashamed of herself. He lowered the paper slightly as she passed by.

'So, have you found your jacket yet?'

Since their jeep ride together, they had hardly spoken and she wondered whether there was something about her that had disappointed him. He was the sort of person who would often find himself disappointed by people, she thought. It was part of his air of unattainability.

'No. I've just been down to the police station to report it missing.'

'They'll be sending out search parties I expect.'

'It was just for the paperwork. So I can get it back on travel insurance . . .' Vanessa said, wondering why she needed to explain herself.

He looked at her, amused. 'Don't worry. I'm only teasing you, Vanessa.'

'I knew that.'

'You should be pleased. It was a very ugly jacket.' He smiled disarmingly. 'It didn't suit you at all.'

'I'm not sure if I should take that as a compliment or not,' Vanessa said. She spoke lightly but, as before, she was aware of being slightly wrong-footed. The man had a knack for it. A way of making her feel as though he spoke to her only on some passing whim. She sat down on the armchair next to him.

'Are all the police crazy here or is it just me?'

'They are all crazy. And they do nothing.'

'Well, they certainly seem to have a stamp for every possible contingency. I've never seen so many –' She broke off. Khusam was staring at her hands with a disconcerting intensity.

'I see you dive.'

'I do *what*? Oh, the watch –' She looked down at her chunky Tag Heuer with some embarrassment. 'Yes, it's a diver's watch, but I don't . . . I've never been diving actually.' How could she explain to him that she simply liked the appearance of the thing? It looked important as though the wearer was equipped – rather like that Superintendent and his wretched stamps, she thought ruefully – for all eventualities. Khusam was the sort of man who would never wear a diver's watch unless he was a bona fida scuba expert. There was nothing inauthentic about him in the least, she thought.

'It's useful for in the bath.'

He laughed at that. 'I never wear a watch,' he said. 'I hate the feeling of being . . . constrained.'

'How do you know what time it is then?'

Khusam ignored the question. 'When are you coming to see the palace?' he said casually.

'I don't know,' Vanessa said, rather startled. During their jeep ride, Khusam had mentioned going to his home, but she had assumed it was a throwaway remark. There had certainly been nothing in his behaviour since that episode to suggest he had meant it seriously. But then, he wasn't the kind of person who bothered with empty conversation. He said what he meant and obviously felt no need to repeat himself. She felt abashed at her own conventionality.

'I'm not really sure I should leave my mother,' she said.

'She seems perfectly all right to me.'

'Yes she is. Of course. She's fine. It's just that I . . . well, I look out for her.'

'I thought it was meant to be the other way around,' Khusam said.

'I sort of feel responsible for her. It was my idea coming here. She wouldn't have come at all if I hadn't practically forced her. I have to make it work out.'

She half expected him to ask what it was she felt she had to do. John Walcott would have done, she thought suddenly. John would have asked her what she was looking for. Quite simply, in that direct way of his. And she knew, as clearly as if this imagined conversation was actually taking place, that she had no answer to that question.

But Khusam didn't seem particularly curious about the situation. He folded up his paper neatly and replaced it on the table.

'Well, think about it,' he said, almost indifferently.

It occurred to her that the matter could quite easily be resolved by him simply inviting Marion to the palace as well. A more polite person would have surely done so. 'Bring her along too,' they might have said. Quite easily and casually. But Khusam was neither easy nor polite. It was not his style.

'I'm leaving tomorrow night,' was all he said. 'If you change your mind.'

That evening, Glenside was full. In the dining room, every table was occupied. At the piano, the fringes of Lily's green poncho, stiffened through accidental immersion in any number of long forgotten foodstuffs, tangled with her fingers on the keys as she laboured enthusiastically over 'Que Sera Sera'. Among the diners there was a mood of great animation, a kind of collective happiness that occurs only rarely and seems beyond explanation. John Walcott, sitting between the two Wests, leaned back in his chair with satisfaction and wondered when he had enjoyed a meal more. He only wished the small brown bear back at the club could have been there to enjoy it too.

He looked at Vanessa, deep in conversation with Greg. She was shaking her head a little as the man spoke, involved, impatient. He did not think he had ever met anyone quite so contrary, so quick to disagreement. It seemed to him a kind of eagerness, as though the world was still an urgent place for her. Behind her argumentativeness was the vulnerability of a person in need of some kind of answer. He wondered whether it had been her idea to ask him to join them at dinner. Probably not. The invitation had come from Marion and it hardly seemed Vanessa's style to get her mother to do the talking for her. He smiled a little ruefully to himself. Mothers always seemed to like him.

As the bearers cleared the last of the coffee cups away, Mrs Macdonald suggested they all went into the drawing room for brandies. It was long past the usual time for her to retire, but she seemed untired, despite a whispered reminder from Dorothy Nichols that she should rest.

They settled themselves in a circle around the fire. John, the two Wests, Alex Khusam and Dorothy, and a sturdy looking man from Colorado who had arrived at the hotel that morning. Professor Kaskusthan, sitting by himself on the far side of the room, looked up as they made their entrance.

'Doctor Kaskusthan,' Marion called eagerly, 'please join us.'

He closed the book he had been reading. 'Well, I had been thinking of turning in –'

'Oh, please,' Marion insisted. 'It's still so early.'

He found a seat between Vanessa and the Prince and settled himself with the slightly apologetic air of an outsider. 'Are you feeling somewhat better?' he murmured to Vanessa.

'Much better. I believe I've got you to thank for that.'

'Not at all. It was a very simple matter –'

Mrs Macdonald's attention was fixed on the man from Colorado. 'This is Jack Hudson,' she announced. 'He's here on a kind of mission. To Everest, I believe.'

'Well, just to Base Camp.' He stretched his legs out confidently. 'On this trip at any rate.'

'Are you a climber?' Marion asked. Hudson had the look of a man used to the outdoors. But his was a well-fed kind of ruggedness, a touch self-satisfied. The sort of man who made a fetish out of gear: his fleece moisture-wicking, his trousers core-vented, his Trek Ready socks miraculously warm yet lightweight.

'I do a lot of climbing,' he said easily. 'Although not on this trip.' In Colorado, he explained, he had been involved in a project experimenting with waste disposal at high altitudes. They'd had some success using solar power.

'Stuff doesn't decompose normally when there isn't much oxygen around,' he said. He glanced around at the group.

'Sorry to bring this up when you've just eaten and all.' He grinned unrepentantly. 'The Waste Disposal Units worked great in Colorado but we wanted to find out how they perform in a monsoon climate.'

The problems had begun the moment he arrived in India. Customs at Delhi had been deeply suspicious. 'I had a letter from the Prime Minister's number two, but it made no difference. They simply wouldn't let the WDUs into the country.' In the end, he said, he had to abandon them altogether. 'Still don't know what's happened to them.' He grinned again. 'Probably got three families living in each one by now.' He had been forced to make the things from scratch which had delayed his plans for weeks. But now he was finally ready to begin the trip to Base Camp.

'By Waste Disposal Units, I take it you mean lavatories,' Vanessa said. 'You're taking two *loos* up Everest?'

'Just to Base Camp. There's a real need for them. You wouldn't believe the mess that expeditions make up there. It's getting like Grand Central Station.'

'I've always wondered at that. The passion to climb,' Marion said. 'Why would anyone do it? Put themselves in that kind of danger. Mountains are such . . . indifferent things, aren't they?'

'Do you climb at all?' Vanessa asked Khusam.

He shrugged. 'Not with any great seriousness. I've done a few peaks. For the sake of the challenge.'

'Like Mallory then. "Because it's there." '

'Yes, I suppose so.'

'Poor Mallory,' Mrs Macdonald said. 'They should never have gone looking for him. When I saw the photograph of his body that the expedition brought back I thought the terrible thing was that he still looked so young. Time had just passed by and left him behind. Such a lonely thing to happen to a person.' She paused. 'He wasn't that much older than me, you know.'

'Can you believe that he tried to get up Everest in a tweed jacket?' interrupted Jack Hudson. 'The man is up there in one of the most inhospitable spots on the surface of the planet and all he has by way of equipment is an extra pair of socks and a tin of meat lozenges. There was this other man, George Finch, who went with him on the 1922 attempt. He invented some kind of down suit to wear and, you know what, the others laughed at him. In their *tweeds*.'

Hudson paused, marvelling at the folly of it all. 'Finch was dropped from the 1924 expedition. And I bet he would have made it up there. With his down suit and all. He might have been the first man on the summit of Everest. Way before Tenzing and Hillary.'

'Ah, Tenzing,' Mrs Macdonald said. 'He visited Ashagiri a few times. He's buried in Darjeeling, of course, but I believe there's a statue of him somewhere around here.' She smiled a little sadly. 'Everyone wants to claim a little piece of someone like that, you know.'

Marion hadn't followed the conversation. She was still thinking about climbing. The terrible cold. The utter weariness of it. And for what?

'Why would anyone do it?' she persisted, looking at Hudson. 'Why do you like climbing so much?'

There was a second or two of silence before he answered. 'I think it's about the thing you said before,' he said, very seriously. 'The indifference of mountains, you called it. I think that's exactly right. When you're up there, you know that you're nothing. An insect. It's a different world, a different universe. You start out with all the right equipment, a plan. You think you're going to beat the thing and then comes the moment when all that is taken away. It's like a burden is lifted off you.' He laughed. 'You're not responsible for the fate of the universe any more.'

'There's a higher power,' Marion said.

'Well, I wouldn't put it like that, but yes, if you like.'

'It's a typical approach in the West,' Khusam said, rather scornfully, 'to disguise a quest for spiritual fulfilment as sport. Here we have worshipped mountains for generations without feeling the need to conquer them. Sherpas have climbed Everest, but they would never climb Khumbila which is far more sacred to them. It would be a desecration.'

Hudson shrugged confidently. 'Well, different strokes you know.'

'One of the interesting things about Everest,' Professor Kaskusthan said a little tentatively, 'is that it wasn't even given that name until the mid nineteenth century. Up until that point it was merely Peak XV on the British Survey of India. Then a clerk took some trigonometric readings of the area and discovered it was the highest point in the Himalayas. After that it became significant, although it had never been considered particularly special by the locals.'

'I didn't know you were so knowledgeable about this part of the world,' Mrs Macdonald said. 'You've been hiding your light under a bushel.'

Kaskusthan looked embarrassed. 'I don't know about *knowledgeable*, but my point is that Everest only became interesting because of the figures. Do you see? If we worship it, it's because we worship the power of the calculation.' He looked at Khusam. 'Another particularly Western habit, wouldn't you agree?'

But Khusam appeared to have lost interest in the debate. 'I suppose so,' he said indifferently.

John, feeling Kaskusthan might be feeling snubbed, turned his attention to the professor.

'What brings you here?' he asked him. 'Are you involved in research too?'

'He does work with memory,' Marion broke in eagerly. 'We've been having such interesting talks –'

'Which reminds me,' Kaskusthan said to her, 'did you manage to remember whatever it was that was causing you so much frustration?'

'Yes. Yes, I did. It was exactly how you said it would be.'

'And was it as important as you thought?'

Marion hesitated. She looked up and caught Dorothy's eye. 'I don't know,' she said awkwardly.

'High altitudes pretty much scramble the brain, right?' Jack Hudson interrupted.

'Oxygen deprivation does have a negative effect, yes,' Kaskusthan agreed.

'When you're *really* high up,' Hudson said with great satisfaction, 'you can't remember squat.'

They were talking and talking but Dorothy Nichols could not hear them any longer. She did not look at Marion again, but sat quite still, her hands on her lap, her mind frozen.

What did the woman remember? That there had been a friendship?

Thin drizzle coming down. Wet white knees below a school skirt.

'Is it time to go back yet? Is it time?'

The girl had her sketchbook stuffed up her sweater in an attempt to keep it dry. It made her look like a box. She toiled up the slope on her short legs, her characteristic willingness tinged by uncertainty.

'Perhaps it's too wet to draw today.'

'Sister Maureen said we could.' Sister Maureen had said a lot of things. You have an eye, she had told the girl. You could develop that, you know. Talent like yours is a precious thing. A special thing.

There had been times before when she had felt jealousy. Always in the weeks leading up to the end of term and then for a few days after coming back from the holidays she had sensed the girl was . . . distracted. Full of thoughts of her family, of reunion and the misery of parting. In the last few days before term broke up, it often seemed as though the girl had left already. Her suitcase packed far earlier than was necessary, her whole being taken up with the yearning to be elsewhere.

It was hard but she had accepted it. The cycle of the school year was a fixed thing, as immutable as the seasons. And, after all, the holidays were merely interruptions. They had each other for the rest of the time.

But this was different. This was new. Sister Maureen with her Four O'Clock Club and her talk of talent and gifts. She took the girl aside one day after lessons and gave her a box of watercolours.

'I've been waiting for someone to give them to,' she said. 'I had them when I was about your age. I knew there was a reason why I had kept them all this time.'

She had felt the girl slipping from her. They were still friends of course, but underneath, everything was changing, losing shape. It was happiness that had done it. Happiness that she had no part of. The girl no longer cried at night and, during the day, when they were together, it seemed that she looked at her in a different way. Still eager to please but less so than before. She made her little notebooks and now she filled them with drawings. A couple of the other girls noticed and asked her if she could make one for them.

She looked up, amazed and delighted. 'Yes, of course I can. Yes, *of course*.'

As if their friendship meant nothing.

'Can other people be Roundheads?' she asked one day.

'Like who?'

'Well ... Ros Conway ... I think she might be a Roundhead.'

'No. She can't be. Nobody can.'

'Why not?'

'It's a *secret*. Don't you remember?'

'I haven't told her anything,' the girl said quickly. 'I just wondered, that's all. She's in the Four O'Clock Club –'

'You told her, didn't you?'

'No. I promise. I promise I didn't.'

She saw then that the girl's friendship had been nothing but the result of a dependent nature. Others led and she followed with no more thought than a leaf floating in a brook. With no more gratitude than a leaf feels towards the current that carries it along.

'Sister Maureen gave me permission to go out sketching after lessons,' the girl said. 'She said it was all right if I went with someone. Do you want to come?'

She nodded. The girl's amiability disgusted her now. A weak, habitual thing, as different from her own fierce love as a shadow differs from a real, living person.

'All right,' she said. 'I don't mind going.'

The rain had begun unexpectedly when they were forty-five minutes away from the school. They were walking up a steep hill in an area little visited by the pupils of St Margaret's.

'Do you think we should turn back?' the girl asked. In the gloom, she looked very pale.

'Not yet. It's only drizzling.' It gave her secret satisfaction to see the look of anxiety on the other's face.

'My sketch pad will get wet,' the girl said, plodding onwards obediently.

'We're nearly at the top.'

'I don't like it here. It's scary.'

'It's not. I bet nobody else has ever been here before.' She looked suddenly at the girl. 'It's a secret place. Only for Round-heads. We mustn't tell anybody else about it. Do you promise?'

But the girl only shook her head.

'Is it time to go back yet? Is it time?'

The top of the hill turned out to be nothing more than a narrow stretch, strewn with large stones. A few steps beyond, the ground terminated in a cliff edge. Below, little could be seen but the brown, wounded side of the hillside. Ripped earth and rocks and far down, at the base of the cliff, a dense line of brush, half obscured by mist.

She peered over the edge. 'Come here and look.'

And the girl, hesitant, but obedient. Her hair flattened by rain. Protected by nothing but the flimsy breastplate of her sketchbook. Knowing no other direction to take.

She pushed her. Not hard.

Not hard at all. It seemed the action was both planned and, at the same time, entirely impulsive. As though she had always meant to do it, but only knew this fact at the very last minute. She felt the small, hard outline of one of the girl's vertebrae beneath her fingers and then she was gone. Only the rattle of rocks marking her passage. No cry of alarm or protest. As if the girl had known how it must be and had accepted it.

It was only later that she saw what it was she had done. She saw it in the shocked faces of those who questioned her and the awed silence of the other girls once news of the accident spread. The world put on hold to listen to her story.

'Sister Maureen said we could go,' she told them. 'She gave us permission.'

She saw it again on the day of the funeral. The girl's parents had travelled through the night. Their faces were not like any she had ever seen before. Features splayed wide by grief like mice on the dissecting table. The mother knew her name. She clutched her, pressing her head against her woollen cardigan, weeping and rocking slightly. The cardigan smelled of violet water and cat's pee.

The whole universe dislodged by a single movement of her elbow.

Later, when everyone had done with the place, she had returned to the top of the hill to create her monument. Not knowing, even then, the true purpose of her actions. But sensing rightness in that careful placement of stone against stone.

Her mark on the earth.

●

Everyone was focused on Professor Kaskusthan. It seemed the subject of memory held endless interest. This did not surprise him. He was used to questions about his work from even the most unscientifically minded of people. But he always marvelled a little at it. At the way memory as an area of study seized the imagination of almost everyone. It was about possession, he thought, and the power to be possessed. He had seen those whom memory had abandoned, and understood that without it a man feels himself nothing. A smear on the surface of existence.

'What is it that you actually *do*?' Vanessa said. 'I mean, how do you study something like that?'

'My work is mostly concerned with a structure in the brain called the hippocampus. We've been looking at ways this structure encodes certain memories. We think it plays a role in the formation of new memories. Patients with brain damage to the hippocampus have trouble remembering recent events. They seem unable to process them in the normal way.'

'Hippocampus,' Mrs Macdonald said. 'That's a seahorse, isn't it?'

He smiled. 'Exactly. Because of the shape of it, you know.'

'Nobody needs to know Latin any more except for doctors,' Mrs Macdonald remarked. She looked at Marion. 'And gardeners, of course.'

'I've always been kind of interested in the idea of total recall,' Jack Hudson said. 'I mean it's all in there somewhere, isn't it? Problem is, how do we get at it?'

Kaskusthan shook his head. 'I'm afraid it doesn't really work like that. Most people think memory works a little like a video camera, recording events and then playing them back, but it isn't like this at all. Quite different in fact. Memories appear to be records not of events themselves, but *how* we have experienced those events. A highly personal selection process. And one which involves many parts of the brain working together.'

'So this hippocampus thing,' Vanessa said, 'can you actually *see* memories being formed there?'

Kaskusthan smiled a little wistfully. 'I wish I could. That's pretty much the holy grail in memory research. Our imaging techniques are still too crude for that, I'm afraid. My guess is that if we could do it, we'd see neurones firing up here, there and everywhere in the brain.'

'Like stars!' Mrs Macdonald said.

'Yes, maybe a bit like that. Like the sky at night, full of constellations. But they'd be always changing. Endlessly different patterns, different shapes.'

'What you said,' John broke in eagerly, 'about memory not being like a video camera, but more a record of our own . . . subjective experiences. It's interesting. I've always tried to paint that way too.' He stopped abruptly, embarrassed at his own frankness. 'It just made me think about it.'

Khusam turned to look at him for the first time. 'So you're the painter,' he said. 'The *miniaturist*. I've heard about you.'

'His paintings are pretty good,' Vanessa said. There had been something in the way Khusam had paused over the word 'miniaturist' that aroused her defences. 'Really amazing actually.'

Khusam smiled at her a little mockingly. 'So, you have been admiring them then –'

'What do you mean when you say you paint that way

too?' asked Marion. 'Just now, you said you painted that way.'

'The old portrait miniaturists painted pictures that people could carry around with them,' John said earnestly, his speech impediment becoming more pronounced. 'To remind them of the faces of loved ones. But they weren't really accurate pictures. They were idealized. Because that's how we remember – how we want to remember people. Then along came photographs and there wasn't any more need for miniatures. But something got lost. How many times have you taken photographs of somewhere beautiful and got home and got them developed and thought, no, that wasn't how I remembered it? I used to do it a lot. Got my photos home and thought, no, that wasn't what I saw. Not at all.'

'It's probably because most people are crap at taking pictures,' Vanessa said.

John Walcott shook his head. 'I don't think so,' he said. 'Photos don't show what we remember, they only show what's *there*. What I do – at least, what I try to do – is paint the way we remember. It's very hard.' He paused. 'I paint small because that's the way memories are. Just bits of things really. Small bits we carry around and look at from time to time. Things that belong to us.'

'That's beautiful,' Marion said.

'But miniatures!' Khusam said again, as though there was something intrinsically unmanly abut the very enterprise. 'One might just as well collect postage stamps.'

'There is a similarity,' John said, stumbling even more over his words. 'But with stamps, you see, they start with something big, a big picture, and then shrink it down. I start off small you see . . . it's different –'

'I'm afraid I still don't follow,' Khusam said. He looked at Vanessa and raised his eyebrows slightly. 'You haven't convinced me why I shouldn't take one of your pictures and simply . . . stick it on an envelope.'

'Well –' John looked down at his hands. 'That's a fair criticism perhaps.'

'No it isn't,' Vanessa said quickly. 'Alex is just being facetious.'

'I think what John is trying to say,' Mrs Macdonald said, 'is that stamps start off big, get shrunk down and that's the end of it. But with his pictures, well, if you reversed the process and blew up their size, who knows what you might find there? You might discover all manner of things too small to have been seen before. A whole world hidden. Am I right? What do you think, Dorothy?'

Nichols shifted uncomfortably. 'I'm not the right person to ask. I know nothing about art,' she said, in the tones of someone conveying a certain disdain, rather than ignorance, of the whole subject.

'Well, *I'd* be interested to see your paintings,' Jack Hudson said suddenly. 'I collect mountain-inspired art. Mostly photographs actually. I've got a couple of Ansel Adams, you know. Worth twice what I paid for them now.' He flashed his customary grin. 'And I've gotta tell you, they weren't cheap when I bought them.'

Mrs Macdonald smiled at John. 'You see, I may have helped you make a sale.'

'He needs a good marketing person,' Vanessa said. 'Don't you, John?'

Beside her, Alex Khusam yawned openly, without inhibition. 'That sounds like an invitation to me,' he said. 'I'd take her up on that if I were you.'

Vanessa looked at him. What must it be like, she wondered, to be so effortlessly attractive? Because she *was* attracted. It was clearly obvious to him. This banter with John was simply his way of showing her he knew. An expression of confidence in his superiority as a rival. But it was a strange kind of attraction that she felt. Not a personal thing at all, she thought. Too automatic for that. None of the usual drama of discovery and suspense. She wondered briefly what it would be like with him. There would be passion, she thought, but it would be of a different sort. Something separate, pre-existing. Not created by either one of them but with a momentum all its own . . .

'I don't think Vanessa meant that,' John interrupted hastily. 'It was just a comment.'

'Don't pay him any attention,' Vanessa said, giving Khusam a reproving look.

John was about to reply when there was a stir around the small circle. Dorothy Nichols had leaped to her feet. 'I *knew* this would all be too much for her,' she cried fiercely. 'Staying up this late, all this talk . . .' She bent over Mrs Macdonald and seized her wrist. The old lady, unnoticed by the guests, appeared to have fallen asleep.

'What's wrong?' Marion said. 'Is she all right?'

Still crouched over her patient, Dorothy made a batting motion with her free hand, as though to ward off approach. 'Keep back,' she commanded. 'Give her air.'

'Has she fainted again?' Marion asked. 'Is it the same as before?'

Jack Hudson and Professor Kaskusthan had both jumped to their feet.

'Should we call for one of those servant guys?' Hudson said.

'Perhaps I should fetch a glass of water –' John said, making for the door. 'A cold towel, something like that.'

'Would it be helpful if I took a look?' Kaskusthan asked. Dorothy turned away, presenting her back to him, and Kaskusthan relapsed into puzzled silence.

Only Alex Khusam appeared unruffled. He leaned forward

in his chair staring at Mrs Macdonald, whose face had taken on a greyish look. 'In my opinion we should all do exactly what Dorothy says,' the Prince remarked coolly, 'and give the woman a little space.'

'I still think we should get hold of one of the servants,' Hudson said. 'Feels all wrong to me to just stand about doing nothing.'

'She has simply fainted,' Dorothy announced. 'Everything is under control. You must leave it to me. It is not the first time this has happened.'

'It's true,' Marion said. 'I was there the last time she fainted. Dorothy knew exactly what to do then.'

'She has worn herself out,' Dorothy said tenderly. She replaced Mrs Macdonald's limp arm by her side and then, very calmly and gently, began to stroke the old lady's forehead. 'She will not do what she is told, you see. That is the way the very old become young again. You must trust me. I have seen it before.'

•

'I hope Mrs Macdonald will be all right,' Marion said.

'I expect she will,' Vanessa said, feeling far from sure.

'She looked so . . . small.' She had been about to say 'lifeless' before she corrected herself. The old lady had only fainted, she had not died. Marion knew what dead people looked like. It was more than just the colour of their skin, their leaden immobility, it was the way they appeared so out of reach. Not people any longer, but simply *stuff*. Seeing Pete lying dead in the bed they had shared for decades, it had seemed to her that he had more in common with the bedside table and the reading lamp and the small pile of pins she had removed from her hair the night before than with her. She had told him goodbye. Saying the words out loud because that was what one was meant to do, meant to *want* to do. But the words had sounded foolish to her. Talking to the dead Pete as absurd as having a conversation with a door.

'Dorothy will look after her,' said Vanessa. 'She seems to have a knack for it.'

After the fainting episode, the group in the drawing room had dispersed awkwardly. The two Wests, feeling the need for fresh air, delayed returning to their room in favour of a short walk to Lookout Point. It was very late and the stars were invisible behind a layer of thick, drifting clouds. The trees, one shade blacker than the sky, were dense and impenetrable. A solitary glow-worm flickered uncertainly in the bushes.

Marion clutched her bag close to her.

'I wonder what's wrong with her,' she said. 'Collapsing like that. It's not the first time –'

'I suppose it's because she's so old,' Vanessa said vaguely.

'But fainting?'

'I don't know. I'm not a doctor, am I?'

'I think I need to make a phone call,' Marion said. 'Back home, to England I mean.'

'Who do you want to call? What about?'

But Marion didn't answer. She stared at the ground as though concentrating very hard on her shoes. In the dim light, the silver leather glowed like pearl.

'You can do it from the hotel,' Vanessa said. 'There's a phone in our room.'

'Haven't you noticed? You can't call out from the hotel phones. They're only connected to each other. You can only call someone else in the building.'

'The lodge then. They must have a line out there.'

'Yes. Yes, that's what I'll do.'

'What do you think of Alex?' Vanessa said suddenly. 'The Prince.'

Marion did not respond, apparently still working out telephone logistics.

'I think he's . . . interesting,' Vanessa said. 'He has this thing, this mission, I suppose you could call it. To restore his grandfather's old palace. He seems completely obsessed with it. Somebody like that . . . he could do anything I should think, but here he is, stuck in the middle of nowhere, spending all his time and energy on the project. *Driven* by it. Don't you think that's remarkable?'

'There's something . . . wrong with his face,' Marion said slowly. 'His mouth.'

Vanessa stopped walking. 'What an extraordinary thing to say! What does his mouth have to do with anything?'

'Nothing I suppose, but you asked me what I thought. I think his mouth looks wrong.'

'In what way exactly?'

'I don't know, Vanessa. Don't keep asking me to explain everything. That's just the impression I have.'

'Well, I think it's a very trivial impression,' Vanessa said self righteously. She should have known better than to ask. Her mother's opinions about everything were based on the most arbitrary of evidence. Almost as if she did it on purpose, thought Vanessa angrily. A kind of perversity.

They had passed through the thickest of the trees and were approaching the open area which, during daylight, allowed sweeping views of the valley and mountains beyond. At this hour, however, the horizon was invisible. One only had the feeling – not arrived at through the usual senses – of great and sudden space. And in the darkness it was possible to imagine that this space had no end, that there was time and room there for a person to fall for ever.

'It's a shame there's no moon,' Marion said. 'It should be full tonight. Almost full, anyway.' She clenched her hands on the cold metal fence of Lookout Point. 'It was almost full last night.'

She was thinking of John Walcott. Of his painting and what Kaskusthan had said about memory. She wished she had found a chance to talk more about that. Perhaps tomorrow, she thought. It seemed she had many more questions, but now, standing in the dark, she wasn't sure exactly what those questions were.

She glanced up. 'Look at the moon!'

During the few moments that they had stood there, the sky had cleared slightly. The darkness seemed to move, thin out, grow heavy once more. Clouds shifted, a few stars appeared. And a moon came into view, full and golden, like no other the two women had ever seen before. It burned like a slow sun, lighting up the clouds which constantly passed over it, swift as rushing water. Like a golden coin at the bottom of a murky river, the moon gleamed, darkened, burned again. It was a moon to fish for, with shirt sleeves rolled up to the elbows and icy fingers among the pebbles and the water making the light of it dance and deceive the eye.

Marion stared at it for a long while. Her moon. Her lucky penny of a moon.

What was it exactly that John and the others had been talking about? Something about memories belonging to us. How the brain worked to make this true. The hippocampus, Professor Kaskusthan had called it. Strange, she thought, that she should find her seahorse again. Not wrapped in cotton wool in the drawer of a school room this time, but tight inside her very own head. Carried unknown by her, like that poor, lost foetus in her friend Ann's brain. The same shape too, tiny backbone braced against the world. How irrepressibly, maddeningly plural life was. How full of discrepancy and blind connection. She turned impulsively to Vanessa.

'I think –' she said, '. . . this trip. I think it will be all right, you know.'

'Do you really think so?'

'I thought, for a long while, that it wouldn't work. That coming here was a mistake –'

'But we still have time,' Vanessa interrupted eagerly. 'I'm so glad you agree with me about this. We have time to make it work. We can still find plenty of things. We haven't been to Sunny Valley or found Dreaming Rock, or really talked properly to anybody who might have old connections.'

'Nobody wants to talk about it,' Marion said. 'Their Ashagiri is not the same as mine. Nobody wants to talk about the past.'

'We just haven't found the right people yet,' Vanessa persisted.

'But that's what I'm trying to say. That it doesn't matter. It's all right.'

'But we haven't even *tried* properly.'

'It's all right,' Marion said again, very gently.

'I can't believe you're just going to . . . give up.'

'No, Vanessa, that's not what I mean at all.'

'It sounds like it to me. Can't we at least make the effort to get to Sunny Valley? I mean, we've come out all this way. If we don't even go there, I don't know what the point of it all was. I really don't.'

'It's not about making an effort.'

Vanessa drew in her breath. All her annoyance at Marion seemed to rise to the surface suddenly. It was precisely this inertia, this apparent willingness to drift with the cruddy tide of circumstance that had dictated all the events of her mother's life. She wanted to beat her fists against her mother's body as she had done as a child.

'Well, tell me,' she began angrily, 'tell me what it's about then. Because I certainly didn't drag myself here so I could potter about in somebody's garden and look at the mountains all day.'

'Why did you then?'

'That's not the point,' Vanessa said quickly. 'You know it isn't. You started this conversation. The point of this conversation and this trip seems to be about you.'

'Then let it be about me.'

Vanessa shook her head. 'I don't believe this. I really don't.'

'Let it be, Vanessa. Just drop it.'

'I won't drop it. I gave up my job to do this trip for you.' Even as she spoke, Vanessa knew that this was only partially true. But she wanted it to be true. The need to blame her mother rising in her with sudden fury.

'Don't you understand that? I gave up my bloody *job*.'

Marion sighed. 'I'm not the mother you would have chosen, am I?'

'What on earth is that supposed to mean? Of course you are. Who gets to choose their mothers anyway?'

'I meant hypothetically, Vanessa.' There was something about the way her mother paused over her name. Drawing the first syllable out in that long-suffering way of hers. Weary tolerance in the tone of her voice. As though it was she, Vanessa, who was the unreasonable one. Who had always been unreasonable. A difficult discontented child, hard to like, a petulant adult, still clamouring with impossible demands.

'I find this *pathetic*,' she said viciously. 'I really do. I find you –'

'Pathetic?'

Vanessa paused.

'I know you think I'm pathetic,' Marion said simply. 'You don't have to say it. From the moment we got here it's been quite obvious.'

'That's not fair. And not true.'

'No. You think I'm pathetic. And I'll tell you the reason why I don't want to go to Sunny Valley. It doesn't have anything to do with the place itself. It doesn't have anything to do with finding the past or not finding it.'

Vanessa didn't think she had ever heard her mother talk in this way. Quite steadily and deliberately, as though she was choosing her words carefully rather than letting them patter out in the usual fashion.

'I don't think you're pathetic, I never said that.'

Marion didn't seem to hear. 'The reason I won't go to Sunny Valley is because I don't want to go with *you*,' she said calmly. 'I don't want to be made to feel useless. I don't want to be like some little dog being taken out for a walk.'

'And that's how I make you feel?'

'Yes. That's how you make me feel.'

'How you can say that, when I came out here with you, organized things, put up with –'

'I didn't ask you to.'

'No, you never ask,' Vanessa said bitterly. 'You never ask, do you?' She paused. 'I don't understand how you can say these things. I don't understand you at all.'

'There's a reason for that,' Marion said. 'The reason you don't understand me is because I'm not myself when I'm with you.'

Vanessa turned away. 'You're right,' she said savagely, unable to help herself. 'You aren't the mother I would have chosen. I would have chosen better. Somebody quite different. Somebody else.'

They walked back to Glenside in silence, Vanessa a little ahead. Her pace was swift and it seemed suddenly remarkable to her that she could walk with such apparent purpose. As though her legs still carried something substantial rather than the shape – mere outline only – that her body had become.

Her mother's words had fallen so lightly, almost easily. As if the wall that lay between the spoken word and everything that was normally left unsaid, the great wall that allowed a person to hold on to the belief that the way they presented themselves to the world was the way the world saw them, was nothing, after all, but a thin line on the ground which could be stepped over in an instant. And yet why not? Why should it not be easy to state something so obvious? That coming here had been just another one of her empty endeavours. Her role self-appointed, her efforts unwelcome.

Pointless then, even in this. The fear that had brought her to Ashagiri; the fear of the emptiness within, of the great cancerous vacuum deep within her, justified after all. Her own mother telling her so. Lifting the covers to show her, yes, in the dark place below the bed, there is a monster. You were right to think him real. Here are his eyes and here his claws.

She walked onwards, dry-eyed, wishing she was home. Wishing she knew where that place was.

PART THREE

The Seahorse

•

She might have been downstairs at breakfast or taking an early morning stroll in the garden, but Vanessa knew neither of these were the case. Her mother had gone. She looked at Marion's unmade bed and at the hook where her jacket normally hung and the space on the bedside table – now empty – where she rested her glasses, and was pierced by the sense that she was all alone.

Her unhappiness of the night before was instantly replaced with remorse. Vanessa cast her mind back to what she had last said to her mother. The terrible thing about words, she thought, was the way they followed you. You spoke them in a time and a place, imagining they would stay there, forever in context. But words knew no borders. They spread, like contaminant through water, tainting everything.

Marion must have risen very early, she thought miserably. Perhaps before dawn. She would have taken her clothes from the chair at the foot of her bed and dressed in the bathroom, in the dark. Had she formulated this plan the night before or had the decision come in the morning? The longing to be elsewhere rising with her waking self. She would have lain there for a moment or two, eyes open, considering how to best make her escape. Then the cautious rising, the groping for her handbag, the soft click of the door closing behind her.

Vanessa dressed quickly. The certainty that she was all alone made everything look different. Shabbier somehow, more scattered. As though along with her bag and coat, her mother had taken something else; a sense of purpose, of justification. She would go downstairs and look in the garden and the dining room, Vanessa thought. And when she did not find her mother there, she would sit down and eat something and think of where else Marion might be. She would not allow herself to worry. She would not imagine her mother lost or hurt or lying dead somewhere at the bottom of a cliff. She had simply gone off on some jaunt or other. She would be back.

Vanessa found momentary relief in exasperation. Wasn't it children who were meant to be the ones who ran away? Even in this, her mother seemed unable to conform to expectations.

It was still early and the dining room was almost empty apart from Dorothy Nichols and Greg, sitting at different tables. Dorothy glanced up as she entered and then looked down at her book again without acknowledgement. It was clear she felt obliged to demonstrate her disapproval at every opportunity, withholding the most ordinary of civilities to make her point quite plain. As if anyone cared in the slightest about the woman's opinions, thought Vanessa savagely. Greg raised his hand in a half-hearted gesture of greeting and it crossed her mind to ask him whether he had seen her mother. But the question would imply she was searching and Vanessa did not want to think she was searching. Not yet. At the same time, he *might* have seen her and perhaps this fact would come out in the ordinary course of conversation. She went over to his table.

'Do you mind if I join you?'

He gestured to the empty seat. 'Yeah. Whatever. I'm just finishing.'

'You're up early.'

'Not for me. I'm always awake by six. Can't lie around in bed.'

'Where's Tish?'

'Tish doesn't eat breakfast,' Greg said flatly.

244

'I was wondering whether you'd seen my mother,' Vanessa said, despite herself.

'Why? Gone and got lost, has she?'

'I just wondered. I mean, I know where she is probably, I just wondered if you'd seen her leaving or anything.'

Greg sucked on the upper hairs of his goatee. 'Nope. She must have sneaked out before me. The Wicked Witch of the West might have seen her.'

'Who, Dorothy?'

'Yeah, she might have seen her. She was down here when I arrived.'

'Why do you call her that?'

He shrugged. 'She gives me the creeps. Every time I look up she's kind of staring at Tish in this weird way.'

'She's probably just concerned. Tish does seem quite . . . ill.'

'I look out for Tish, you know? It might not seem that way, but I look out for her.'

'Yes. Yes, of course you do.'

'I hope you find your mother,' Greg said, in a changed tone. 'She's all right, you know, your mum. She's been really kind to Tish. Brought her out of herself a bit. It's made a . . . difference.' He caught himself abruptly. 'She's filled all the pockets in my backpack with those beads of hers. Makes me sound like a fucking rattle.'

'Don't you think you should take Tish home?' Vanessa said gently.

'We saved for two years to get here. Tish will be all right.' He pushed back his chair and stood up. 'I'll see you around.'

After he had gone, Vanessa began to think of the places her mother might be. At the top of her list was the idea she had simply gone shopping again. To Avari's perhaps or another of the many curio shops in the town. She poured herself a cup of tea, making an effort to drink it slowly, as if this was an ordinary morning. But eating anything seemed beyond her. She fiddled with a piece of toast, stared at the wall opposite and wondered what she was doing. Time was passing while she was engaged in this pretence of normality. Half an hour already since she had woken up and seen her mother gone. She looked at her watch. Closer to forty minutes. Panic stirred inside her. She fought it back and tried to organize her mind.

Avari's then. That was the first place to look. She would not think about what she would do if her mother wasn't there. She would simply go.

The shop was quiet. Avari caught her eye as she stood in the doorway, scanning the interior, half hoping that Marion might emerge from behind one of the piles of rugs. He smiled and gestured for her to come in. 'The daughter of my favourite customer!' he cried. 'Please, have some tea, a seat . . . there is always room here.'

'I can't. Has my mother been here this morning?'

He shook his head. 'It's still so early. No customers yet.'

'Are you sure?'

'Of course. I know your mother. We have so many nice chats.'

'Well, I'm sorry to bother you,' Vanessa said, turning to go.

'My favourite customer,' Avari sang out as she left. 'Please give her my regards.'

Vanessa continued her search. Ashagiri was laid out in tiers like a wedding cake. At the top of the cake – its crowning decoration – stood Glenside with only the hill and Lookout Point above it. Slightly further down, but still part of the topmost layer, were most of the landmarks of the old Ashagiri, the Raj town. The Anglican church, abandoned Grand Hotel, the cottages with their Deco-style balconies, Fountain Square, Klein's and the other more upmarket eateries. Continuing downwards, one entered Ashagiri's middle layer, the municipal district. Three large banks, a post office, cinema, a multitude of moderately priced shops selling shoes, groceries, hardware and fabrics. Below this, sprawled the largest section of the town. The market, bus station and endless ragged buildings that housed the majority of Ashagiri's inhabitants.

Moving from the top of the town to the bottom one passed by slow degrees from the hushed to the fervid. From empty spaces, trees and mountain views to teeming, jostling streets, full of haphazard connections; a crush of colour and gesticulation, of broken shadows, shouts and dusty feet, whirling scraps and things half glimpsed. Vanessa took several hours to make the journey. The morning had already passed by the time she found herself in the market, with a basket of cackling chickens at her feet and no clear sense of where she should go next.

She had been to Lookout Point and around Fountain Square twice, walking slowly and looking in all the shop windows as she passed. Then down to the club, through the courtyard and into the gloomy reception area. The dining room and lounge had both been empty. Klein's next. She had turned away from the doorway in disappointment even as one of the waiters was hastening to show her to a seat. She had been into all the banks and the post office and had even stopped by the Museum of Natural History, although she had no real hope of finding her mother there. The exhibits seemed more wretched than ever on a second inspection and she walked quickly through the building, tainted by their redundancy.

Loneliness gripped her. She visited the fabric shops stacked high with shiny nylon and netting, crossed and recrossed the street, making small forays down alleyways and into dimly lit restaurants. After an hour or two it became clear to her that she was not going to find her mother in any predetermined location. She had been to all the places she could think of.

Now all she could hope for was that she might spot her by chance in the street.

She walked onwards, moving downhill.

Vanessa had been to the lower part of the town before, but not alone and never with the sense of vulnerability that now overtook her. Today it seemed that every shout, every shove of the crowd, every madly fluttering scrap that caught her eye was like another blow, beating at her self possession. One of the street vendors rattled a chain in her face. Whistles blew. The chickens squawked and fluttered, releasing small white feathers through their wicker cage. Her right hand was covered with some red powder from when she had reached out to steady herself against the wall of a building. She wiped it on her trousers feeling utterly disorientated. It was past lunchtime. Early afternoon already.

She reached the edge of the market and took a small path leading further downhill towards a cluster of wooden houses about half a mile distant. The path was very steep and narrow, and full of activity. There was a profusion of washing and strings of children with dirty ribbons in their hair who called out 'hello! hello!' in reedy, excited voices. Men sitting together by the side of the road played *karom* on great polished wooden boards, with hammered bottle tops as counters. Deep within the bushes which spilled out between the sides of houses, the yellow, incurious eyes of foraging goats glimmered briefly and were gone again.

Everything, the houses, the women, the assorted animals, the schoolchildren, the coloured cotton banners of a small temple, the clusters of morning glory, the dirt, the drying washing, the rivulets of water running down drains and tiny streams by the side of the path, the rocks, the makeshift shrines stained with ochre and crushed flower petals, the metal counters speeding across the *karom* boards, the boards themselves, everything was tumbling together down the slope in a great incorrigible wave of dirt and noise and movement and Vanessa moved with it, helpless and fearful, without purpose or resolve.

Her mother was not here. She did not know what she was doing any longer or where she was going. She sat down suddenly on a low wall by the side of the path and covered her face with her hands. She had caused all this trouble by her cruelty. Wanting to make everything better for her mother, but instead only making things far worse. And now she was on a hillside somewhere, far from everything, with no plan. Worn out, undone by guilt. From amidst the hubbub, she could hear the grunting of pigs. A soft, revolting sound that amplified her remorse, transforming it into self loathing. What would she do if she couldn't find her mother? How would she ever explain it? She pictured herself going to the police station to make a report. Not a stolen jacket this time, but a missing relative. The Chief of Police would make her write out another statement; sitting over her, criticizing her phrasing. 'I do not think "missing" is quite the right word,' he would say, 'I think *driven away* is closer to the mark.' And then he would stamp everything in sight with those little rubber stamps of his and she would have to go back to England alone. With two suitcases.

Somebody touched her very gently on the shoulder. She looked up.

'Prasad! What are you doing here?'

He smiled shyly and gestured towards the houses further down the hillside. 'I live here,' he said simply. He paused. 'Are you looking for somebody?'

'My mother,' Vanessa said unsteadily. 'I'm looking for my mother.'

He was dressed in his club uniform. The dark green Nehru-style felt jacket buttoned up smartly, his cap at a correct angle.

He was going to work, she thought. They had often joked that Prasad knew everything. That you could ask him anything and get the right answer. She knew that it was childish to believe this was actually true, but she was too exhausted and unhappy to care. 'You haven't seen her anywhere, have you?' she said.

His face lit up. 'This morning!' he said. 'I saw her this morning.' He pointed upwards towards the top of the town. 'Getting into a jeep. With a gentleman.'

'A man?'

'Yes. With a jacket. A red jacket.' He paused, as though searching for the right word. 'Not red ... lighter, like this flower –' He pointed to a clump of cosmos flowers by the wall. 'The jacket this colour.'

'Pink?'

He nodded. 'This morning. Very early.'

Bharani! thought Vanessa. It had to be. Only Bharani was possessed of such sartorial enthusiasm.

The realization that Marion had absconded somewhere with Bharani deepened Vanessa's mystification, but it reassured her too. Of all the adjectives one could apply to the man, sinister was not among them. She walked back up the hill with new energy. Where could the two of them have been going? Obviously somewhere one could only get to by jeep. A suspicion began to form in Vanessa's mind. She reached the taxi park and stopped, considering. If she was right, it made no sense to return to Glenside. Her mother could not possibly be back already. She approached one of the taxis.

'How much to Sunny Valley?' she said.

'One hundred rupees,' the driver said, very daringly.

'Okay, whatever.'

He took off with a swirl of gravel and dust. One hand on the wheel, the other dangling out of the open window, fingers drumming casually against the side of the vehicle. 'Twenty kilometres,' he said, as though to justify the exorbitance of his fee. 'Long way.'

'Yes,' Vanessa said indifferently. 'A long way.' She leaned her head back against the seat, fixing her gaze on a small green and gold elephant hanging from the rear-view mirror that swung to and fro as the car barrelled along. It had a smug look, she thought. Tiny glittering plastic eyes, trunk curled up in a smirk. Why Bharani? she thought. Of all the people in the world, why Bharani?

The jeep rattled along without further comment from the driver. They passed through two small towns and then turned off down an unmarked road, with low bushes to either side. Vanessa sat up and stared about her. They were driving through tea.

It was beautiful, the place where her mother had been born. It looked like a garden. The tea bushes spreading down the gentle slope were softly damp and in the thin mist they glimmered with a silvery sheen on their dark leaves. Each bush was low and round and satisfyingly dense. Trees outlined the hills beyond and rose at intervals between the tea, seeming to float above the bushes, the bases of their trunks invisible.

In the middle distance, a small group of women worked the crop, picking the leaves and tossing them into huge panniers strapped to their backs. Each woman had an open umbrella tied to the back of her pannier to shelter her from the elements. Everything was rounded in this landscape. The curved umbrellas, the bushes, the gentle rolling hills, the winding path traversing the slopes by slow degrees.

The taxi bounded down the hill, rocks bouncing off the undercarriage, gears grinding. 'Road no good!' the driver announced with great cheer. 'Old. No tarmac.' Vanessa looked about her without answering, trying to protect her head from banging into the roof of the car. There was no sign of her mother's jeep. She had been so certain this was Marion's destination.

They arrived finally at a cluster of buildings at the base of the small valley. A group of low outhouses surrounding a larger structure; the tea factory itself. 'One hundred rupees,' the driver said.

Vanessa reasserted herself. 'That's there *and* back,' she said. 'And it's a complete rip-off.'

'It is the going rate, madam,' the driver said with great bravado.

'Just wait here. I'll pay when I get back.'

The nearest building had a sign on the door that said Manager's Office. She pushed it open without hesitation and stepped inside.

Her mother, Bharani and two other men were sitting together around a rickety table. There were four or five small teapots on the table and a cluster of cups, each half full of dark liquid. One of the men had his head tilted back, making a low, gargling sound. Another was holding a cup in both hands and sniffing at its contents with great absorption. At Vanessa's entrance, Marion, who had been laughing, stopped abruptly. All four of them turned and looked at her.

There was a large tea leaf stuck on the end of Bharani's nose.

Marion had taken to Mr Bharucha and Mr Karanth straight away. Both assistant managers of the tea estate, they complemented each other perfectly. Mr Karanth was tall and merry. He laughed a great deal and wanted to cut the tour of the factory short so that they could all repair to his living quarters where he kept a supply of tea liquor. Mr Bharucha, on the other hand, was small and intense. He insisted they see every detail. He was determined that the visitors should learn everything there was to know about the cultivation of tea at Sunny Valley.

When Mr Karanth informed them that one hundred kilograms of freshly harvested leaves shrivelled down to a mere thirty after the process of withering, Mr Bharucha was quick to correct him. 'The actual figure is twenty-nine kilograms,' he said, making sure that Marion wrote the number down on a piece of paper he had supplied for the purpose.

'During the fermentation procedure,' said Mr Karanth, with a casual wave of his hand, 'the room is kept at about seventy degrees.'

'The perfect temperature is in fact seventy-one degrees,' Bharucha corrected. 'And it must be kept perfectly constant at all times.'

All this talk of facts and figures made Bharani's eyes glaze over somewhat. He was not used to being on his feet for such long stretches of time. Karanth's mention of tea liquor had brightened him for a moment or two, but when it became clear the drink was not forthcoming, he seemed to sag a little

253

at the knees. But he was a good sport, thought Marion. A kind man.

Going by herself to Sunny Valley had not been planned. It had just happened. She had woken before dawn with nothing on her mind except an overwhelming urge to be alone. She wandered for a while in the garden, and then, crossing the empty lobby of the hotel, her eye had been caught by one of the photographs on the wall. A row of women with heaped baskets resting on the ground in front of them; tea bushes behind and the long, low roofs of buildings. It was not a picture of Sunny Valley, but another estate whose name she did not recognize.

The idea of making the trip had come to her then. Partly a desire to get the much talked about visit over and done with. Partly to show her daughter that she could, after all, act independently. But mainly because of a longing that came over her at the sight of those smiling women. A sudden desire to go back to the place where she had begun.

People liked to imagine a circularity to existence, she thought. Of beginnings meeting endings, of journeys that always returned to source. Life as a ring with reason for all loss contained within its mathematical eternity. She had read somewhere that the instinct of new-born babies to root – to turn at a touch to their cheek and blindly suck – returned in extreme old age. Everything else gone except this first, last, primitive impulse. A homecoming of a sort. Out of such random quirks, patterns could be made and consolation found.

Of course, it meant nothing, she thought. Life wasn't circular at all, it just went onwards. But still, one should be allowed a few sentimentalities. It didn't seem much to ask. She turned from the photograph abruptly, her mind made up. Coming out of the entrance to the hotel, she met Bharani. There was a pained expression on his face. He had been unable to sleep, he said. All night, tossing and turning. It was his indigestion. A family weakness, he told her. All the other members of his clan suffered in the same way.

'But where are you going?' he asked. 'You cannot go alone.'

'I shall be perfectly safe, Bharani. I will be back in time for supper.'

He tagged along beside her anxiously. 'You will need someone to bargain with the jeep driver. These men are like wolves. They are quite utterly ruthless.'

'I shall be fine.'

But he was so eager to please; beaming at her despite his gastro-intestinal woes. 'I am an excellent bargainer,' he insisted. 'I will get a good price for you. And we will drink a lot of tea. It will be good for my condition. Tea has excellent medicinal qualities.'

'Are you *sure*, Bharani? It's a long way away. We'd be gone most of the day –'

But he was already darting back inside the hotel. 'I will be back in a jiffy,' he called happily. 'I must first fetch my jacket –'

Mr Karanth and Mr Bharucha had seemed delighted to see them. Particularly when they discovered that Marion had been born there. They explained that the old living quarters on the estate had been torn down some time ago and new ones built. 'It was a problem with subsidence,' Bharucha said apologetically. 'They are not the same any longer. Not as grand.'

'They are bachelor bungalows now,' Karanth added, with a rather naughty look.

But the tea factory itself was the same as it had been in the days when her father had overseen production. The same stone floors, heaped with tea, the same humming machines. The machines had been operating without interruption for over a hundred years, running on fan belts and the movement of sturdy cogs with a steady, wonderfully smooth action.

'People knew how to make things in the old days,' Mr Karanth said fondly. Carved into the silver metal were their names. Here was the Maguire Patent Packer and there the Britannia Balanced Pucca Tea Sorter; the manufacturers now forgotten, outlived by their products.

The progression of raw tea leaf to breakfast table was a complicated and enchanting journey. Only the youngest part of the bush was harvested – two leaves and a bud, plucked between finger and thumb, and laid out in long wooden withering troughs. 'These troughs are six feet long and the tea must be no more than four inches deep,' Bharucha said reverently as they gazed at the long strips, stretched out like swathes of some precious fabric down the length of the upper floor of the factory.

The tea was withered and then rolled and then laid on marble slabs to be fermented. It was put on a slow conveyor belt to be dried and then it was graded. The grading machine was Mr Karanth's favourite. 'You see this chute? We put the tea in here and it is caught in this fan. The lighter pieces are blown to the back. The larger particles remain at the front.' He stroked the metal. 'There are twelve routes for the tea to take, according to size and weight. You see, they arrive here.' He pulled open one of a dozen small drawers at the base of the grader to show them the heaped tea inside. 'The first three drawers are our finest grade. The last three, we discard to maintain quality.'

'And then there is the packing,' Bharucha said. 'The crates must be vibrated a little to allow the least possible wastage of space. We stamp each one with the date and the grade. Seventy crates leave this factory each day. Seventy!'

Marion thought she had rarely been anywhere nicer. There was nothing dirty or artificial in the entire factory. Just pale wood, silver metal and piles of dark tea. The sun had come out during the tour and it streamed in through the windows, casting a golden light over the tea scoops, faded sacking, discarded panniers and neatly swept floors. It caught the dark-brown tea and made it glimmer russet like the highlights in hair. It shone on Mr Bharucha's face as he explained the workings of yet another machine. 'This is a thirty-six-inch double action,' he said earnestly. 'This is a forty-six double action.' The whole place was suffused with the heavy smell of tea; warm and dusty and sweet and the sun seemed to intensify this smell, giving it an even greater richness.

Beside her, Bharani shifted wearily from foot to foot. 'Will there be a tasting?' he asked plaintively. But Bharucha was rushing them to look at the furnace. 'You must stand close,' he ordered, steering Marion towards the fiery hole. 'A great deal of coal is needed to keep it going. I do not have the precise figures on the tip of my tongue. But it is a great amount.'

Karanth was determined to find someone on the estate who might have been alive during Marion's father's time. Just beyond the furnace he spotted an old man. The man spoke no English and seemed bewildered by Karanth's rapid questioning, but he nodded his head.

'Temple,' he said vaguely, still nodding. 'Mr Temple.'

'Ask him how old he is.'

'He says he is sixty.'

'That's too young,' Marion said. 'He couldn't possibly remember.'

'Oh, don't listen to *him*,' Karanth said rather scornfully. 'These people don't know their age. They never get old. They stay sixty years of age until they die.' He laughed. 'It's a miracle!'

'Will there be a tasting?' Bharani said again, more loudly than before. They turned to look at him. 'The hours have *flown*, you know,' he said. 'I am quite certain it is lunchtime already . . .'

Tea tasting was an art, like wine tasting, and the assistant managers were proud of their skills. They found two extra chairs in the Manager's Office and arranged a dozen or so different grades of tea on a tray, each with its own pot. What a joyful procedure the tasting was, thought Marion. And how extraordinarily noisy. They must first smell the dry tea and then smell it again once water had been applied, all the time marking the paleness of the liquid, a sure sign of quality.

'Not like that!' cried Karanth, observing Marion's hesitant sniff. He bent his nose to the table and snorted loudly. 'One must catch the full aroma. Absorb it thoroughly!'

After the sniffing, came the sipping. A cacophony of gurgling. Karanth and Bharucha held the liquid in their mouths and whistled with it. They pursed their lips and sucked it. They made it bubble in the backs of their throats. Then they spat it out with great, appreciative hisses and thrust their noses into the wet leaves that remained to smell again the lingering aroma.

'Now you try,' commanded Bharucha, handing Bharani a cup.

He blinked nervously. 'It is all most delicious –'

'Come on, Bharani,' Marion said, 'get gargling. It will be good for your stomach.'

'There you are!' Vanessa said, in a loud, angry voice. 'I've been looking for you all morning.'

'Oh, Vanessa,' cried Marion, 'you came all this way –' She realized, with a stab of remorse, that she hadn't thought of her daughter once all day. 'You didn't have to come. We were leaving soon anyway.'

'You might have left a note.'

'Didn't I? I meant to –'

'I had no idea where you were.' Vanessa knew she sounded sulky and this made her even more furious. 'You can't just go gallivanting off without telling anyone, you know. Have you the slightest idea how –?'

'Please, Vanessa. Not here,' Marion interrupted. 'We can talk about this later.' She looked at her companions apologetically. 'I'd like you to meet two new friends of mine. This is Mr Bharucha and this is Mr Karanth. They run things around here.'

Vanessa shook both men's hands unwillingly.

'You've missed the tour,' Marion said. 'It was so lovely.'

'Educational!' Bharani chipped in.

Vanessa gave him a withering look. 'You've got something on your nose,' she said.

He brushed it off sheepishly.

'It's not Bharani's fault,' Marion said. 'Don't be angry with him.'

'Would you like some tea?' Mr Bharucha said. 'We are sampling assorted grades.'

'No thanks. I'm fine,' Vanessa said tightly. 'I've got a taxi waiting outside.'

'Please, Vanessa. Sit down for five minutes. Just five.' Marion smiled, hopeful, placatory. 'I know I shouldn't have gone off like that.'

'I have been gargling,' Bharani announced importantly in an attempt to pour oil on troubled waters. 'It is the correct way to taste the tea, you know.' He tilted his head back and gave her a demonstration.

'The factory is lovely,' Marion said again. 'I wish we had more time to show you. Everything so calm and really, just the same as it must have been when I was a baby.'

'Well, I'm glad you got something out of it anyway,' Vanessa said, making an effort.

'Oh, I have. Such a lot. Mr Bharucha and Mr Karanth have been so kind –'

'I asked the taxi to wait for me. I don't know when you were planning on leaving. You can stay here if you want, of course.'

'No. We'd better be going too.' She rose, regretfully, and turned to the two managers. 'We've taken up too much of your time already.'

'It was a pleasure!' cried Karanth. 'Please come again.'

Mr Bharucha left the room briefly and returned with two silver foil packages. 'A memento,' he said proffering them shyly. 'This is our very best grade. To enjoy at your leisure.'

They were mute in the taxi returning. Vanessa, in the front seat, stared ahead. Marion, who wanted to be friends again, was daunted by her daughter's rigid posture and could think of nothing to say. Even garrulous Bharani was forced into a nervous silence. Marion felt sorry for him.

'Is your indigestion better?' she asked in a low voice.

He smiled heroically. 'A fraction. Although I expect it shall return in full force.' He patted his silver package. 'I shall fend it off with continued infusions.'

The taxi driver resumed his habitual drumming on the side of the car, indifferent to the troubles of his passengers.

'I don't think I'll be around for dinner,' Vanessa said suddenly. 'I'm going away for a while.'

Marion leaned forward anxiously. 'But where?'

'I don't see why I should tell you, but if you must know, I'm going to Rupkhand. With Alex. He asked me to visit his palace and I've decided to take him up on the offer.'

'Do you think that's a . . . good idea?'

'Of course I do. I wouldn't be doing it if I thought it was a bad idea.'

'But where is the palace? How will you get there?'

'He'll drive me. He has a jeep. It's quite a long way off. I'll be gone at least for the night. Perhaps longer.'

Marion stared at her daughter helplessly. Vanessa still had not turned her head.

'Can't we talk about it at all?'

'I'm talking about it now.' Vanessa spoke to the window, eyes fixed on the left-hand windscreen wiper.

'Are you *sure* you want to go?'

She did not answer.

'At least stay for supper. Go tomorrow.'

Bharani stirred on the seat. He seemed agitated. 'Mrs West,' he whispered, 'Mrs West. This is not above board. Not at all.'

Marion patted his knee. 'It's okay, Bharani. Vanessa knows what she's doing.'

'The prince lives a long distance away,' Bharani said unhappily. 'And he is . . .' He paused. 'I don't like to say it, but I must. I must speak out. He is not a gentleman.'

Vanessa laughed abruptly. 'I'm a big girl. Ask my mother.'

'She can take care of herself,' Marion said, sounding unsure.

Bharani shook his head.

'You're not just doing this because . . . because I went off today, are you?'

'Of course not! I've been meaning to go for a while. There's no reason why we shouldn't do our own thing, is there?'

She turned and looked at her mother for the first time in the conversation. During the course of the day Vanessa had swung from resentment to fear and remorse. Now, following the relief of finding Marion, resentment had taken hold of her once again. It was Marion's apparent lack of concern about the worry she had caused. The fact she had chosen Bharani as her companion for her trip to Sunny Valley. But most of all, it was the knowledge that her mother had no intention of discussing their row, either now or in the future. 'We'll talk about it later,' she had said. But they wouldn't. It was not her mother's style. Marion never *dealt* with anything, thought Vanessa. And this passivity seemed suddenly utterly selfish.

'We're not joined at the hip, you know,' she said. And any private doubts she may have had about her proposed trip were silenced by the satisfaction of seeing the unmistakable worry in her mother's face.

•

The night was very still and full of insects. Large bodied things, beating against the headlights of the jeep with small, lethal thuds. They swarmed frantic around the street lamps, wings blurring the air with a numb insistence like the broken crackle of faulty electricity. Vanessa glanced at her companion. As always when she was with Khusam, she was acutely aware of his presence, but tonight this awareness was sharper, charged with expectation.

She had found him already loading up his jeep, making ready to leave. 'Got any room for an extra passenger?' she asked lightly.

He seemed amused. 'I thought your mama wouldn't let you come.'

'Well, I'm here, aren't I?'

'Are you sure you don't have her stashed somewhere?' He made a pretence of looking in the back seat.

'Very funny.'

He swung himself into the driver's seat. 'Well, come on then. Unless you've changed your mind again.'

He drove more carefully than usual, slowing as they left the lights of the town behind, his eyes fixed ahead in concentration. Before, in the daylight, she had been frightened on this road. Now, in the dark, it was even more dangerous. But she was too wrapped up in her own daring to be alarmed. As though the taking of one kind of risk protected her against all others.

'Actually my mother probably *is* worried about me. She's

been listening to Bharani. He seems to think he's her new best friend.'

'Ah, Bharani – '

'He told her you aren't a gentleman. Whatever *that* means.'

'But I have been to all the best schools,' he said mockingly. 'I went to Harvard no less.'

'What was it like?'

'I learned nothing there,' he said shortly.

'Why not?'

'I studied Government. It was a waste of time. I could have learned more spending the time here, among my own people.'

Again that note of possession in his voice. She ignored it, watching his hands on the steering wheel, the way the loose cuffs of his shirt slipped back, exposing his wrists. They were fine boned, unusually slender.

'Bharani has the most bizarre ideas about everything,' Vanessa said. 'Do you know what he told me the other day? He's planning a trip around the world. Some cousin or other of his is getting married in London. In Dalston of all places. So he's flying out there, spending a day at the wedding and then flying back. Via Chicago. He changes planes there and then flies around the other side of the world to get back to Calcutta. God knows why. A whole week it's going to take. The whole time on various planes with one day in Dalston. I don't suppose you've ever been there. You wouldn't want to go.' She leaned her head back and laughed out loud. 'You know what he said? "It will take six days but I will actually be travelling for seven due to the fortunate circumstance of time difference as I circle the globe." He's actually looking forward to sitting on a plane for a week. It must be the prospect of all that airline food.'

Khusam smiled a little absently, apparently thinking of other things.

'The more I think about it, the more appropriate the trip

seems,' Vanessa persisted. 'I mean, it's perfect for him. World travel without the hassle of ever leaving your seat and an endless supply of meals right there. It's perfect!' She laughed again.

But Khusam seemed bored by the topic. 'Are you comfortable?' he asked. 'You can shift the seat back if you need more leg room.'

'No, that's okay, I'm fine.'

They lapsed into silence. Vanessa thought of her mother, back at the hotel. Dinner would be almost over. 'Please stay,' her mother had said as Vanessa packed a small bag for her trip. 'Just stay for dinner. John is coming again. I asked him to. Last night.'

Vanessa shook her head. 'I can't. Alex is leaving in a few minutes.'

'But John will be so disappointed. It's you he comes to see, you know.' She moved to the window. 'It's dark already. I don't like the idea of you driving in the dark.'

'I'll be fine. You know I will.'

'I still haven't made that phone call,' Marion said abruptly, as though the approach of night had jolted her suddenly.

'I've left it so late. What time do you think it is in England?'

Vanessa shook her head. 'I don't know. Leave it to the morning. Who do you need to talk to all of a sudden anyway?'

'Tracy. Tracy Fuller. I *meant* to call her earlier. I really did.'

Vanessa gave up trying to fathom the erratic shifts and turns of her mother's thought patterns. 'Whatever it is, it can wait. Go to the lodge in the morning. Or wait until I get back. I'll sort it out then.'

'I don't know. Perhaps I should do it now. I just don't know what time it is there.' She sat down on the bed. 'It's nine hours difference, isn't it? But is that nine hours ahead or nine hours behind? I don't want to wake her up in the middle of the night . . .'

Vanessa paused, wondering whether she should leave after all. Her mother seemed more than merely distracted. She looked almost distressed. Then she remembered the scene at the tea estate. The four of them sitting there in the office. Her mother laughing unrepentantly. Quite unaware of the torment she had caused. Or perhaps simply indifferent to it. Vanessa turned away. 'I don't have time for this right now. I'll see you tomorrow. Or the day after.'

'There were bears in these woods once,' Khusam said suddenly.

Vanessa stared out into the dark. It was wild terrain. 'What happened to them?'

'Deforestation,' Khusam said, his voice dull. 'Half the trees gone. In the daylight, you can see it. Whole hillsides without cover. They just came in and cut them down. They're still doing it.'

'Can't it be stopped?'

'There have been no bear sightings for a couple of years now,' Khusam continued. 'But I think they are still out there somewhere. Just a few of them left.'

'It makes you angry, doesn't it?'

He ignored the question. 'When I was small we were forbidden to go into the woods behind the palace because of the bears. There were so many then. Of course we went anyway. We would sneak bread from the servants and go out with it to try and lure birds. I had a bow and arrow I made.'

'To shoot birds?'

'Yes,' he smiled at the recollection. 'We got into such trouble. Because it was so dangerous.'

'Did you ever see any bears?'

He shook his head. 'They will come back,' he said, suddenly fierce. 'Somehow we will find the ones that are left and bring them back. I will see to it.'

'Yes,' said Vanessa, 'I really think you will.' She looked at him admiringly. 'You'll make the woods wild again.'

They had been travelling for almost two hours, always climbing, before Khusam slowed and turned right on to a dirt road. The incline was very steep. Vanessa held on to the door handle to steady herself. The wheels of the jeep spun a little frantically against loose earth and then they were passing between two pillars. The gates, Vanessa thought. These must be the famous gates. A few seconds later and they had stopped in front of a large, unlit building. Khusam leaned on the horn and, a moment later, a light flickered in the entrance.

'Come,' he said, leaping down from his seat.

In the dim light she saw the doors of the palace, vast and wooden. Deep-red lacquer, a few shades darker than blood. Above her, the outline of a long, pagoda-style roof cut into the sky. But there was little time to get her bearings for now the great door was opening and a man with an angular, unsmiling face was greeting Khusam, his head nodding in brusque deference as they stepped over the threshold.

Khusam said something to him very rapidly in a language Vanessa could not understand. The man was clearly a servant of some sort. He wore an embroidered waistcoat over shabby trousers and his feet were bare. The waistcoat hung a little crooked, as though he had put it on with some haste.

'Come,' Khusam said again, 'he will bring us food.'

She followed him into a large, empty lobby. Stone floors, doors to the left and a wooden staircase at the far end. A smell of burning. Not the smoky, singed aroma of recent fire, but cold, like something long extinguished. Vanessa hesitated. But Khusam was already going up the stairs. She followed him uncertainly. At the top, he paused before a second pair of large, double doors.

'Welcome to my home,' he said, swinging them open. He stood back and let her pass in front of him.

Her eyes swept the large interior. 'Alex, it's *gorgeous!*'

The room, long and high ceilinged, was a dazzling sight. A maze of colour and pattern. The walls, painted with lotuses and spiralling clouds, the floors and benches covered with thick-textured carpets, red and gold and green. Carved wooden dragons set above the tall windows, blue mouthed, rampant, breathing fire. Instead of chairs, the floor was heaped with cushions embroidered with silver and gold threads that glittered as they caught the light. It might have been overwhelming, this blaze of colour, but for the utter simplicity of the room's few furnishings. The benches were Spartan in line and the low tables, lacquered a deep black, were unadorned. Three plain earthenware pots stood on a narrow stone shelf and, beside the fireplace, nothing but a simple wicker basket for kindling. Vanessa thought she had never seen anything so sensuous and at the same time serene. Relief heightened her delight. She turned to her companion.

'Downstairs, I thought –'

'That it hardly looked much like a palace?'

'Well, I suppose so. I suppose I thought that. It's so empty down there.'

'You wondered what you were doing. Perhaps your mother was right about me after all.'

'No. No, I didn't –' She stopped. It was exactly what she had been thinking. 'But this. It's so lovely –'

'I haven't restored all the rooms yet. Just this one and part of the sleeping quarters.'

'I had no idea it would be like this.'

He smiled proudly. 'It's all local craftsmanship. But not the stuff you find in the tourist shops in Ashagiri.' He swept his arm around the room. 'These things were not made for sale. They were made to furnish a palace. By people who remembered how it used to be.'

'Tell me about it. How it used to be.'

'First we must eat and drink. I have some very good wine. Indian wine.'

'I didn't know there was any good Indian wine. I assumed you had to import it.'

'Not true,' he said, very seriously. 'India produces excellent wine.'

They settled themselves on a pile of cushions in front of the fire. Here, in his own domain, Khusam looked different, Vanessa thought. Utterly at ease, even more beautiful. The firelight on his cheekbones, his pharaoh's lips. She looked up at the ceiling quickly. There were lotuses painted there, curling, running wild.

'It's amazing how comfortable it is sitting on the floor.' She had removed her shoes at the door to the room and, under her bare feet, the carpet felt warm and very soft. 'I don't know why the rest of the world bothers with furniture.'

The bearer entered the room with a tray of several dishes and a bottle of red wine. He set them down on one of the low tables nearby. 'What are these things?' cried Vanessa, peering at the food.

'These are ferns,' Alex said, pointing to a cluster of green whorls. 'Very tender and good. And these are steamed mo-mos.'

'Mo-mos?'

'A little like dim-sum,' Alex said. 'But far better.' He held out the plate. 'Try one.'

He poured the wine. It was better than Vanessa thought it would be. And the ferns were extraordinarily nice. A light, woody flavour, tasting of the forest and new growth.

'I love the way they're curled up like that,' she said. 'Like little wheels.'

'They collect them from the forest. In the morning, while the dew is still wet –'

He was looking at her now. He reached out and took the wine glass from her hand and then he was kissing her. She lay back against the cushions. For a moment or two, all she could think of was the fact that there was a fern still held between her finger and thumb. She wondered whether she should put it down. It would make a mark on the carpet but what was the alternative? To keep holding on to it? Close up his face looked very broad. He was kissing her and following the shape of her head with his fingers as though he was examining it. She lay very still, feeling nothing but strangeness.

'I like you,' Khusam said, pulling away for a moment, 'because you don't know how attractive you are.'

'Oh,' Vanessa said, rather feebly. She felt dizzy. It was the wine and the lotuses tangled above her and the surprise of his contact although she had known it would happen all along.

'Tell me something I don't know,' he said abruptly.

'What do you mean?'

He rocked back on his heels, watching.

'Anything. Tell me something I don't know.'

The request cleared Vanessa's head. She sat up. 'What a peculiar thing to ask. Something you don't know. How do I know what you don't know?'

He shrugged, amused. 'Surprise me.'

'Okay. What I'm thinking. You don't know that.'

'Oh, I think I can guess.'

'What I'm thinking,' Vanessa said, 'is why on earth would you ask me something like that. Perhaps it's a test. Or perhaps you simply like gathering random bits of information. No, it's a test.' She frowned, trying to work through the logic of it.

'But why test me? Are you bored perhaps? Not very flattering. And now I'm thinking, perhaps I've failed the test. Was I meant to say something else?'

He laughed. 'You talk too much.'

'I was just trying to answer your question,' Vanessa said with some indignation. He put his hand on her shoulder and pulled her to him. 'Be quiet,' he said.

'Okay. I will. I'll be quiet.'

He kissed her again and then, moving to the back of her neck suddenly, began to bite her there. Very hard and gentle at the same time. His teeth bearing down with great urgency, almost ferocity. As though he might break the skin, but then pulling back a fraction at the instant of contact. Almost hurting her, but not quite. The two forces of abandon and restraint meeting at a single point on the very threshold of pain. Up until this moment, Vanessa had felt distanced from events, her mind separate from his touch. Now, with the biting, she felt herself trembling, slipping. She thought of the fabled bears in the woods beyond and felt them come close. Up to the walls of the palace itself. Dark haunched, incorrigible. Her eyelids flickered. Around her, the colours of the room broke and swam.

He stopped and looked at her suddenly with an expression both calculating and amused.

'You like that, don't you?' he said.

She stared at him, speechless.

'Animals mate that way. With the male's teeth at the back of the neck.' He smiled a little cruelly. 'It is the primitive in you.' He bent towards her again. 'You must give in to it, you know.'

She hesitated for a moment, suddenly uncertain. 'I hope you don't think that I do this kind of thing all the time. Because I don't. It's not like me at all.'

He threw his head back and laughed. 'Vanessa, Vanessa.'

'What?'

'It's not as though I'm lining you up as a candidate to bear my children, you know.'

She bit her lip, pulled up short. Of course it was true what he said. She would have been a little alarmed if she thought he was thinking about such things. It would have been inappropriate, peculiar. But still, for him to state it quite so bluntly, as if the possibility, however far-fetched and premature, was quite beyond the bounds of credibility, irked her dreadfully. It felt like an insult.

'I know that. I wasn't implying . . .'

'Don't be so defensive.' He reached for her again. 'Where were we?'

She moved away. 'What's wrong with my childbearing potential anyway? While we're on the subject.'

He looked bored. 'Nothing of course. That I know of. That's not the point.'

'Well, tell me, what *is* the point?' Vanessa said, irritated by his tone.

'This is stupid.'

She raised her chin. 'What *is* the point?'

'My children will be the heirs to the throne,' he said slowly, as though explaining something to a simpleton. 'The woman I marry must be a member of the nobility. She must come from one of the old families.'

Vanessa laughed. 'The throne? Nobility? Come *on*, Alex!'

He said nothing, his face fixed, suddenly savage.

'I can understand why you want to restore the palace and everything, but continuing the dynasty? That's taking it a bit far, isn't it? I mean, there's no kingdom any more.'

'You're ignorant,' Khusam said. 'It's not your fault . . .'

'But I'm right, aren't I? There isn't a kingdom.' Vanessa was beginning to think her mother had been right about Khusam's mouth. It had an ugly look to it. 'I mean, India took over *ages* ago.'

The Prince's face had flushed a deep red. 'You are a . . . tourist here. A guest in my house. What do you know about anything?'

'I didn't mean to upset you.'

'I'm not *upset*,' he said, lingering over the word, as though he considered her incapable of provoking such an emotion.

'Angry then. I'm sorry, if I've made you angry.'

He said nothing.

'Perhaps I should leave.' She stood up. 'I think it would be best if I went.'

But Khusam made no move to assist her. He remained seated on the floor, his face no longer angry, but fixed, almost blank. 'It's a long drive back,' Vanessa said, awkwardly.

'Yes, a long way. And now I suppose you think I'm going to take you.'

'I'm sorry,' Vanessa said again. 'I don't have any other way . . .'

'I am not your hired driver.'

'No, of course not. I didn't mean that.'

'I'm tired,' he said. 'I don't feel like driving any more tonight.'

'Then your servant perhaps . . .'

He looked at her and she saw that she had been wrong to think him no longer angry. Her words had simply intensified his contempt.

'I may need him,' Khusam said flatly. 'And anyway, we haven't done what you came here for.'

'What do you mean?'

'You know very well what I mean.'

She wished she could move, but sitting down again seemed

like an acknowledgement of defeat. She could go to the door but what then? What if Khusam simply watched her with the same immobile, furious expression on his face and made no further move? I do not know this man, she thought, and felt fear run through her.

'I didn't come for . . . that,' she said. 'I came to –'

'See my etchings?' He laughed.

She had come for the adventure, she thought, but what kind of adventure did she have in mind? Of course he was right. The lateness of the hour. The fact that her mother had been excluded from the invitation. The way that servant of his had stared at her on the doorstep. She had turned her eyes away from that look which now seemed to her to have had nothing welcoming or courteous about it.

Khusam was watching her with something like amusement on his face. 'Come,' he said, patting the seat next to him, 'sit down. Have some more wine.'

For a moment, Vanessa considered doing what he said. Of simply resuming where they had left off, disregarding their argument and the cruelty in Khusam's face which she had always seen but had chosen to ignore until this moment. She could pretend that she believed it was another of his games. Like standing on the outside of his jeep. A dare, nothing more. She might even come to believe it herself. She might, in time, believe it enough to make it into an anecdote to be recounted at a dinner party back home. The night she had spent with a Prince. Evidence of her own daring. It would be easy. Easy to let him continue, to tell herself no, there had been no coercion. Safer too. He would drive her back the next day. They would not need to talk much.

How easily she had stepped from what was known and certain into this place without landmarks. She did not know where she was – not even what the outside of the palace looked like. It was night and she was in a strange country and even if she went to the door and opened it and simply left, jeep or no jeep, would he allow her to go? She did not know him, she did not know what he would do. She looked down at her bare feet, realizing that she had forgotten where she had put her shoes, and felt the first prickle of tears behind her eyes.

He was still watching her. Sipping his wine now, quite relaxed. He is enjoying this, she thought. Wondering perhaps how long I can go on standing here. And she was caught by something quite unknown to her. A sense of humiliation that seemed to belong not merely to her present helplessness, to these alien walls and Alex Khusam's mocking face, but embraced everything that had brought her to this place. Her mother's silence, her father's death, the whole misguided enterprise. She had thought, in her self-importance, to find meaning here and now, now she could not even find her own shoes.

'Stop sulking, Vanessa,' Khusam said. 'It doesn't suit you.'

She looked at him silently for a second or two. It was not the first time she had come across a bully. They were common enough after all.

'If you won't take me in the jeep,' she said evenly, 'then I'm going to walk.'

Marion delayed speaking to Dorothy Nichols until dinner was over and everyone had returned to their rooms for the evening. She told herself she was waiting for the right moment, but she was nervous about the encounter. Dorothy had hardly been friendly to her and what Marion needed to talk about was an awkward matter, something over which Dorothy might well take offence. Marion had the feeling that all sorts of things caused Dorothy offence. But there was no way around it. When she had finally got through on the phone, Tracy Fuller had sounded concerned. Marion had been hoping her friend would dismiss the whole thing, but Tracy seemed worried.

'I think you should at least *ask*,' she had said. 'Although it's probably a coincidence. At that age . . . well, old people are unpredictable.' Tracy had been a nurse before she got married and spoke with some authority. 'But you should check on it. It does seem a bit strange.'

'How are you, by the way?'

'You mean, apart from having been woken up in the middle of the night?'

'Oh God, I'm sorry,' Marion said. 'I couldn't work out the time difference.'

'I'm fine. I'm doing well. Are you having a good time?'

'Did you get my postcard?' There was a beeping noise on the line and then silence.

'It has a panda on it,' Marion said. She listened to the silence for a second or two then replaced the receiver. 'I think we were cut off,' she told the hotel receptionist.

'Yes,' the woman said. 'Would you like to try again?'

'No,' Marion said slowly, 'there's no need.'

It was almost eleven before she summoned up the resolve to approach Dorothy's room. She hesitated before knocking. From inside, she could hear a faint, grinding noise. Like stone rubbing up against some kind of metal with a grating, wincing persistence. At her knock, the noise broke off abruptly and there was a moment of complete silence.

She knocked again.

The door handle turned from the inside. 'Dorothy,' she called, 'it's Marion.'

Dorothy was wearing a violet dressing gown with a high collar bunched around her neck. The gown ended at her knees and her feet were bare. She stared at Marion without the slightest movement of her face, a rigid immobility that became more disconcerting as the seconds passed.

'I'm so sorry to disturb you,' Marion said. 'May I come in?'

'I've been expecting you,' Dorothy said expressionlessly.

'I know it's late and everything. I should have come before. But it's important. I do need to talk to you.'

'Yes. I suppose you think you do.' With an abrupt, ungracious movement, she turned aside and let Marion enter.

On her previous visit to the room, Marion had been struck by how orderly everything had been and she was now surprised by the disarray that met her eyes. The bed was scattered with clothing, jars and bottles littered the table by the window, some with their lids off, others lying on their sides. The trays of grass were still on the window ledge, but now they sprouted wild and unkempt, the tips turning brown. On the table, a pestle and mortar full of a dark brown grit had spilled part of its contents over the floor. Dorothy must have been grinding at it when she knocked, Marion thought.

'Are you going to get to the point,' Dorothy said, 'or do

you have another little book to show me?' She gave a small, scornful smile.

'No, nothing like that.' Marion was a little shocked by the other's rudeness. Dorothy had never been particularly amiable, but up till now she had always been civil enough. Marion decided to dispense with preliminary chit-chat.

'It's about something else . . .' She paused. 'Look, this whole thing is a bit awkward so I'm just going to come out and say it. The last time I was here, I saw a drug bottle. The label said Propranolol. I saw it quite clearly.'

Dorothy seemed surprised. Her hand flickered towards her mouth and away again.

'Did you?'

'Yes, I did. I recognized the name because that's one of the drugs my friend Tracy Fuller had to take after she had her stroke. She said she needed it to help prevent another one.'

'How very sad for her.' The sarcasm in her voice was impossible to ignore. Marion took a deep breath and ploughed on.

'If you take too much of it, Propranolol can cause a person to lose consciousness,' she said. 'It makes you faint. I remember Tracy explaining that to me. Because she's so forgetful, you see. She had this little box with the dose and the day marked on it. So she didn't take it twice.'

'Is this little lecture getting to any kind of point?'

'I know it's late and I'm probably fussing over nothing but I wanted to make sure,' Marion continued nervously, aware that she was beginning to babble. 'As I say, I'm probably completely wrong about it, but Tracy said I should ask. She was a nurse, you know.'

'She was a nurse and she had a stroke. Is there anything else I need to know about this Tracy?'

'I don't mean to upset you. Please don't think . . . I just wanted to ask, that's all.'

'Ask me what?'

Marion stared at her pleadingly. She had known this encounter would be tricky, but she had never imagined such open hostility. She wished she hadn't come. It was clearly a mistake. But it was too late to turn back now.

'I wanted to ask whether there's a chance that someone – one of the servants perhaps – could have got hold of the stuff and be giving it to Mrs Macdonald. I thought maybe you could check and see if you noticed any missing.'

Now that she had said it out loud the suggestion suddenly seemed quite preposterous. What had possessed her to come barging in to Dorothy's room with her far-fetched suspicions? But Tracy had said she should ask. Tracy had agreed with her. Marion took strength from the thought.

'I just thought I should ask,' she said again. 'Just in case.'

Dorothy threw back her head and laughed. A loud, ragged sound.

'Poor Mrs Macdonald! Poor, poor Mrs Macdonald. On top of all her other troubles, now she is being poisoned. And she is such a very nice old lady.'

Marion was speechless.

'But who could it be who is doing it? Colonel Mustard in the drawing room? Miss Scarlet with the rope?'

Marion flushed. 'I suppose it does seem a bit silly . . .'

'Has it ever occurred to you that bottles can hold different things from what their labels say?' Dorothy asked. She darted to the bedside table and rummaged among the items scattered there. 'I collect containers of many different kinds. To keep my ingredients in.' She held up the offending bottle and shook it. 'This one, the one that you saw, originally came from my mother's medicine cabinet. And yes, it once contained Propranolol. Can you see what it contains now?'

Marion shook her head. 'I've been rather stupid, haven't I?'

'Go on, take a look,' Dorothy insisted. She came up and shook the bottle in Marion's face. 'What can you see?'

'They look like . . . some kind of . . . twigs.'

'Cloves. Just cloves. From the market here in Ashagiri.'

'I've been stupid,' Marion said again, helplessly. 'I just wanted to be sure. I hope you understand.'

'But I do.'

Up until this moment, Marion had felt a variety of emotions. Dismay, embarrassment, concern. Now, for the first time, she felt the beginnings of fear. It was the way Dorothy spoke. The satisfaction in her voice. It was the way she was standing, a little too close.

'I understand very clearly,' Dorothy continued in a calmer voice. 'You have come here making accusations.'

'No,' Marion said in protest. 'No. You misunderstood . . .'

'You have made accusations. It is a matter that should be made public.'

'What do you mean?'

'I think Mrs Macdonald should be told that one of her guests believes there is a poisoner at large. Here at Glenside, where everything seems so very warm and kind. A worm in the apple so to speak.'

'But I don't think that,' Marion said in great distress. 'That's not why I came. I didn't really think someone was doing it to cause harm, but maybe trying to help. Not knowing what the drug was perhaps and thinking it would do some good. I just wanted . . . I was just thinking about Mrs Macdonald.'

'Yes, a worm. But who is that worm? It is you, Mrs West. With your suspicions and your accusations.'

'You're turning everything around. I don't understand why you're being like this.'

'I am looking after Mrs Macdonald. I am the one who has her best interests at heart.'

'I shouldn't have come.'

'No. You shouldn't have. And now it is time for you to leave. From Glenside. You will not be welcome here once the facts are made known. There will be no more cosy little chats in the private room. Neither for you nor your daughter.'

Marion, who had been reaching for the door, turned back abruptly. It was the mention of Vanessa that did it. Something rose in her. A fierceness.

'My daughter has nothing to do with this,' she said. 'You leave my daughter alone.'

The other woman, still sure of the upper hand, smiled slowly. 'Ah, that worm again. It has turned at last.'

'A few minutes ago, when I knocked on your door, you said something,' Marion said slowly. 'You said you'd been expecting me. I think I know why. I've known for some time. I wasn't going to say anything about it. I didn't think it was my business. We all have our . . . secrets.'

Now that the matter was finally out in the open, Dorothy felt a strange sort of relief. It was tinged with triumph. The woman could do nothing to her. It was weakness that had kept her silent.

'I wondered just when we were going to get to that,' she said easily.

'I thought you had your reasons,' Marion continued. 'I still don't intend to tell anybody. I don't want trouble.'

'What is there to tell? What proof do you have? It was a long time ago, Mrs West. She died a long time ago.'

'Yes. It was a long time ago . . .' Marion said with sudden uncertainty.

'You know, I could have done it without touching her at all,' Dorothy said almost conversationally. 'She always did everything I told her to. At the end, when she was standing there, I could have simply told her to jump. I could have told her she would fly off that cliff and she would have believed me. I thought of it. But it would have taken persuasion and I was getting cold. So you see, you have nothing to tell. Whether I touched her or not it would have been the same.'

An expression of nostalgia had crept over Dorothy's face. As though she was recalling some memory, long familiar, which never failed to bring pleasure.

'What you remember, Mrs West, means nothing now.'

'What I remember? But it wasn't that. How could I remember that?' Never before had Marion experienced the kind of aversion that now possessed her. Her hands felt cold as if even her blood was in retreat.

'All I remembered was the name. I dreamed of her, you see, the girl in the . . . in the accident. But I couldn't remember her name. I wasn't really friends with her, you see. And then I met someone. A man giving food to the beggars for his sick brother. He wanted his brother to have the benefit of that act of charity, I suppose. So he was doing it in his brother's name. That's when I realized that you couldn't be Dorothy Nichols. That was the name of the girl who wrote in my autograph book. The one who died.' She stopped. 'The one you . . . *killed*.'

'You're somebody else,' she added. 'Somebody different.'

The other looked away, either in fear or simply indifference. 'Who are you?'

'Prudence,' she said suddenly. 'Prudence Jebb.'

An ugly name. The name a person might give to a daughter because nothing any prettier seemed quite appropriate. Prudence. Often shortened to a single syllable. Prue, Prue, *Prew*. Like the sound of somebody spitting.

'I don't remember you,' Marion said. 'I knew everyone there but I don't remember you.'

'No,' Prudence Jebb said savagely. 'No, you wouldn't. Of course not.'

'Even dead she was more real to you, wasn't she?' Marion said wonderingly. 'She had more . . . existence. I didn't say anything. I didn't think it mattered.'

'What *does* it matter? What business is it of yours or anybody's?'

The woman turned away from her. Marion looked down at her bare feet covered with spilled grit from the floor of the room. How eager Vanessa had been to find some key, she thought. Some meaningful connection between the past and present here in Ashagiri. Poor Vanessa, so full of hope, so desperate to please her. As though she could, by force of will, make a circle of her mother's life, where no circle existed. And here it was after all, the connection. In this terrible, unkempt woman and her confessions.

'What does it matter?' Prudence Jebb said again. 'This business of names is an irrelevance, Mrs West. As for the . . . other, there is nothing you can do about it now. It is simply my word against yours.'

Marion closed her eyes, seeing again the words of the name, scrolled so carefully in her autograph book.

Dorothy Nichols.

The little bluebirds flying aloft. The homilies of her half-forgotten classmates. *Think of me in all your wishes, Think of me when washing dishes, If the water be too hot, Cool it but forget me not* . . . Dorothy was dead. Her parents dead too. Her school, the clothes she had worn, the toys she had loved, all gone. Maybe the only thing left of Dorothy Nichols – the only evidence that she had ever existed as a real individual rather than just a name in a record – was her drawing in Marion's autograph book.

A feeling rose in Marion. Deeper than tenderness, older than love. The urge to protect. It was Dorothy she had come all this way to find. All the time thinking she was coming for herself, to get away. But she had never needed an escape. It had taken the mountains to see that. An old lady's kindness and the sweet smell of drying tea.

It was Dorothy Nichols she had come to save. Fifty years after the event but not too late.

'It matters,' she said very steadily. 'It matters because Dorothy was a real person. She wrote her name in my autograph book. It must have taken her hours.'

Prudence Jebb stared at her. She looked smaller to Marion, somehow diminished. But she felt no pity.

'She was such a little girl,' Marion continued. 'Somebody's *daughter*. Not yours to take. Not then or now.'

She paused. 'It's you, isn't it?' she said. 'You've been giving Mrs Macdonald Propranolol to make her faint. To make her worse. All this time caring for her and all this time making her worse.' She nodded. 'Yes, I can see by your face it's true. I won't ask why. I'm not sure I want to know the reason. I wonder if you even know it. People who do these things never have the reasons, do they? We want them to have the answers but they never do.'

'Do you know how many hours I have spent with that old woman?' Prudence burst out shrilly. 'Do you have any idea of the time, the *energy* I have devoted? I have made myself ill over it. I have made myself *ill*.'

'I think you have been ill for a long time.'

'I have cared for Mrs Macdonald as I cared for my own mother –' She broke off abruptly, her face white.

'Your mother?' Marion repeated in an appalled voice. And now curiosity finally rose in her. It was a strange fascination,

horrified beyond measure. 'Your mother? What kind of . . .
thing are you?

'How dare you? How . . . dare you?' Prudence said numbly.

Marion turned for the door. 'I'm going now,' she said
tiredly.

'You can't go. Where are you going?'

'It's over. This whole thing.'

Prudence Jebb watched her leave. She should stop her, she
told herself. She should stop her. Why couldn't she move?

Her throat ached. She had a balm to ease that, she thought
automatically. But where was it? Everything was out of place.
She stood motionless, her hands empty. Even if she knew
where it was, could she reach it? Could she unscrew the small
lid of the jar or would her hands, spirit like, pass straight
through as insubstantial as breath? It was too great a chance
to take. She must remain very still. Only her stillness stood
between her and nothingness.

Outside she heard the sudden cawing of rooks. She listened
intently, thinking of the bird's dark, circling flight and the wet
woods of her childhood.

●

Vanessa and Khusam stared at each other for a moment in silence.

'You can't walk,' Khusam said at last, almost lightly, 'the bears will get you.'

'I thought you said there weren't any left,' Vanessa said, relieved at the bantering turn in the conversation. But her reply seemed to infuriate him again. He rose abruptly to his feet and grasped her shoulders as though he would shake her.

'Stop messing around,' he said savagely.

Up until this moment, Vanessa had not properly understood what might happen to her. She had known it in her head, but she had not yet felt the certainty of it. Now, at his touch, she saw that there was perhaps nothing she could say or do that would change the course of things. That his anger was a part of him, something he clung to along with that title of his which would have meant something if he'd been born fifty years ago but was just a nickname now, a kind of joke. A moment before, it had seemed as though he was enjoying himself and now she saw she had not been mistaken. It gave him satisfaction – almost pleasure – to have a focus for his anger. But it was too late for insight. The time for that had long gone.

There was a place she must reach. The road going back. Sometime in the next few hours. She fixed her mind on it. Imagining the way the morning would look with everything that happened here already over and done. The wheels of the jeep taking her back, every second widening the distance between then and now. Nothing else mattered. She must put everything else aside. Somehow vaulting over the terror and shame of what might lie ahead so that she was already in that moment of safety. On the road, going back. Still herself, under another sky.

Khusam grabbed at her around her waist suddenly, pulling and pushing her at the same time so that she was obliged to do a little dancing shuffle in order to keep on her feet.

'Don't. Don't *do* this.'

He wedged a thigh between her legs and lifted her, propelling her forward. In a minute she would fall. She clutched instinctively at his shoulders for support, momentarily confused between the desire to resist him and the need to keep her balance.

'Please, Alex. Please.'

His hand was on the back of her neck, twisting her head towards him like someone trying to angle a mirror. He smelled different from before. Sweaty. The aroma spiked with the faint, unpleasant tang of his excitement.

I am on that road, she thought. I am already there. This is a thing of the past.

In a minute I will fall, she thought. He will be on top of me. And I do not know if I will be able to breathe. There is something wrong with him. Yes, with his mouth. Mother saw it. Oh, Mummy.

Her eyes filled with tears. Please let me just be able to breathe. Make him let me breathe.

There was a sound at the door. Khusam, still gripping her, paused and turned his head. The sound came again. Raised voices, then a clattering, as though someone unfamiliar with the workings of the door was attempting to enter.

Khusam uttered something. A command. Very loud and angry. Vanessa could hear his servant on the other side of the door saying something with great agitation. The door banged open.

'Hello there!' John Walcott said loudly. His eyes took in the scene. Khusam, flushed and astonished. Vanessa's arms braced against him, her face wet. 'I've come for Vanessa,' John said with great cheerfulness. 'Promised her a lift.'

Khusam stared at him, mute with surprise.

'Got all your stuff, Vanessa?' John said in the same, affable tone. 'We'd better be off. I borrowed Mrs Macdonald's jeep, you know, and I ought to get it back before morning.'

'What are you doing here?' Khusam said furiously. 'How dare you –'

'I expect they'll get rather worried if we're not back by morning,' John interrupted. 'It's not an easy road to drive at night, is it? We don't want them sending out search parties, do we?'

Khusam's eyes flickered to his servant who had entered the room behind John and now stood in the doorway as though to block it. He paused for a second. Then let his arms fall to his side.

'So, the painter arrives,' he said evenly. 'The painter of small things.'

John smiled. 'Did you have a bag, Vanessa?'

She looked confused for a second, then remembered her small backpack lying by a pile of cushions. She picked it up woodenly.

'The painter of small things,' repeated Khusam, ignoring her. 'I wondered the other night, when we were talking. I wondered whether he painted small because his vision was also . . . very small.'

'You've got me there,' John said amiably.

'Yes,' Khusam persisted. 'A vision no bigger than his pictures. The size of a postage stamp.'

'You're probably right. That's always been a problem of mine. Can't help it, I'm afraid. Always looking at the details.'

Khusam curled his lip with scorn.

'Well, we'd better be going,' John said, gesturing to Vanessa. She joined him silently, without looking again at Khusam. At the door she stopped suddenly.

'I can't –' she whispered to John. 'What about my shoes?'

'I don't think you should worry about them right now,' John whispered back, glancing at Khusam's grim-faced servant. 'Bare feet are okay. We don't have far to walk.'

His pace was steady as they descended the stairs and crossed the lobby to the doors of the palace. Nothing in his posture suggested flight. Once inside his jeep, however, he started up the engine and was backing out of the courtyard before Vanessa had time to fasten her seatbelt.

'Watch for the gate posts!' she cried.

'Bloody things. They look like gallows.'

'Yes. That's what they are. Bloody. Literally bloody.'

John looked at her sharply.

'It's a long story,' she said dully.

Back on the road, neither said anything for several minutes. John drove slowly, face bent towards the windscreen, his hands tight on the wheel at every bend.

'How did you know where I was?' she said at last.

'Your mother and Bharani. At dinner. The Prince has something of a reputation apparently. They were worried about you. Mrs Macdonald too.'

She started to cry then. The tears coming so fast there was no point in wiping them.

'I feel so stupid. So stupid and useless.'

'Did I ever tell you,' John said conversationally, 'that I'm an only child too? My parents had me when they were quite old. But they were the sort of people who must have seemed middle-aged even in their twenties. It was just the way they were. They seemed to me to have always been old.'

He spoke without looking at her and there was something immensely companionable in this. As though he didn't want to draw attention to her crying, but at the same time wanted her to know that there was nothing whatever the matter with it.

'We went on holiday every year,' he continued. 'Always in England. We never left the country. We went to places like Cumberland and Devon. Places with names of food attached. Cumberland pie. Kendall Mint Cake. I suppose it was comforting to them, something they were familiar with. My parents weren't big on risk taking. We stayed in Bed and Breakfasts. I remember there being a lot of talk about the quality of the various different breakfasts. How difficult it was becoming to find a really good, old-fashioned English breakfast as opposed to the Continental sort. My mother was particularly outraged by the Continental sort. She said if she wanted a Danish pastry she would have jolly well gone to Denmark, thank you very much.'

Vanessa looked out into the darkness as he talked. There was nothing to see but the wash of her own tears.

'I don't think I was bored exactly,' John said, 'but I was alone. I seemed to spend a lot of time looking out of windows. I remember once, in Cornwall, we stayed in a b&b right on the sea. You could see the waves from the window of the front room. There was a small garden and a road between the b&b and the sea, but the land sloped a bit, so that when you looked out, you couldn't really see the road at all. Just the tops of the hedges on either side of it and the water beyond. I was standing there, looking out, and I heard this drumming noise. I must have been six or seven. I didn't know what it was to begin with. It was very loud and getting louder all the time.

Not like the beating of a drum. Too chaotic for that. Like thunder broken up into little pieces.'

'What was it?'

'Horses. Three horses came around the corner suddenly. Galloping down the road. Two brown and one black. I could see them very clearly because the hedge was low. And because they were so big. At least, they seemed that way to me. It was a very windy day and they were running right into the wind. With their manes blowing back and broken ropes trailing from around their necks. I had never seen anything so beautiful.'

'Where had they come from?'

He shook his head. 'I don't know. They must have escaped from somewhere. I wanted them to go on running for ever. My father said, "Someone's going to catch it," and then he shut the window.'

'I should have known,' Vanessa said, 'not to go off with Alex. I should have known.'

'No,' John said. 'No. You were just trying to make a break for it. Like the horses.'

She started to cry again. Softer this time.

'I didn't mean to upset you.'

'No, it's okay. Honestly.'

'Look, it's getting light already,' he said. 'Before we go back, I think there's something you should see. A place you should go.'

'All right,' she said limply. It seemed she had lost the ability to make any kind of decision for herself.

They drove for a while and then John turned off down a sandy pathway that led for a few hundred yards downhill, before widening into a clearing, surrounded by trees. He cut the engine and sat still. 'The path goes on over there,' he said, pointing.

'Aren't you coming?'

He shook his head. 'I think you should go by yourself.'

'But where?'

'It's called Wishing Lake. At least, that's the translation. There's a legend about it. They say the water can't hold anything impure. The proof of this, they say, is the fact that there's never anything floating on the surface. No leaves or debris of any kind.'

'Is that really true?'

'Why don't you see for yourself?'

She smiled for the first time since leaving the palace. 'This is like before, isn't it, John? When you wouldn't let me look at the mountains until I was really close. You like surprises, don't you?'

'I don't have anything else to give,' he said simply.

She looked at the distant opening between the trees. 'I can't go. I haven't any shoes to wear.'

'You can borrow my flip-flops.' He leaned behind him and rummaged in the back seat of the jeep. 'They're in my bag somewhere.'

'They're almost new,' he said, rather anxiously. 'Honestly, I haven't worn them much. I bought them when I first got here because they seemed, well, the thing to wear in India. Never got into the habit of it though.'

'But they're way too big. I won't be able to walk in them.'

'It doesn't matter much with flip-flops, does it?' He turned them over thoughtfully in his hands. 'Amazing things. Half the world wears them. I've always wondered who invented them.'

Vanessa took them from him. 'I suppose I should give it a go.' She opened the door of the jeep. It was cool outside. The sky silvery with dawn. Without looking behind her, she began to walk towards the path. She could smell water. A green smell that intensified once she was amongst the trees. The path was stony and, despite John's assurances, she slipped a couple of times as she went, the flip-flops slapping clumsily against her heels. It was darker here. Even at midday, the sun must barely penetrate the leaves. Her feet squelched into a muddy puddle clogged with twigs. She hesitated and looked back the way she had come, then pushed onwards, head down, concentrating on the placement of her feet.

A hundred yards or so further, the path turned a gentle corner and she saw she was walking now on wooden boards. She looked up. She stood at the top of a small jetty leading into the water. Vanessa stopped. A single breath came up through her body in a great sigh.

The lake was set in a natural bowl, several hundred feet in diameter, surrounded by dense forest. Around the water, a band of sedge, blonde in colour and very thick. Circling the shore on three sides, hundreds of wooden posts set at ten-feet intervals bearing white prayer flags that flapped in the slight breeze. The water was very still. Across its shining expanse floated not a single twig or leaf. There was no sound except the slight flap of the flags, the small shiver of the sedge and a single bird, too far off to be sighted, somewhere in the trees, that cawed steadily with haunted, solitary insistence.

She walked a little unsteadily to the end of the jetty and looked down. The water was neither blue nor grey nor brown. It was simply transparent. Unsullied, untouched. She could see right through it to the sandy bottom of the lake. Vanessa sat down with her feet dangling over the edge, almost touching the surface of the water, but not quite.

She wanted very much to wade in it; simply slip in, still wearing her jeans, and feel it against her. She wanted this as much as she had ever wanted anything in her whole life. Wasn't this the sort of thing one was meant to do in India, she thought, a touch self-mockingly. Weren't people always throwing themselves into places like the Ganges? Tourists trying to find enlightenment in water so filthy they'd barely flush their loos with it back home. It was the sort of thing Greg and his kind got off on. And what would getting wet achieve anyway?

She thought of the summer she had turned thirteen. She was up to her neck in the ocean, treading water, looking back towards the beach. The family were on holiday. Her mother and father distant specks on the sand. She loved the water. On the way to the beach she had longed for this moment as she always did. The first sight of the ocean piercing her with a joy she could never quite articulate. And then the scramble into her swimming costume. Fumbling under the towels on the beach with new-found modesty because of the tiny breasts that had sprouted, seemingly overnight, and which filled her with such embarrassment. She hated the half-wayness of them. If only they would disappear or else hurry up and grow.

And now here she was, up to her neck. Waiting for the usual pleasure to engulf her. But the pleasure never came. It was lovely in the water, of course. Cool, exhilarating, filling her with a sense of freedom, but something was missing. The old abandon was gone. Like her child's body. Quite gone for ever. In that moment she saw that she was not inside the sea at all. The water never let you in, it did not join with you. It simply parted for your shape as it was obliged to do, keeping its own secrets after all. She was overcome by a kind of desolation. Her pale legs beating below her, her heart full of inexplicable sorrow. In a little while, when she grew tired, she would return to the shore, and the water would close up again behind her as though she had never swum there at all. And it would always be like this, no matter in what seas she bathed.

No, it would be quite pointless to get wet. Besides, she would make a mess of Mrs Macdonald's jeep. Compounding the humiliation of her encounter with Alex Khusam with a miserably soggy passenger seat.

But the lake, it was so very lovely. And there was nobody to see her.

She leaned down and took off John's flip-flops, placing them carefully side by side next to her on the jetty, then rested her hands on the wood and levered herself smoothly forward into the water. It was cool and very silky and almost waist deep. She stood there for a second, getting used to the sensation, then took a few steps out. Her feet made small yellow clouds as she walked. In a few seconds she was up to her chest. She stopped and spread her arms out over the top of the water and looked up at the sky.

Wishing Lake. She supposed she should make a wish. What did she want? What was it exactly that she wanted? How to turn the mashed, unspoken longings into neat request? There were rules to wishes. Her mother had a few. A wish could go on for ever, her mother had told her once, as long as you leave out the full stops. If you just used commas, you could go on wishing until you ran out of breath. In fairy stories you were usually allowed three wishes. It had always seemed to her an open invitation to cheat. Even if you wasted the first two, you could always wish for three – or five – or ten more with your third. The fact that nobody in the stories ever seemed to grasp this simple fact had always seemed quite inexplicable to her.

But now, standing there, up to her armpits in the water, Vanessa was overcome by a feeling of tiredness. The problem with wishing, she thought, was that it took up so much energy.

What she wished for suddenly was not to wish any longer.

Instead, for once, for just once in her life, to be wished for.

To be wished for was the same as being blessed. It was blessing that she wanted. Given not because of anything she had said or done, but as a gift. Wasn't that what everyone secretly hoped for? To lay down the burden of wanting, the endless struggle of wanting? She closed her eyes.

She felt a sensation around her ankles, the smallest and softest of touches. If she hadn't been standing so still she might have missed it. She looked down. In the water around her ankles there were goldfish swimming. A long time ago, perhaps years and years, someone had once slipped a few into the lake and they had thrived. Unnecessary, beautiful. Once, a long time ago, someone had dreamed of gold in that water and now there was gold there. She would never know the reason.

Vanessa watched them for a long time. If blessing comes from a place beyond our will, she thought, then it cannot be prayed for. It cannot come at our request. Instead, what we must pray for is something else. That there will be moments in our lives – few and short perhaps – when we see that we are blessed. When we understand that recognition is all we need.

In water that could hold nothing impure, goldfish kissed, she rested her brow against the cool palm of the sky and felt herself grow still.

•

John was asleep when she returned. His head tilted far back, his big hands still resting on the wheel. He woke when she opened the door and looked at her without comment. As though the sight of her dripping appearance did not surprise him in the least.

'I think jeans must be the worst thing to go swimming in,' she said, hoisting herself up on to the seat beside him. 'I'm going to make a terrible mess, I'm afraid.'

'I don't think so. Not too much. The seats are all plastic anyway.' He smiled. 'Ready to go?'

'Not quite. I think I just need a moment or two.'

They sat for a while in the silence, watching the light change. Vanessa thought of the lake, hidden now behind the trees and wondered if she would ever find it again. If she would know the road to take, recognize the turning that led to that single path. It must be marked on a map, a place like that. She might find a local map in Ashagiri if she hunted.

She was cold now. The water drying on her. Her chilled hands resting on her lap were paler than ever, almost silvery. Almost the colour of her mother's party shoes before she got them muddied walking up to Glenside that first night. There is no map, she thought suddenly, no key. No pattern to the stars, no sign.

The world is beautiful, she thought, because it does not explain itself.

'We'll be just in time for breakfast,' John said, starting up the engine.

She pictured them all, sitting around the table in the dining room. Her mother, Bharani, Mrs Macdonald, Greg and skinny little Tish. 'I hope . . .' she began, 'I hope I won't have to –'

'Tell everyone what happened?'

'Yes. I don't want to have to go through it all. It's hardly something to be proud of, is it?'

'I shouldn't worry. I don't think you'll have to tell anybody anything unless you want to. Khusam's hardly going to be saying anything. I doubt he'll be hanging around Glenside for a while.'

He looked angry for a second. His face fixed, stubborn. She had not seen this in him before and felt obscurely grateful for it.

'The trouble with Alex,' she said slowly, 'is that everything has to go according to his plan.'

John's mouth tightened.

'Don't you see? Everything has to be just so with him,' Vanessa said, almost sadly. 'That palace of his. He's locked into it. Into his idea of the way the world should be.'

'I don't know about any of that,' John said shortly. 'It seems pretty clear to me what sort of a person he is.'

'My mother has this story about a seahorse,' Vanessa said. 'I keep thinking about it. She was a little girl who'd never seen the sea and she thought seahorses were like horses on land. Like your horses perhaps. She thought there was one inside a chest of drawers in her school. My mother's not a very logical person, you know. Even now. Rational thought is not a strong point. She wanted there to be a horse inside and the wanting made her believe it was true. And then one day she saw the seahorse and it was so tiny and nothing at all like a real horse. She was so disappointed.'

He laughed. 'Yes, I can see that.'

'But that isn't the real point of the story. The point is that she looked at the seahorse and she loved it anyway. Despite her disappointment.' She paused. 'Sometimes I think that sums my mother up. Her high hopes. And in the end, made happy by so very little. I think Alex . . . well, Alex is as unlike that as it's possible to be.'

'Something should be done about that man.'

'You mean, I should report what happened?'

'Perhaps . . . it's up to you, of course.'

'I have the feeling it wouldn't get me very far.'

'You do have a witness,' John reminded her. 'I would back you up.'

'I know you would, John. It's just that we're leaving in a couple of days. I'm not sure I want my last few hours in this country to be ruined. Things have been difficult enough for my mother as it is. God, it sounds as though I'm making excuses, doesn't it? I never thought I'd be the sort of person to just *take* something like this without kicking up a fuss. Perhaps if it had . . . gone further it would be different.'

'I don't think you're making excuses at all.'

'The truth is that I really should have known better. Respectable women simply don't behave like that here.'

'I think your mother will be glad to see you,' John said. 'She was trying so hard not to be worried.'

'We parted on such bad terms,' she said sadly. 'We had an argument and I never said sorry.'

'You'll be able to when you get back.'

'Yes,' she said, although she knew that what had been said between them would never be brought up again. But now this seemed more comforting than anything else. Being without justice, forgiveness knew no limits.

'I haven't thanked you yet. For rescuing me.'

He looked embarrassed. 'Well . . . it wasn't very much. Although there was a moment by the door there when I thought it could go either way.'

'With the servant? What would you have done . . . would you have fought him?'

'I'd have had to, wouldn't I? I've never been in a fight before. I'd probably have been completely crap.'

'Yes, I think you probably would.'

'Anyway, I didn't have to.'

'I've never been rescued before so I don't have anything to compare it to, but I think it was pretty brilliant. Even if you didn't have to fight anybody.'

'Let's just say I think I'll stick to painting. Painting is far easier.'

She looked at him very steadily for a second or two. An unusual man, she thought. Not like anybody else, with his stammer and his odd enthusiasms. Doomed perhaps, to always walk a little out of step with the rest of the world. She had asked herself what it was about her that attracted such men and now the answer came to her. It was because she was attracted to them. She always had been. To the loners, the freakish. Michael the confused, Martin Sorenson the lonely, Theodore Christmas, all eyes and shiny shoes. Even Bharani who, now she thought of it, had made her laugh in a way Alex Khusam could never hope to have done.

And now John. A boy who had spent his childhood staring out of windows and was still staring, though the windows had all been opened.

'I've been thinking about your painting,' she said abruptly, as though making up her mind. 'About the problem of exhibiting your stuff. I think what you need is a website. I could set it up for you, if you like. When I get back home.'

'Could you?' He turned to her, his face alight, his eyes as clear as wishing water.

'Easy,' Vanessa said.

PART FOUR

Dreaming Rock

It was breakfast time when they entered the dining room at Glenside, but Marion, Tish, Greg and Bharani, who were sitting around a single table, didn't seem to be eating anything. Instead, they were talking together in low, worried voices like people facing some collective, impending crisis. Even Bharani, who could normally be relied upon to make short work of half a dozen pancakes, appeared to have lost his appetite. He was slumped forward, elbows on the table, a picture of dejection.

'There you are,' Marion cried when she saw John and Vanessa come in. 'I'm so glad you're back.'

'Were you all waiting for me?' Vanessa asked, bewildered. 'There wasn't any need. I'm fine.'

They looked at her in surprise.

'Where is Mrs Macdonald?'

Bharani sighed and shook his head dramatically.

'Of course we were worried about you,' Marion told Vanessa. 'Of course I was –'

'It is Mrs Macdonald we are waiting for,' Bharani informed her. 'The bearer will be bringing her in shortly.'

'Poor Mrs Macdonald,' Tish said plaintively. 'After everything she's done . . .'

'She will have been told, of course,' Bharani said. 'They will have told her as they told me.' The others nodded.

'Told her what? What are you talking about?' Vanessa was beginning to feel a little annoyed.

'It is Dorothy Nichols,' Bharani said importantly. 'She has

disappeared. It turns out that she was not what she seemed to be.'

'She was a con woman,' Tish broke in excitedly.

'It is true,' Bharani said hastily, keen to hold on to his role as storyteller. 'It is true. She was not Dorothy Nichols at all. It was an assumed name.' His voice lowered. 'She must have been planning everything from the start. It is possible she had an accomplice, that she was, one might say, working from the inside. A member of a ring.'

'But what has she *done*?'

'She has run away with Mrs Macdonald's thangkas,' Bharani announced. 'The precious thangkas from Alexandra David Neel. They are worth a fortune. A small fortune.'

'I knew she was a fake,' Greg said. 'I told you, didn't I, Tish?'

'You just said you didn't like her. You didn't say she was a fake exactly.' The drama of the situation seemed to have put new spirit into Tish. 'I always thought she was quite nice.'

'You always think everyone's nice. I wasn't taken in by all that caring stuff. It was obviously part of her plan.'

'Yes,' Bharani said. 'She only pretended to care. It was an act.'

'Sit down,' Marion said to Vanessa. 'You must be exhausted. John too. Have some tea. We're waiting for Mrs Macdonald to come down.'

'So we can commiserate,' Bharani chipped in. 'To show her she still has friends.'

'God,' Vanessa said. 'I thought Dorothy was strange but I didn't realize she was a thief.'

'Are you all right?' Her mother spoke in a low tone. 'You know, I really *was* rather worried about you, Vanessa.'

'I'm fine. Nothing happened. John brought me back. Does anyone know if the thangkas were insured?'

'It is their sentimental value that can never be replaced,' Bharani said. 'It is not the money for Mrs Macdonald –'

He was interrupted by the arrival of the old woman herself. 'Oh, Mrs Macdonald,' Bharani sang out anxiously. 'I am so very sorry. They will find her. She will be apprehended by the police. I have utter confidence in our police.'

Mrs Macdonald settled herself on her chaise with a quick smile of thanks to the bearer. She looked around her at the faces of her guests.

'Oh, Bharani,' she said sadly. 'Everyone . . .'

'The head bearer gave me the information this morning,' Bharani said. 'He wanted to know if I had seen Dorothy. The thangkas were gone, he said, and so was she, and putting two and two together . . . Then Mrs West tells us that Dorothy was not Dorothy at all. She was somebody else altogether. Somebody Jebb. It has all been rather confusing.'

Mrs Macdonald sighed. 'Poor Dorothy –'

'But it wasn't Dorothy. It was somebody else. It was a somebody Jebb,' Bharani persisted rather wildly. 'And she is not poor at all. Those precious items are worth a fortune, Mrs Macdonald.'

'Yes. I know.' Mrs Macdonald exchanged a long look with Marion. 'I know all about it. Marion has already told me everything. You really mustn't worry about me, you know.'

'Bummer about the thangkas though,' Greg said. 'There's a black market for that kind of stuff. It's not meant to leave the country, but it does all the time. It's amazing what a little bribery can do in this place.'

'I don't think Dorothy will have much trouble leaving the country with my thangkas,' Mrs Macdonald said. 'I imagine customs will merely assume she bought them in a high quality curio shop.'

'But they are priceless, Mrs Macdonald!' Bharani said. 'They are from the city of Lhasa . . .'

She shook her head. 'No. I sold those a long time ago. We hit a bad time, you see, with the hotel. It was during the fifties, before tourists really discovered India. Glenside was falling apart. We needed to make renovations . . .' She smiled with great happiness. 'I think Alexandra David Neel would have been so proud of me. She was never one to hold on to material things after all. She made me a gift when I was only thirteen and I turned it into this place. I'd have lost Glenside if it hadn't been for her. In a funny sort of way she gave me my life. That's why I was so fond of the thangkas. I had them copied exactly, you know.'

Vanessa laughed suddenly. 'I love it. The fake Dorothy and the fake thangkas. They belong together.'

'I shall miss them, of course,' Mrs Macdonald continued. 'But old age is a funny thing. One loves one's small treasures more than ever and yet when they are gone, it doesn't seem to matter much at all . . .'

'I'd love to see her face though,' Greg said, 'when she tries to flog the things.'

'She will be laughed at,' Bharani said with great satisfaction. 'Everyone will laugh at her.'

'Yes, I suppose they will. I do wonder though whether we were right to let her go.'

'What could we do?' Marion asked her. 'There was no real –'

'No,' Mrs Macdonald agreed. 'We couldn't stop her. But I do worry about where Dorothy will go to next.'

They had packed everything a good hour before the jeep was due to arrive for them. Marion in particular was anxious to leave plenty of time for the task. 'I don't know why this zipper won't do up,' she complained, struggling with her suitcase.

Vanessa made no offer to help. 'You have too much stuff. You brought too much in the first place and then you added to it with all your shopping. Avari will be sad to see you go.'

'Buddha is such an awkward shape,' Marion said. 'I didn't realize how much his knees would stick out . . .'

'Do you really need the tea?' Vanessa picked up the silver foil package.

Marion grabbed it away from her. 'Yes. It will go in my hand luggage. I have to have the tea.'

'You won't drink it. I know you won't.'

'I have to have the tea,' Marion said firmly. 'It was a present.'

She stood for a moment by the window, looking out. The morning was cloudy and the topmost peaks of the mountains invisible.

'I hoped we'd see the snows,' she said. 'On our last day.'

'They're there. We saw them, remember?'

'Yes.' She thought then of how much of life was like that. The hidden spaces, the silences, filled by remembered things. The world made complete by memory's eye.

'Well,' Vanessa said, 'we've said goodbye to everyone. What shall we do now?'

Marion looked at her watch. 'Come on. I think we've still got time.'

They took the path around the church again. Past the graveyard full of children and up the hill to St Margaret's. They walked easily this time, with thoughts of departure on their mind, expectation behind them.

'What did Mrs Macdonald want to see you about?' Vanessa asked. 'When we were saying goodbye. She took you into that room of hers.'

'She wanted to give me this.' Marion reached into her pocket and pulled out something wrapped in tissue paper. 'Her jade necklace. It's very old. Isn't it the loveliest thing you ever saw?'

Vanessa took the string. 'It's gorgeous. Really generous of her. I know you two are friends, but I wonder what made her give it.'

Marion took back the necklace and wrapped it up carefully before answering.

'I expect she wanted to thank me.'

'What on earth for?'

Marion paused and looked at her daughter. She put the necklace back into her pocket and carried on walking.

'I think she thought I had helped her,' she said at last.

'I got a present too. From John. One of his paintings. The one he was working on when we went up to see the sunrise. He didn't want to give it to me yet because it isn't quite finished, but I made him.'

'You're so bossy, Vanessa.'

'Somebody has to be.'

'You never told me about your trip the other night. Whether you had a good time or not. I was hoping Alex would be around so I could say goodbye. I didn't talk much to him, but I'd have liked to say goodbye.'

Vanessa thought briefly of telling her mother everything.

'It was okay,' she said. 'Nothing to tell really.'

They saw the roofs of the school and then the gates and old quadrangle.

'It was behind the main building. Higher up,' Marion said. 'I wonder if there's still a path.'

'But will you recognize it again? It was only a rock after all. There must be a lot of rocks around.'

'But it was the largest. Nobody would have moved it unless they wanted to build on that land. And anyway, I'd remember it. I can still see the shape of it. It was the place where I spent the happiest moments of my whole life, you know.'

Vanessa stopped. 'Oh, Mother. That's so sad. You shouldn't have had the happiest times so long ago.'

Marion smiled. 'But that's the best time of all to have them. That way you keep them for longer.'

St Margaret's was behind them now and the woods thick. 'I hope we won't have to hack our way through,' Vanessa said, peering into the foliage. 'It looks totally wild in there.'

'No we won't. There's a path. It's been paved. They must have done it recently.'

'I wonder if Dorothy ever went up to Dreaming Rock,' she said. 'The real Dorothy I mean. I expect she did. I wonder what she thought about.'

But Vanessa was plunging ahead.

'Come *on*, Mother,' she called. 'Why are you going so slowly?'

'It's *steep* and I'm over sixty.'

Vanessa looked back at her abruptly. Marion's face was red and she moved with effort. Her mother couldn't be tired, thought Vanessa. She couldn't be *old*. Not yet, not yet.

'Come *on*,' she said fiercely. 'We're nearly at the top.'

'You're so mean. How did I have such a mean daughter?'

The path levelled out finally on to a small paved space surrounded by trees. It was misty up there and very silent. Vanessa and Marion stood quite still.

'There it is!' cried Marion suddenly. 'Dreaming Rock.'

To the little girls at St Margaret's, the stone had always looked like the summit of something. A pinnacle. It was the reason they had made a shrine of it. A place of solitude, almost of worship. And others must have seen this too. Years later, choosing this place for their statue of Tenzing Norgay. One bronze foot on the top of the rock, climber's axe held aloft in triumph. Tenzing on Everest. On the very top of everything.

In photographs of the climber, caught in his moment of glory, he wears a balaclava, goggles and an oxygen mask. He has just made a small hole in the snow and buried pieces of chocolate and biscuits as grateful offerings to the gods. He has just shaken hands with Edmund Hillary and thrown his arms around him and thumped him on the back with triumph. But on Dreaming Rock, Tenzing stands alone, bare-faced. No need for oxygen, joy is all he breathes. A slight wind ruffles his hair. From where he stands he can see the whole world and he likes what he sees. It is his moment and he will never leave it.

Marion ran forward. 'I *told* you it would still be here.' She touched the statue's legs reverently, then bent and stroked the rock itself.

'I expect that's where Tenzing spent the happiest time of *his* life too,' Vanessa said. 'He looks like it, doesn't he?'

'Yes he does. I really think he does.'

•

Their jeep driver was employed by Glenside and drove with unusual care back down the road leading to the plains and the Calcutta train. He told them he was a Gurkha. A soldier. He had fought in the Falklands War for the British.

'Goose Green,' he said. 'Stanley.' He repeated the names of these places in a wondering voice as though unable to quite believe that he had seen them with his own eyes. It had been years and years ago and the islands were so far away.

Vanessa rolled down her window and caught the scent of marigolds growing on the hillsides.

'What was it like there?' she asked. 'What did it feel like?'

'Cold,' the driver said. 'With white in the water.' He might have been describing a place in a dream, whose landmarks, once so clear and unambiguous, were slipping now into confusion. In the dream he had understood this place he found himself in. He had known a hundred facts about it, could describe a hundred features. But now, waking, he remembered only two. It was cold there. There was white on the water.

They were nearly at their destination. The road had lost much of its steepness and wound through jungle now. It was very quiet beneath the trees and, despite their tangled branches, the unruliness of the undergrowth below, the two women had the sense of arrangement, of mysterious order. As if they passed, not through jungle, but across some great parkland, carefully tended, though invisibly.

'I hope we get a sleeper again,' Marion said. 'We will, won't we, Vanessa?'

refresh yourself at penguin.co.uk

Visit penguin.co.uk for exclusive information and interviews with
bestselling authors, fantastic give-aways and the
inside track on all our books, from the Penguin Classics
to the latest bestsellers.

BE FIRST

first chapters, first editions, first novels

EXCLUSIVES

author chats, video interviews, biographies, special
features

EVERYONE'S A WINNER

give-aways, competitions, quizzes, ecards

READERS GROUPS

exciting features to support existing groups and
create new ones

NEWS

author events, bestsellers, awards, what's new

EBOOKS

books that click – download an ePenguin today

BROWSE AND BUY

thousands of books to investigate – search, try
and buy the perfect gift online – or treat yourself!

ABOUT US

job vacancies, advice for writers and company
history

Get Closer To Penguin . . . www.penguin.co.uk